H. A

Off Course

A Cathy Prior Thriller

FUTURE BOOKS

Copyright © 2024 H.A. Fowler
All rights reserved

The characters and events portrayed in this book are fictitious. Any similarity to real persons, living or dead, is coincidental and not intended by the author.

No part of this book may be reproduced, or stored in a retrieval system, or transmitted in any form or by any means, electronic, mechanical, photocopying, recording, or otherwise, without express written permission of the publisher.

TO MARK

One

WORKERS DRESSED IN dirty construction gear were already dismantling the port's wall and ceiling fixtures when I finally got there, someone scraping at sticky-looking sockets with a putty knife, which was surely dangerous (although the guy doing it seemed fairly relaxed), someone else prising off facings from the panelling before letting them crash noisily onto the concrete floor, jarring my head and making my entire body wince in protest.

The upturned cones of new bamboo culms were already poking up through the floorboards and cement, defiant, determined and, unfortunately, also deadly - not that you could have guessed from just looking at the wooded stems.

The workers didn't look bothered by the invader plants, whistling as they took the place apart. Perhaps they just hadn't noticed the stuff or didn't know how it was taking over planet after planet, though it'd have been tough to miss. Maybe no-one had bothered to warn them about how fast the stuff grew, not thinking a crew of workers important enough to worry about. The planet was full of nasty attitudes like that. I certainly wouldn't be missing any of the snootiness if this flight happened as hoped and I managed to leave Earthen.

A noisy rattle of letters on the board changed the mood, adding urgency and immediacy to the collection of passengers who'd been hanging around looking bored. As the metal flaps turned they revealed a fresh carousel of destinations from around the universe. Yes, good, Aballonia. A relief. It'd probably always be the black sheep of interplanetary relations, might as well have a skull and cross bones next to it, really, given its current standing. At least the flight was happening – that was something.

The port flues were blasting out a perfume of fetid, stale sun protection; the stench somehow underlining my doubts as to the wisdom of this trip. I shook my head, hoping to dispel my fears. It didn't work.

"Heat's not helping much," said one of the workers, mopping at his brow with theatrical relish. I couldn't tell if he was talking to me out of kindness, because he could see my exhaustion. Or maybe because he was feeling grotty too and hoping for sympathy from me.

"No, not easy," I replied, pathetically grateful for even a crumb of human solidarity, almost tempted to stop and chat, despite my lateness, but aware I couldn't risk it. Missing this flight would mean curtains for my career, I had to make it. "Slept through my alarm, running a bit late." I grimaced.

"Too much to drink, was it?" His manner remained jocular but had acquired a judgemental edge too. He wouldn't meet my gaze. Even my red-gold quilted jacket made from recycled saris wasn't enough to stop me feeling quite sick and rather cold, though I was wearing the side with delicate strips of gold running across it, in some no doubt ludicrous attempt to magic up good luck for myself. It wasn't really working. Ed used to laugh at me for my "very silly" superstitions, as he put it, and he'd pretty much dictated my clothing choices for me when we were together, but he wasn't here, so I could wear what I liked. Theoretically, anyway. The red-gold seemed to go with my dirty blonde hair I'd noticed so, in a fit of giddy new-found freedom, I'd put that on before leaving the flat.

"Too much to drink? Goodness, no. Hardly touch the stuff." Sometimes it was worrying how easily the lying came to me, though he didn't look like he was buying my nonsense.

"Whatever you say, dear." He still wouldn't meet my eyes, though, and shame rushed through me like a meteor shower moving fast in deep space, altering the lighting and appearance of the asteroids, clapped-out old satellites and assorted rocks in its path.

With relief, I spotted a moving walkway about twenty metres ahead, not yet dismantled, unlike just about everything else in the spaceport. Stepping onto its rollers, I felt my body properly relax for the first time in many hours. Shrugging off my backpack, I propped it up on the handrail, leant against it. Breathed in and out deeply.

The fragrances wafting toward me from Orbit Free smelled cloying, artificial. Fake. It didn't matter, I couldn't afford them anyway. I was probably feeling critical of the scents because I knew funds wouldn't stretch to buying perfume. One was the inevitable Eau de Bamboiades, decorated with pictures of slanting sticks. Like we didn't already have enough of the wretched stuff.

I glanced at the ceiling; sure enough, shoots were poking down through it. The stuff was unstoppable.

We were approaching the end of the travellator before I became aware of rapidly cooling wet cotton clinging to my skin under the jacket. Unpeeling it, I flapped it a little in the air, foolishly aware that wouldn't help much.

Disembarking, I pounded past empty gates, fearful of being seen by anyone I knew – they'd have sneered at me for travelling what they called 'cattle class', a horrible expression that, in fairness, I'd never used myself, even at my worst.

As I stumbled along, my black webbed gilet slipped from my fingers, wrapped itself around my thighs and nearly made me fall. I picked up both the garment and what was left of my dignity before scurrying on, trying not to let myself look at the sleek bamboo doors leading to 'executive' lounges.

The pain of job loss felt physical at times like this, though it was several months since I'd been kicked out. Queueing, worrying, waiting, living off pasta with a few drops of olive oil left over from the old life; it was all taking rather a lot of adjustment, much more than I'd expected. It wasn't much fun seeing what an arrogant bitch I'd been in the past either, even though, in fairness, I'd never used the odious term "cattle class".

Back then, he'd have flown me here. Probably while complaining about money wasted on my drinking, like in that conversation when we broke up.

Never mind, except I did mind. Rather a lot, in fact. But no time to waste if I was going to make the flight. Aballonian Spaceways had a reputation almost as mixed as my own; they'd want this to happen – and promptly, too.

I shouldn't have drunk so much last night. The Eau de Bambusia had been difficult to resist; at this rate, I might need to inspect the porcelain again.

Bangles jingling, I pushed at a grubby wall panel to access the gate's economy lounge. I must have forgotten to put on deodorant, my nose was registering an unpleasant, acrid smell mingling with stale alcohol. Me.

Never mind. I'd get a few squirts of Jolie Poaceae from a tester when I could, my own supply had run out.

Lack of expenses was proving to be, well, expensive. I wasn't used to travelling on my own account. If I could find the snapper - Kolya? - he might pay for a few things. Drinks, food, snacks. Cabs. I'd no idea where he was though. He'd probably heard of my fall from grace, didn't want mixed up with me.

Never having worked with him before, I was relying on a single, blurry image in his crystal signature to know what he looked like. Not promising, going by the pic. An intense pair of dark eyes beetling out from under craggy (and untinted) eyebrows. Problem was, none of the élite were even prepared to take my calls, though they'd sucked up to me plenty back in the day.

In fairness, my own mugshot wasn't much of a guide either; taken twenty years previously, it showed me looking . . . relaxed. As anyone would after a bottle of Valpol. Not quite sober, but, in fairness, not close to puking, either.

Even if I couldn't find this Kolya, I'd have to board. I'd a lot invested in the trip. Stuff like my credibility, identity, self-worth and income. I had to prove my story about the discovery of this so-called miracle food true. Despite those bloody scientists denying it.

I needed that old job back because, well, because it was my identity, my everything, the one bit of me worth anything; the rest of me being so defective, so hateful, so horrible. Only my work had redeemed me a little bit – while it had lasted. It hadn't lasted long.

There weren't many actual passengers in the lounge; mostly just a few workpeople, dressed in protective kit and hard hats, already unfastening seating from where it was screwed into the floor.

As if stressing why I had to make this flight, I watched as they prised off wall panels, chucking them down onto the wooden floor with a noisy clatter that jangled my nerves. Other signage, plating and fixings followed, drilling into my aching head as they fell. There wouldn't be any more flights on this route. Not now, possibly never. Under the signage you could see where the bamboo was making inroads with small yet tough shards. I turned my head away, not feeling strong enough to watch, even in microcosm, how bamboo was taking over the universe. Our universe. Our homes, our dreams, our pastures and prairies – devoured by a grass.

With dismay, I watched one of the workers wince as he hit his thumb with a hammer. "Poor you," I mouthed at him. He acknowledged my look of sympathy before unearthing a greyish cotton hankie from his trouser pocket and wrapping it around his thumb.

"Is there somewhere I can get a glass of water?" It was a member of spaceport staff I asked. She looked overworked and hassled but nodded towards a drinking fountain fixed to the wall. Underneath were tiny conical paper cups, stacked one upon another. Filling one up, I walked back over to the worker who'd hurt his hand and held it out to him.

"Thanks," he said, sounding slightly surprised anyone was bothering to be kind to him.

"Okay? I'd get that looked at if I were you."

"Last call for Aballonia." The voice came over the tannoy. "Last call."

Hurrying over to the boarding queue, I thought again about my photographer and fixer, who should have been here by now. Damn. He was going to be difficult to replace; the journey meant several weeks in deep space. No more flights at all after this

The story wouldn't get much of an audience if we didn't have compelling visuals. Unless I could prove there really was a miracle food being created in Aballonia, I'd be lucky to be travelling anywhere at all, might even face trial.

Panting from effort and nerves, trying to make my breathing quieter, I eventually got to the top of the queue. The Aballonians didn't want journalists poking about, asking questions; so, officially, I was an 'academic'.

Kolya would be my 'research assistant'. If he ever turned up . . .

It didn't just feel like it was taking forever to get to the front of the queue. More than half an hour passed before I got to a member of staff.

"See your ticket?"

I straightened out my crumpled papers, pushed them towards

him; the judgemental look on his face making me squirm.

"Bit of a rush, sorry."

"That's not a valid ticket." He sounded pleased with himself, possibly because he knew the news could only upset me.

"No, no, it isn't, you're right."

He looked smug about his powers of acumen, and I began to hate him a little bit more.

"But this is a letter from your head of marketing saying I can have two seats on the flight." I pushed the papers back towards him, trying not to look defiant. "As long as we're okay with galley jump seats."

"Hmm…" He stroked his face before stretching out a hand to pick up the comms crystal. Tilting his head to one side, he drawled into it, as if determined to put me in my place by deliberately taking his time about 'helping' me.

"Wants to hitch a couple of galley places. Her and a researcher, she says."

Whoever he was talking to must have made a caustic, witty remark; the gate guy snorted and turned his head away so I couldn't properly see him contorting his face into what looked like a sneer.

Putting the receiver down, he ran a hand through beautifully-coiffed hair and turned back to me, looking as if he could smell something bad when he turned in my direction. In fairness, there may have been some truth to that, I probably did smell fetid.

"I'm researching the pre-Aballic settlements there for a thesis."

"Are you indeed." He wouldn't meet my gaze, instead focussing on his crystal as if it might explain everything.

"We'd a group of academics here last week." He didn't sound like he approved of such goings-on, maybe jealous of anyone who got better jaunts than him. Scrutinising my face, spaceline guy looked even more suspicious, though that barely seemed possible. "From the university. There a reason you weren't with them?"

"Marketing said I could have two seats." I tried to stay calm.

"Did they indeed." He sounded unimpressed, disbelieving.

"Not planning on going home again, then?" He still didn't meet my gaze as he spoke.

Even if the trip meant travelling on a dustbin with a mouldy toilet as my seat, I'd go for it, never mind about return flights. I'd sort all that out later.

Judging by the state of the spacecraft I could see sitting out on the runway, our vehicle might not be a million miles from refuse disposal.

"Last flight from Earthen to Aballonia, my love," he said, surprising me by actually looking at me at last. I hadn't been expecting concern for me. "Thought how you're gonna get home?"

"Of course." Not in much detail, admittedly.

He held my papers under a security light, scrutinised them, looked at me again and waved me through. It wasn't the triumphant relief I'd been expecting on getting onto the flight. The experience was more making me wonder if Aballonia had a few extra secrets I'd only find out about once I got there. And once I got there, there wouldn't be an easy way back home, as space line guy seemed keen to impress on me.

Seeing another queue next to the spacecraft door, I placed my bag on the floor and sat down next to it, folding my legs into each other.

"You'd think there'd be a bigger fanfare, wouldn't you," said a woman nearby, sipping something from a polystyrene cup. Maybe bamboo and bergamot, going by the piquant aroma. "Last flight out there and that."

I'd have liked a drink too. Funds didn't permit.

Neither of us was travelling light; the knuckles, ears and neck of my fellow passenger were glistening with jewellery; I felt burdened too, though maybe not exactly in a lapidary form. Glancing out the window at the rolling fields and hills of Earthen, I felt a wave of sentimental emotion wash over me. Maybe my career wasn't the be-all and end-all I'd thought, though it felt sacrilegious just thinking that. What else could matter as much as my work?

She shook her head. "Normally they'd make a big fuss about something like this. Makes you wonder, doesn't it."

"What do you mean? Wonder what?"

"What they're trying to hide."

Stretching my neck and shoulders, I thought ahead. Aballonia was tearing itself apart through war between government and rebels, who claimed people were being denied food so extra-planetary folk could scoff it instead. Journalists weren't meant to set foot on the place, so henceforth I was an 'academic', like Istvan.

Officially, the nearest you could get to Aballonia was a neighbouring planet called Eyelash. It was said to be close enough for mainstream news stations to pick up voice traffic, but I was hoping being an academic would let me explore the planet itself. I'd even invested in imitation horn-rimmed glasses and a moth-eaten thrift cardigan for the part.

While I hadn't expected the trip to be easy, it was getting off to a bad start. Someone on pictures had recommended this guy, but snappers were an odd crowd. Dave saying he was okay didn't mean much; and Kolya was already late. I hadn't met him before the flight, not having the money to take him out for a drink like I'd normally have done; I still needed him for the trip to work. It'd be impossible to sell a story without visuals. Words alone wouldn't attract anything like the same interest – or fee.

Kolya's crystal was going straight to voicemail. I'd have to board, see if I could find another snapper once I made it to Aballonia. If I made it there. Or take what pictures I could myself, even if they wouldn't be winning any prizes. At the ship door, I felt a deep weariness slide over me, the bag slung over my shoulder cutting into my flesh with the weight of my remaining belongings. Some of the water in my cup slopped onto my sleeve.

The thunder of engines joined the soundtrack of desultory chat, a tired-looking greyish light lingered in the dusk. The soldiers standing at the cabin door were fingering greasy, dust-marked weapons, their steel helmets fractionally askew, making me think they might shoot me by accident. Or at least pretend it was an accident.

With relief, I watched as someone looking like a snapper – dirty flak jacket, glancing around, taking in all the angles, calculating and acquisitive like a young fox scenting the night air for his supper - left the terminal building and crossed the tarmac. When he joined the queue at the foot of the steps he did so with an impressive insouciance. I was surprised by his appearance, though; nothing like his photo. This guy's eyebrows were positively tame.

Once he was on the ship, we managed to speak to each other.

"Hi, Istvan, your photographer," he said, quietly, sticking out his leather-clad arm with a verve, precision and force that unsettled me.

"Istvan?" Not the name I'd been given. And his accent . . . Hard to place. His Earthen perfect, but, somehow, maybe too perfect? His inflection odd too.

"Nice to meet you." At last . . .

Shaking hands, I registered a jolt of attraction with dismay.

"Don't forget we're here as academics, remember?" Being bossy seemed a possible way out of sexual entanglement, men didn't generally like that.

"Academics? Uh, oh. Yes, of course."

His hair was long, like that guy in The Young Ones. Hippyish. A central parting suggesting an unworldliness or disregard for more conventional concerns, though he'd smart sunglasses in the breast pocket of his newish-looking fatigues. A neatness, cleanliness and tightness that belied the limpid blue eyes and hair braids.

"I'm here to replace Kolya," he began. "Didn't he explain that? Typical Kolya." He chortled to himself, without explaining anything more to me, although he must have known I'd never met this man whose behaviour he found so predictable.

"No. But not to worry."

He looked discomfited; I laughed in a manner intended to put him more at ease. "It's been a bit of a day," I said, rearranging my hair so the linen holding it back from my face wouldn't stick into my head as I leant back.

I watched him search inside his jacket. With an air of calm efficiency at odds with the scattered hippy I'd initially taken him to be, he unearthed a cellophane packet and held it delicately between his thumb and forefinger.

"Best to plan ahead," he said, holding the packet out to me. For a brief, terrifying moment I thought he might be offering me drugs – on a pan-galactic flight where that kind of behaviour could earn you long-term incarceration.

"Go on, take it, it won't get you into trouble."

Something about the way he spoke made me begin to wonder if he was, in fact, on close terms with all kinds of trouble. Had already been so, would almost certainly be so again.

But I stretched out a hand to take the little packet – roughly the same size as a condom in its foil wrapper. On the cellophane was an eighteenth-century lady with an elaborate hairdo. To my relief, (and slight disappointment, too, if I were to be honest) inside was nothing more sinister than a toiletries set, with ear plugs.

"For later, if you can't sleep."

"Thanks." I tried to hide my feelings of being underwhelmed by his gift, not wanting to be ungrateful. It was hard, though, to escape the feeling he was playing me in some way, though I wasn't yet sure how or why, so I tried to sound slightly ironic, fearful he was privately laughing at me.

Setting off for the unknown, I glanced through the steamed-up porthole at the asteroids, stars and planets we could now see hanging in the sky, suspended by mysterious forces I didn't understand, reminding me of decorations on a pine tree fast losing its needles.

"Did Kolya not tell you I was replacing him?"

I pushed stubborn hair out of my eyes again.

"No, no, he didn't." Had Kolya said something? Maybe I'd been drinking . . . And had just forgotten . . . It was horribly possible.

"Speak with Kolya. He'll vouch for me." He raised his chin, tilting it, looking as if he was preparing to joust for someone's honour.

"I can't get hold of him. Or Dave, who suggested him."

The papers on my tray table spewed out from the crystal lay neglected, each of them with writing coded to appear like pieces of academia, relaying words and figures, addresses, times and dates in loopy, messy handwriting.

"You've got me, not Kolya." He shifted against the faded orange upholstery of his seat in a way that made me wonder if he was sexually excited. He turned to look out the greasy porthole, blotted with splotches of something looking horribly like bird poo.

"I'm a professional, you know. You don't need to worry. I can show you some of my work, if you like, And I'll tell you more about how we're going to play this once we're through the dark matter." He paused. "If you're okay with that?"

"Yes, of course. Fine." My voice quavered. When would we be through the 'dark matter'?

Through the cloudy plastic, it was just possible to see a small blue circle receding further and further into the distance. "Goodbye, Earthen," I whispered to myself. "I'll be back as soon as I can."

As the ship sped across dusty stretches of star-dotted universe, our already-limited reserves of energy depleted even further with every weary day that passed. The ship's interior offered the same depressing view of seating and fixtures carved out of plastic and bamboo blends. The spaceline was claiming all its craft were grass-free, but I felt sure I'd seen a something that looked horribly like a rhizome growing in the ladies.

The noisy thrumming of engines was to become our soundtrack for the next few weeks. The world outside, if it even still existed, was mostly invisible through the infamous mid-planetary mist storms. Even there, the nodules of bamboo hanging in mid-air made progress slower than it should have been.

I turned to look at Istvan, who was flossing his teeth after a tough lunch we'd both struggled to eat.

It was a boring afternoon; the day wasn't going well. We'd struggled to chew and digest our lunch of Asiatic corms. Not only had they been tough as only leathery old bamboos can be, but they'd also come complete with a feathery outer coating that had tasted like an especially toxic anti-depressant.

Istvan shook his head, as if hoping to clear away any potential distractions – physical and mental – preventing him from concentrating on something in his hand. Ah, yes, his boarding manifest.

A soft glow backlit the planets, it felt as if my work world was coming alive again.

I began to look through my bag to check for communications on any of my devices. I was rather proud of the bag, an ethnic affair bought back on Earthen and adorned with dangling tassels onto which someone had threaded gold-coloured rings.

On the spaceship the bag felt simply lame, out-of-place, like Christmas decorations glimpsed by mistake in mid-summer. Never mind. I snuggled into my seat, trying to rest and gather my strength for whatever lay ahead.

The days passed, albeit slowly, until one afternoon I began thinking guiltily about the man who'd been meant to be my snapper.

"Is Kolya okay?"

He'd a young daughter with health problems of some kind, I vaguely remembered. Maybe he'd had to stay on Earthen to look after her. We were out of range now for communication with Earthen, I couldn't get hold of him to ask him myself.

"He's fine."

I gave him a look meant to indicate a certain distrust.

"And his daughter's okay?"

"Everybody's fine."

"That's good." I dropped my gaze, aware Istvan wouldn't be elaborating on how he'd obtained this information.

"You're very kind, asking after all these people."

"It's normal, isn't it?"

"Not for everybody, no."

Feeling a little flustered, I began picking at some loose skin on my thumb, scratching until it bled; I clutched at it in a doubtless futile attempt to stop Istvan seeing.

The tabletop creaked as I released and lowered it, sounding as if it needed oiling. On its plastic surface were circular purple stains, memories of other journeys, other libations. Wine was such a rarity nowadays; I hated the idea of anyone wasting even a few drops of the precious liquid.

The handful of other passengers aboard the craft had shrunk into themselves, now a fretwork of bones and blankets lit up by the usual spacecraft paraphernalia of lights, sensors and orbital equipment.

Repressing a desire to sigh deeply, I glanced at the small basket I'd brought with me, stowed under the seat in front. At least I could enjoy a good drink now I didn't have Ed nagging me. I didn't even bother open it slowly, just unbuckled the basket straps fast as I could, felt myself relax with pleasure at the creaking sound as I lifted up the lid. Inside, unopened, was temporary release from the shame, anger and fear: a ready-mixed gin and tonic.

"Any more news on this miracle food?" I didn't want him complaining about my drinking, so was steering onto what I thought were fairly neutral subjects.

"Miracle food . . . There's no such thing." He folded his arms across his chest, looking outraged I could even suggest such a thing.

"But you read my stories? The ones that got me sacked?"

"Of course."

"My story was true, that's why I'm going to Aballonia. To prove it. To prove there is a miracle food."

Istvan shook his head angrily, as if I'd said something blasphemous.

Trying to focus on opening my can, I felt a sharp jag of pain in my hand. Yelping, I jerked backwards, knocking the can onto the cabin floor. The contents landed on my jeans, making the fabric cling uncomfortably.

"I will help you, if you give that to me. But, please, don't forgot. We're academics on our way to investigate pre-Aballic settlements, no?"

"Of course we are." No, we weren't. He was taking our cover a bit too seriously, wasn't he? But I couldn't get into this at that exact moment.

Looking down, I could see a redness trickling down the top part of my finger, reaching as far as my beloved Celtic cross ring. I wanted to put the finger in my mouth there and then, and give it a quick wash that way, but didn't want him to see me doing something potentially sexual. So instead, I curled my finger into my hand, trying not to worry about deep-space cuts and their possible complications.

"You okay?" He sounded genuine in his concern. This felt new, very new, being with someone who – at least as far as I could tell – was being kind to me, though in a confusing way. I was reluctantly aware of paying him to work for me. Still, it felt good to enjoy attention, my turn in the warming spotlight of kindness.

"I'm fine, fine, thank you. Absolutely fine." The metal had cut two of my fingers, which were now bleeding even more profusely than before, I realised.

"Shall I get help?"

Help? The way he spoke made me think of a knight charging off to joust for his lady's honour. Something about him – a reserve? A hidden power? A deliberate quietness? - hinted at depths I longed to understand. I got a sense of a pledge of honour taken somewhere along the way, firm and irrevocable. It was only a can of gin and tonic at stake, though. I didn't want to get carried away.

"No, it's okay, thank you." I paused, embarrassed. "I've never been to Aballonia before. I'm just nervous."

"Not many people have. You're not alone." He inspected his fingernails, neatly clipped and clean. Mine felt even mankier in comparison.

"That's partly why I want to go there."

Not totally true, but I wasn't going to tell him that. My aim was to act more like Muscardinus avellanarius, a creature said to be secretive, nocturnal and rarely seen. Progress so far was mixed.

"You're going there to put yourself on the map again, no?"

"Covering wars and famines is – unfortunately – what we do."

"I know."

"Yes, we trade in misery." I turned my head, checking nobody could have overheard me. Better, wittier replies kept occurring after I'd delivered my response. I began whispering. "You're a photographer, you know how we earn our living." I wasn't sure why he thought himself so saintly, he made his living preying on disaster, same as me.

I allowed myself to doze, still wary of letting down my guard, but also exhausted. Everything might feel better for a rest, so I tried to ignore the crisp wrappers on the floor and odour of stale sweat. The air freshener smelled like it might once have been meant to suggest lavender; somehow it just underlined our distance from anywhere the stuff might actually once have grown.

It wasn't immediately obvious why our ship was speeding up. I was just aware of not being asleep any more. For a moment, I wondered if we'd nearly collided with an asteroid or passing moon and were trying to get away from it. My stomach lurched as we accelerated even more on the downwards slope, the angle steeper than anything I'd ever tackled before.

Gripping the arms of my seat, I tried my meditative breathing routine. In through the nose, aligning our chakral senses... The voice drifted back to my memory. And out through the nose. Silly chakral senses, not much help at a time like this.

The shuttle was speeding downwards so fast my palms were sweaty as I clutched the arm rests. It was hard not to feel we were speeding to our deaths, a final resolution of all our torment. The anguish would at least be over, after this. Or maybe, despite everything, I did want to survive. With fumbling, shaking hands, I tightened my seat belt.

Without saying anything, he stretched out his hand to me. Wordlessly, I took it, despite my reservations. Turned and glanced at him. He nodded at me. Despite myself, I began to feel better, as if together we might be able to survive. Stars shot past us. Blurred. Disappeared.

We slowed and, as I watched through the porthole, I saw another ship draw up next to us. The new vessel had a piratical bent. Dishevelled. Erratic. Lawless, yet purposeful. Dirt that belied its official markings. Metal patchings fixed to the rigging. Space gulls swooping and cawing around the vessel's walls, loud enough for us to hear at this distance. It wasn't difficult to imagine someone being required to walk the plank on that ship, in fact something jutting out of the craft looked like it would fit the bill rather well.

Thudding. Thumping. Walloping. Trembling.

The porthole shuddered at the docking collision. Although I'd little idea what the craft and its occupants wanted from us, I couldn't help feeling uneasy. Our crew remained worryingly silent.

The soldiers who began clumping noisily aboard our craft were leaden, purposeful. Their language sounded coarse underneath the plastic defences. Making a loud, clumping noise, their boots looked as if they'd been hand-made by an apprentice cobbler as yet unskilled in their craft. That wasn't bothering them. There was a smell of foreign detergents, and they'd that uncanny appearance of being replica models of themselves, better fitted to sitting in miniature on a window sill or mantelpiece.

Wordlessly, I slipped my hand out of Istvan's, embarrassed at anyone seeing my cowardice and neediness.

Recoiling at the sight of their guns, though, since I was still afraid, I pushed myself further back against the stickiness of my seat, my muscles straining. Istvan, too, pulled his legs in closer to his body. The wished-for effect, I think, was one of cool insouciance; I was frightened enough to feel grateful to him for just trying to act as if things were okay.

Too nervous to drink anything, I tried to sink deeper into my seat and escape attention, but my legs wouldn't stop trembling, fluttering jerkily as messages from brain to limbs diverted elsewhere in my fear. Where the gin and tonic had landed on my jeans, the fabric was now sticky, I noticed with annoyance, registering that the material was still clinging to my thigh through a large wet patch on my right leg. The smell of stale alcohol wasn't enhancing either my mood or perfume.

Two

LOOKING AT THE guns held by the spaceport soldiers, a sliver of unease slithered through me like milk curdling in a jelly. Sure, the weapons looked like plastic toys, the kind my neighbour's son used to play with. Bigger, though. Deadlier. Angrier.

Through the port's tinted windows, I could just make out remains of bombed-out buildings; above them the planet's famous trio of suns were performing a rondelle under assorted flotsam and gases.

When I noticed a guard beckoning to me, I shuffled forward, pushing my bag along with my feet. It was hard not to feel uncertain about the reception awaiting us, especially after being taken off the ship early by the planet's authorities. It didn't feel like any of this boded well for the trip, but maybe they simply wanted to frighten us, or this was the quickest way for them to log our details.

Somehow, I couldn't imagine them nodding us through while wishing us a pleasant stay in their delightful, war-torn capital.

When it came to my turn, the guard leafed through my papers, glancing up every now and again as if having difficulty matching the dark-haired, serious-looking girl in the picture to the present-day me. I'd been younger back then, but it was still me – maybe I looked different because they hadn't let me wear my glasses for the picture. I'd lost a lot of weight on our peregrinations, too, living off powdered drinks and little else, so I was taking a perverse pride in his doubts over the picture.

"Take off your hat."

Electricity made it stick to my hair, as I removed it, strands of hair fanning outward and upward. Embarrassed, I patted at my head, which disconcerted me more by pushing jolts of electricity through my ink-stained fingers.

Every so often the guard raised his right forefinger to his mouth, licked it and returned to using it to leaf through the pages, before closing up the document, pushing back his chair and standing up. I watched with dismay as he opened the door from his station and stepped out. Him taking a personal interest in me didn't feel like good news, a bit like how you never wanted doctors to be that interested in you. Far better to be dull to doctors, and probably to customs officials too.

"Come here."

"Tell me what's wrong?" I must have sounded hysterical, but a three-week-long space flight and being taken by force off your own ship could do that.

Istvan looked worried for me, and I loved him for being protective. His attitude made me think he saw danger ahead for me, though, but it was hard to be sure, he wasn't the talkative type; I'd already learnt to be patient in waiting for his input. It could mean a long wait – sometimes days, but one that was usually worthwhile. I did privately hope that he wasn't going to be one of those guys who acted as if any slight to 'their' woman was a personal affront to them, but you never knew; it was early days for us.

When he stepped forward, so he was standing next to me, I had a stern word with myself to avoid reaching for his hand. He was wearing a wedding ring, as I'd clocked within moments of meeting him, though he hadn't yet mentioned a wife. Maybe keen to keep work and family separate?

"Let me go with you."

"Not you, no." The guard looked like he might double as a traffic cop in his spare time, holding up his hand to Istvan with a bored calm that suggested hours spent reminding angry drivers they weren't the kings of the road some maybe imagined.

"Don't hurt her." He sounded genuinely concerned for my welfare, though that might have been wishful thinking on my part. More probably he was thinking about the salary I was meant to be paying him - and what would happen if I got banged up to rights in an Aballonian prison cell.

It was still difficult, though, to be sure of exactly what he was doing. Maybe money explained it but dicing with spaceport security seemed risky; the place had a human rights record that might best be described as 'patchy'. I remembered him saying he was originally from here, so perhaps he thought they wouldn't hurt one of their own. Personally, I wouldn't have banked on it, not with their track record.

Ignoring Istvan, the guard took me by the arm, and began escorting me away from the main spaceport, opening a gate that led away from the central thoroughfare. Outside, a crow hopped down from a fence and ferreted about on the tarmac, looking slightly perturbed by events, but only slightly - not enough to pause for long in his hunt for food.

"She hasn't done anything wrong." Istvan was calling over to us.

Half-turning to look back at him, I became aware of the hold on my elbow tightening. Tension ran up the back of my arm, squeezing the muscle from elbow up to shoulder.

I hadn't known Istvan long, it was tempting to think he was maybe fond of hamming things up, because that could cause diversions, make things happen. Journalism and show business; they weren't really all that different to each other. The other possibility was that he was fond of me, although he seemed too together to be interested in a loser like me. It was a shock to watch him dump down his bag, put both hands on a security bollard and rather nimbly clamber over it. He leant back to where he'd started, picked up his bag and took that with him.

"You're not allowed here," said the guard. The Aballonian landscape outside looked primitive and forbidding, despite its corona of suns. The kind of place where you could all too easily imagine witches appearing before psychotic Shakespearean kings, muttering warnings made all the more alarming for being unfathomable and mysterious.

Other passengers were turning to look at Istvan; maybe hopeful he'd supplement whatever in-flight entertainment had been missing.

Followed by Istvan, the guard steered me toward what looked like a nondescript cupboard. A scuffed and dented plaque on the door said in capital letters 'CLEANING'.

"I'm calling for back-up," said the guard, sounding as if he hoped to reassure himself with his words.

Istvan looked undeterred, knocking his foot against the scuffed and dirty door kicker plate. There was no window or even just a panel of thickened glass anywhere on the rectangle of wooden door.

Overhead, the planet's national anthem – I'd done some research - crackled across a thick, fetid-smelling atmosphere. Clashing chords made it sound angry, aggrieved – as if its composers were determined to apply vengeance to anyone foolish enough to wrong them.

Guards came in and marched Istvan off. "Be brave," he whispered to me. "It'll be all right."

The place was putting me in mind of that torture cell back on Earthen, the one where no-one larger than a dog could lie down or rest.

The holding pen wasn't far removed from what I'd half-expected, half-feared. Large, unidentifiable blotches of something – dirt? – sprawled across flooring, walls, even the ceiling.

More disquieting than the dirt was the speed with which I shelved the old version of myself. I felt naked, without any outer personality whatsoever. The more so for Istvan no longer being with me; he'd grounded me in my old self, however fragile that now felt. The Aballonians must have taken him off to question on his own – and prevent us from comforting each other or comparing stories.

The trappings of my life had defined me, as had the different milieux where I'd lived and tried, however unsuccessfully, to operate. Not any more. Problem was, there hadn't been much under the surface. I was a Potemkin village, me, all show, little substance. The old me, the journalist who'd cross the universe (while pretending to be someone else) if it meant a story as a result, she was gone. Had maybe never even existed in the first place, except in my imaginings. And, with her, also what remained of my self-confidence. It was deflating, to register how quickly it had all happened; stepping into a cleaning cupboard had stripped away all I'd been stupid enough to think composed me. Identities were more fragile than I'd realised. A mouse scuttled along where clay floor met whitewashed walls, paused, looked at me, and scarpered. I wished I could do the same. Everything in my life was hand-to-mouth, hurried, desperate, much more temporary, provisional than I liked to accept. Or had even realised. Whether I liked what was happening or not (I didn't) had little bearing on what was unfolding, I'd lost not just my freedom in this accursed place but also myself, too. And in losing myself, it felt as if I'd already lost everything else too. Even more than I'd already lost in the old life with Ed. At least the bleeding had finally stopped; there was no longer the physical reminder of our sundering and the trauma, hurting me every time I urinated, every time I dressed in the morning, undressed at night. The emotional memories would take longer to go, might take more than soap and water to remove.

Henceforth, I was in this prison cell, decked out with a macabre bunting of spiders' webs, and I was whoever and whatever they told me to be. There was no Cathy left, she'd begun disappearing back in mid-space, them seizing me at spaceport control was just another step in the same process. Had she ever even properly existed in the first place? All I could do was be a compliant pleaser. A weirdo. There'd never been any 'me'; I existed only in as far as I could mould myself into meeting the needs of other people. The idea of having needs of my own felt ludicrous, self-indulgent. Just travelling to the end of the universe wasn't going to change those feelings of being incomplete, empty. I couldn't see a point to me, just me, unless I was in the role of either dutiful daughter or sexual partner. I was a hollowed-out woman, a projection of others' needs, fears and wants

Being trapped in the dirty little room, it was hard to avoid dreadful imaginings, the kind involving sexual abuse and life imprisonment. That human rights watch… why hadn't I paid more attention to it? Made more donations?

The ceiling hung low, the lighting harsh and inconsistent, flickering as if the power supply was precarious. At no point did I see anybody in there who looked like a spaceport cleaner. In fact, there was no-one else in there at all, though the place could definitely have done with some cleaning.

It was a shock when Istvan reappeared, looking oddly calm. I'd fallen asleep in one of those awkward naps that leaves you aching, sore and wiping dribble off your chin. Opening my eyes, his face was the first thing I saw.

"I've come to see how you're doing. Can't leave you on your tod." He smiled and spread his hands out to either side of him, as if hopeful the dusty and dry spaceport air might provide the answer to our quandaries, before glancing at me with what looked meant to be a reassuring look. "We're in this together."

Were we?

A security guard went into a curtained alcove on his own. It was impossible to hear what he was saying, even Aballonia had woken up to sound-proof curtains; all that was audible was a clipped, brisk flurry of what sounded like instructions or orders. I didn't understand enough of the language to get even the gist.

Coming out of the booth, the man gazed at us both a moment.

"That's it," he said. "We don't want to see either of you again."

Istvan turned to me.

"All right?"

I didn't feel even remotely "right", but nodded and made a jangling noise with my handcuffs as I tried to reach out my hand to him.

"We're letting you both go. We've searched your luggage, nothing of interest there."

"Here's your handbag." He held the velvety creation out, keeping it as far away from him as humanly possible.

"We don't want any more trouble from either of you. Next time you're space-hopping, make sure your paperwork's in order."

What was wrong with our paperwork?

Rubbing a hand over his face, the guard returned to the uncertain solace of pages of crystal work covered in his planet's alphabet.

"What did he mean, about the paperwork? I mean, sorry, crystal work?

Istvan shrugged. "No idea. I wouldn't worry. They're letting us go."

He took me by the elbow as we walked away. I was expecting him to let me go once we cleared the cleaning-cupboard-cum-prison, but he kept hold of me until back in the main spaceport.

"Bit strange, wasn't it?"

"What?"

"First they take us off the ship and then make us go through control with everyone else?" Although the flight hadn't exactly been packed, I'd counted only a dozen of us: several women in their sixties or maybe seventies, presumably heading home and not bothered by maybe getting stuck there, a hitchhiker, possibly young and hippyish enough to be reckless in his travel plans. A few business types. A soldier, maybe drafted back into the Aballonian army, who were said to be looking for reinforcements. And me and Istvan, just two bookish, young and unworldly academics swotting up on the place's history.

"Yes, see what you mean."

With some misgiving, I gripped the handle of my rucksack, pulling it along as if it were an unusually obedient dog toward the exit sign. I winced as I misjudged my step off the kerb, my ankle twisting and cold rainwater splashing up from a puddle, soaking and darkening my trousers.

Three

A FEW STARS were radiating what light they could, diffusing and reflecting the depleted energy left at this distant end of the universe. Standing in the spaceport's pod park, we could see from the sky that all three suns had long ago set for the evening.

Water vapour warm from my lungs rose in a steamy cloud into the darkness, my body shaking from the stress of the last few hours. I knew as soon as I spotted it that our space pod would be the dirty, shabby one at the end of the line, not that I felt happy to be right about that. My rucksack and bag felt even heavier than they had twenty minutes earlier. With dismay I gazed at the dirt encrusted on the vehicle's fenders, aware of the backpack's straps digging into my shoulders.

A further glance at the craft suggested it was almost certainly not of a recent vintage, while also not old enough to have acquired the patina and status of age; not even 'retro charm' would have applied to its grubby, tarnished veneers. Sadly, exhaustion made me forget to school my features into neutrality and the driver scowled, maybe he'd noticed my doubts about his jalopy.

"What a beautiful pod," I began, loading my rucksack into the boot, aware of sounding unconvincing in my praise, but happy to feel the pressure on my shoulders ease off as I dropped the bag down onto the muddy, dirt-smeared plastic.

Our driver didn't reply, instead grunting in a martyred way. Silently, with only the briefest of eye-meets, Istvan and I got into the pod and strapped our belts over ourselves. The fabric on mine was fraying and damaged, as if a hungry rodent had enjoyed a tasty feast from it. I felt a quiver of fear as the driver kicked our vessel into flight mode.

Although I was mostly just relieved to be free again, my recent incarceration was still on my mind.

"How could they know?" I felt frightened, incomprehension sharpening the fear. "About me, about me being a journalist, I mean. It's not on my passport."

I paused, afraid of angering him, but determined to get some answers.

"Did you tell them?"

He reared backwards and forward in his seat, agitated. "Of course not." He sounded angry as he exploded at me. "How can you even suggest that? I've no idea why they suspected you." Returning his gaze to the pod window, he looked out at rain-spattered darkness. "This is nothing to do with me. How could it be?"

"I don't know," I said. "It's strange, though, isn't it." Somebody must have tipped off Aballonian security. Told them to expect a visit from me, even I could work that much out. Otherwise, why would they have taken me and Istvan off our original flight?

Looking as if he was refocusing on his reflection in the window, Istvan said nothing. Perhaps he found fault with the square, tough-looking face there, now illuminated by passing street lights.

It was hard to work out how I felt about him, so soon after everything with Ed. Istvan was good-looking, intelligent, appeared composed (sometimes unusually so, in fact), measured, decent. But every so often he became wildly angry, usually for reasons I didn't understand. The thought of asking him if I was doing something to offend him had crossed my mind; I didn't much fancy the explosive rage that might meet my request.

The air in the pod smelt of stale tobacco smoke. As we passed bombed – out ruins, just enough of their old shape surviving to draw a poignant comparison with how things used to be, there was a bad, icky feeling in my stomach. The feeling grew worse as I became aware of the space pod slowing to a halt.

"We're here," said our driver, sounding dourly triumphant.

It was hard to be sure where 'here' was; the streetlights were out and the gappy lettering in a foreign alphabet on the street name wasn't giving away much either. But at least there were buildings, complete, recognisable ones in which you could imagine people living.

"I've got to get the key from the neighbour," I announced, anxious to fill the silence. "She looks after the flat. We arranged it that way."

Arranged it that way back when I was reckless enough to

embark on this foolish expedition, I thought, clambering out of the pod, struggling to get my footing on the rubble and detritus littering the road, aware of pain shooting across my ankle. Getting back my career in journalism was feeling less and less important with every fresh set-back we encountered. If I could get just a safe evening's sleep and a shower, I'd be happy, never mind about fame and journalistic glory.

Picking my way across the columnar bamboo plant stems pushing up through the concrete paving stones, most of them already waist-high, I checked through the instructions Lyudmila had sent me. Nice of her, too, to have sent over the Aballonian convention for naming streets, flats and houses, but it looked so complex I might never master it; I was reluctant to ring the wrong bell and risk waking up one of the neighbours. One of bamboo's side benefits was it was supposed to be helping with climate change, but judging by the loss of feeling in my frozen hands and toes it had a way to go before effecting meaningful improvement on Aballonia.

Feeling uncertain, I jabbed at the button corresponding most closely to the code in my instructions.

"Hello?" The voice sounded foreign, as if unused to speaking Earthen.

"Hello, it's Cathy. The academic. From Earthen, I booked an apartment with you."

"Ah, yes. Let me see." The voice – female – sounded more quivery, older than I'd been expecting after conferencing with her back on Earthen. "Welcome. Come in."

The disembodied voice went silent, a buzz reverberated through the door's metal plating. Taking that as my cue, I pushed at it. It was still surprising, though, when the door yielded. I didn't want to get my hopes up, start imagining the place meant shelter or kindness.

Underneath a collection of keys on the wall in the front lobby was a woman in her fifties or sixties, wearing a garishly coloured headscarf in pinks and reds and dressed in a grubby white plastic jumpsuit that made her look like an extra from Star Wars. But she'd a kind smile and a firm (though not bone-crushing) handshake.

"You've made it at last," she said, squinting at me from behind outsized spectacles. "And brought company too." She glanced at Istvan, her gaze lingering on his nose studs. I'd wondered about those myself, but hadn't liked to say anything.

She rifled through a rack of keys on her desk, selected two and passed them to me.

"One for you, one for your friend." She sounded as if she thought we were more to each other than pals.

"Brilliant, thank you." I blushed with fear I might come across as sarcastic.

The first thing we did once inside the apartment was look in the fridge; there was hardly anything in it.

A wizened and purplish potato-style tuber. A pot of soured (not in a good way) cream. Bits of indeterminate, yellowish gloop coating the metal trays for holding food that might have once been butter. On the floor was a half-empty box of washing powder, sadly inedible.

"Hope you're not feeling hungry." I wasn't sure how he'd respond to discovering there was nothing to eat.

Looking unconcerned, he got up off the sofa, where he'd been reclining, legs wide apart, and padded through in socked feet to the kitchen.

"Got any bouillon?" he asked.

"Ah, yes. Bouillon. Let me see." I didn't want to admit I hadn't a clue what he was talking about.

"You don't know what I'm talking about, do you."

"Don't be ridiculous. Everyone knows about bouillon." I caught his eye and laughed. "Okay, it's a fair cop, I haven't a clue."

To my pleasure, he laughed at my feeble sally. I opened the nearest kitchen cupboard, unsure what exactly I was looking for. All I could see was a small and dirty ceramic pot painted with purple five-petalled flowers holding salt and a tiny spoon for dispensing it, various herbs in brown plastic sachets and sell-by dates from the previous century plus a glass containing a few mismatched forks, knives and spoons, along with a corkscrew still holding a wine-stained cork liberated from its bottle. It smelt pleasant in there, though, making me even hungrier. Aromatic.

Herby. Like at my granny's. Or on a foreign holiday.

"Nothing in here," I announced, trying to sound jaunty. "We can manage without." I wasn't sure we could, though. Not in the slightest.

Looking doubtful, he wandered closer to the counter and picked up the potato. It was no longer difficult to understand why so many in the city and at the spaceport had looked thin, underfed.

"This'll be all right." He picked it up and looked at it with distaste before putting the potato back on the worktop.

"Getting on a bit, isn't it?" I gazed at the shrivelled-up skin.

"What?"

"The potato. Not sure it's edible."

"Yes, it is. We'll have potato soup. I'll make it. We'll be fine."

"If you say so." I wasn't letting my hopes get too high, but was beginning to feel confident enough to risk teasing him slightly.

Despite his promise, dinner was a lacklustre affair. I brought out some bowls with the clearish liquid in them we'd just made. The stuff looked (and, as I would later discover, also tasted) not unlike how I imagined water from a washing-up bowl might.

"We could use straws to drink it." He mimed using a straw, making me giggle.

I didn't like to talk about how at least I'd be losing weight, that didn't seem right, not when most of the planet was facing possible starvation. I could be sensitive, despite what Ed had claimed.

Putting down the straw, Istvan picked up his spoon and began drinking the colourless liquid.

It was all we had on offer that evening. A little reluctantly, I joined him.

As the next few weeks passed, we struggled to settle into the new place. It was filled with scruffy toys belonging, I assumed, to the owner: a dog-shaped pyjama case that always seemed to be raising a quizzical eyebrow at me, as if it silently shared my secret doubts as to the wisdom of this trip, a crocheted hippo made in a medley of blue, yellow and black bamboo-strengthened yarn, whom I mentally christened Happy. The name occurred one afternoon in a fit of no-doubt-absurd hopefulness that I could change our karma through efforts at manifestation. Somehow, though, the presence of someone else's cuddly toys only underlined my sense of alienation, emphasising our current distance from where I considered my real home to be.

My mood usually lightened in the late mornings, though, when the sun arrived on our side of the valley, light bouncing off the beech leaves shivering in the breeze like ping pong balls in a fast-moving game of table tennis. In the square under our flat, we watched as newer leaves eased out the desiccated older ones, which the tree had guarded jealously all through winter, unsure about weathering the cold without a covering of some sort, no matter how aged and decayed.

Most of my time I spent in face-to-face meetings, trying to find out more about the famine, the war and this so-called miracle food that had cost me job and (in a round-about way) my relationship too. Whole weeks passed searching for clues as to the whereabouts of my missing contact, whom I would need if I were ever to prove my story true. I was hampered by not speaking or understanding Aballonian very well, making me almost totally reliant on Istvan for interpreting, although I was swotting up on the language as much as I could.

"I need more detail on the food, as well." We were sitting together by the window that opened out onto the square, eating a meal only slightly more satisfying than the one we'd had on our first night there.

"You mean on whether rice tastes better boiled and then roasted or just boiled? Or maybe marinated in herbs first?"

"You know why I need to track Zoltan down. I'm getting worried he might be a figment of my overactive imagination."

"Hey, come on, you interviewed him, you know he's real. Even if he is elusive. Maybe we'll find out about this new food and it'll be tasty, so we can start eating that." He paused. "If it exists, that is."

"Our cups will runneth over." I couldn't help smiling at my own silly joke. Pathetic of me, really.

As the weeks passed, I came to see Istvan as more fallible, more human, than I'd first thought. I grew used to him loping around the flat, meditating and making long, rambling calls, conducted in rapid Aballonian. Despite my studies, I couldn't yet understand enough to follow what he was saying.

In general, I found the Aballonians guarded in their dealings with me, hardly surprising, given the civil disturbances and food shortages. I was also hampered by having to pretend, at least at first, to be an academic in my dealings with possible sources.

Often while in the flat or out interviewing we could hear sporadic bursts of gun fire, with the distant sound of shouting and smoke from explosives rising above the buildings.

Aware of my clothes gradually feeling baggier and looser, secretly I was pleased with the weight loss from the watery soup diet, but stayed guiltily silent about it, aware others were facing life-threatening food shortages. It wasn't the time to be boasting about weight loss, not when so many were suffering. Even I knew that.

One morning I travelled out to the university, where I was hoping to interview a couple of tutors. Outside the building were two or three wind-chafed protestors. I felt aware of judging them; they were the type who'd have been labelled weirdos at school, the ones whom the cool (for which, read 'cruel') kids would have shunned. The demonstrators were standing their ground today, though, chanting and shouting at the foot of some wide, stone steps leading up to the porticoed entrance of the library. All of them did look a little chilled and desperate, even the boy in the fur coat and balaclava.

I tried to navigate past them, glancing only briefly at their home-made placards with Aballonian writing daubed on them. Wood smoke drifted across from a large metal container serving as a kind of heater and cauldron, reminding me of happier times back home spent camping and making bonfires with Ed, cooking up the fish we'd have caught earlier. I gave myself a little shake to dispel the memories. The fire didn't look as if it was spreading much in the way of warmth; despite the few sparks flying into the morning air, everyone was still stamping their feet and breathing onto their fingers.

Giving the protesters a half-smile, I went to the main university entrance. Walking towards the reception, I began fussing at strands of hair blowing about my face, pushing them back under my hat as best I could.

The receptionist wouldn't make eye contact with me, instead gazing at ledger entries in a crystal in front of her as if seeking a runic, secret knowledge.

"This was arranged weeks ago. Really. I phoned only yesterday to confirm. It's about a joint-research project with a university on Earthen."

The two men in uniform surprised me by their strength and speed, unexpectedly appearing next to me. A practiced aggression to their movements permitted no dissent.

I felt myself lifted off the floor and up into the air, their arms under mine. Solidity on both sides, unshakable.

"What . . . what . . ." I faltered, struggling to locate my voice.

"Go along home, dear," said one of the men. "We don't want you coming here again." They put me down outside the door where I'd just come in.

I walked out unsteadily, aware of my cheeks burning. It felt as if the drumming of the protestors had abated a little, at least enough for me to ask a few questions or strike up some kind of rapport, so I walked over to them, paused and listened for a few moments, shuffling my feet in an attempt to stay warm.

"What's your game plan, then?" one of them asked me. "Police don't want observers around. You not understand that?"

"I want to help you," I whispered to him. "I want to get word out of what's happening here. Please, will you help me? Will you help me and help the people being harmed?"

"No, no, you let them be. Sure you're not a journalist? Certainly sound like one."

"I'm not a journalist," I hissed back, aware I might be betraying myself with my strength of feeling. "I'm trying to help you."

"Help us? Don't make me laugh. I know your type. Only person you're interested in helping is yourself. Number One."

He had a point, horrible though it felt admitting that to myself.

"Okay, this is helping me, but it'll also help you. I can get your message a lot further than a few passers-by. So why don't we work together? You help me with details of this new food and I get word out about what's happening here."

His expression looked less mutinous than before.

"I'll need to think about it, see what the team says."

"Will you tell them I can get word out, help you all?" I paused, feeling genuinely uncertain. "If you'll let me . . .

"I'll need to talk with the others. And we're getting a lot of attention ourselves from the goons." He nodded towards the line of oddly immobile helmeted gentlemen standing guard over by the university. None of the policemen came across as bibliophiles, but sometimes you just couldn't tell with people. Quite why a place of learning should need such strong defenses was another source of mystery.

"Is there somewhere we can go and talk? Privately?"

"This is my apartment." He scribbled words and numbers in Earthen on the back of a cigarette packet, tore off the piece of cardboard and handed it to me. "Meet me here this evening about six. We can talk more then."

We were on our way home from yet another dead-end interview that yielded no fresh information, when the pod came to an unexpected halt. Feeling it slow and lurch to a stop, I turned round to see what was happening. Our driver lifted his hands up from the wheel, then slapped them down again rather too vigorously for comfort.

Getting out of the pod, the first thing I noticed was the unexpected smell of seasonal festivities in the air. Not that there was anything particularly festive about the scene of devastation in front of us; it felt wrong even to be thinking of day-lengthening celebrations faced with so much destruction and loss.

Immediately in front of me were what looked the remains of what might once have been a house for relatively prosperous members of the middle class, now sticking up out of the ground like damaged teeth that not even the most sophisticated dental work could have saved. Effectively, the housing was missing its enamel; the front wall was torn away and collapsed, now just ruined plaster and bricks. What might once have been a large, blue ceramic vase had shattered into pieces. A dog was nosing around in what might have once been the kitchen, pausing in its hunt only to howl mournfully every so often, giving voice to a wider, more collective grief. The smell of marzipan hovered in the star-speckled night, giving a clue to what must have wrought this damage.

Every step I took made a horrible, crunching noise: broken glass being ground into smaller pieces. A few, brave owls were hooting with a low, melodic thrumming, and those leaves left on the sycamore by the road were shaking out their hair, arranging and rearranging it, rustling, whispering and susurrating. In the distance I could hear a pod accelerating further away, doubtless keen to avoid the scene in front of us.

"What's going on?" I tried not to sound as anxious as I felt. Inhaling through my nose, exhaling through my mouth, just like the meditation chip was always saying. Bloody meditation chip.

"What's happening?" I was a journalist, after all, despite denying it, and despite the mistakes I'd been wrongly accused of making. Asking the same question I'd already asked moments earlier, while of course trying to make it sound different, was part of my (former) trade. Sometimes it worked. More often, it didn't.

A crowd of masked protestors was swarming over the road, blocking our way.

"Do something." I was ashamed to own the outdated belief Istvan, being male, should be the one to take action, but not ashamed enough to abandon my pride and beg.

"Press the horn," he shouted to the driver, who did as he was told. The noise made no difference to what was happening.

Bombing and demonstrators had made the flight route impassable, that must have been why we'd stopped. I twisted round to get a better view. Maybe we could simply reverse out, take a different route home. Too many protestors, though, we couldn't have reversed out without the risk of hurting them.

In front of us, I could see a young child – maybe seven or eight? – sitting on a pile of broken stones, dressed all in pink, from her hair band down to her trainers, her thumb inserted into her mouth. In all the destruction, she must have got separated from her parents, no doubt they'd be back soon for her.

Something about her was worrying me, though, but I knew I wouldn't be able to help. I hadn't the beginning of a clue about how to comfort a young child, I'd have been a bad parent, even if things had worked out differently with me and Ed. If this child in front of us thought I could help her, then, seriously, God help her. Because I couldn't.

Breathing out heavily, I watched my sigh make a plume of white smoke in the cold darkness, framed by a concertina of circling hill tops snaking around what yellow squares of light were left in the city.

"Are you okay, sweetheart?" I asked her, crouching down to her level.

She made an audible glooping sound as she took her thumb out of her mouth, and rubbed at her eyes.

I took off my hand-knitted scarf, offered it to her. Her eyes lit up warily at the sight of it. I felt a pang of loss; I'd been fond of that scarf, but her need was greater than mine.

"It's okay. You're safe. I won't let anyone hurt you."

It was an odd sensation, saying those words, feeling that what I was saying was true. I would keep her safe, I would rescue her from whatever danger she faced.

She was shivering like a baby deer in the spring thaw. No jacket to ward off the cold, which was nipping at us. I took my own jacket off and wrapped it around her.

Tears were running down her face and I felt bad for her, though at the same time I couldn't help wondering if this was a scam designed to lure us into a trap to fleece us.

"What are you doing here? Where's your family?" My Aballonian wasn't great, but, like I said, I'd been working at it.

Looking upset, she turned and pointed with her hand at the broken line of houses behind her. "Gone," she said in Aballonian.

Gingerly, I put my arm around her. I couldn't let her down. Just couldn't. And some primitive memory, one I couldn't even properly remember, was making my chest tight with pain.

"Who's looking after you?"

She shrugged with a humility that again made me want to cry.

"Nobody. I am looking after myself."

It was hard to believe she was even close to being up to that job. She couldn't have been much older than eight or nine. Her hair was in pigtails, from which strands of hair had detached. The shadowy light of rescue lanterns dotted about the site was giving her an otherworldly aura. Her dress was thin and dirt-marked, the kind of dirt that looked many days, if not weeks, old and well-nigh impossible to shift.

"The bombers came. They don't like us." Tears ran down her face as she offered me this depressing summary of events, leaving dirt-free vertical rivulets to highlight how dirty the rest of her poor face was. "But now it will be okay, now you are here."

For somebody so young, she'd a tough grip; holding onto me with the ferocity of a spacepod accelerating for take-off.

"Any family nearby?"

She started crying again. She was so thin, her bones were practically jutting out through her clothes. And fragile, too. "I don't have a family," she said, gesturing to the bombing. "Maybe I could come with you?"

That didn't sound great, the idea of looking after her myself. I hadn't a clue how to look after a child. Didn't know how Aballonian social welfare operated either. Byzantine, all-powerful, under-funded, I'd guess. If it even existed . . . Surely there was someone else who could help her? Yes, we were at the farthest possible end of the galaxy, but they'd still need a safety net of some kind?

"I'm Oxie," said the girl.

A good name, I thought. Strong but not weird.

"Cathy."

We shook hands, which felt weird under the circumstances.

I didn't feel like much more than a child myself most days. Maybe my body privately agreed with that assessment, maybe that was why it had deprived me of the chance to be a mother myself. All that blood . . . I shuddered at the memory.

"We'll take you to the police, see about getting you help." I tried to think of something cheerful to say; nothing came to mind. "Some warm clothes."

She didn't look as excited by this idea as I'd hoped. Her face fell and she slid her hand out of mine. I smiled at her and took her hand again, squeezed it gently. She didn't smile back, didn't show any emotion at all. Just a frozen fixity.

"I could stay with you?"

"It'll be okay," I whispered aware that things might be anything but all right, reluctant to say she couldn't stay with me.

"We need to find the police." I really wasn't sure about letting her stay with me, even for just the evening. We needed to find her parents, fast. And get the family back together.

If I took her in, even just for an evening, the Aballonians might accuse me of kidnapping her, send me off to a murky far-away orbit from which I'd never return. She might steal all my stuff. Or have a horrible, communicable disease. Fear got hold of me, lodging somewhere between my chest and tummy. Or she might be a con artist, employed by a gang to play the forlorn orphan.

Maybe my landlady would know what to do.

She took my hand again, hers cold, small and clammy.

"Shall we go now? To your house?"

"No, sweetheart, no. We can't do that, I'm afraid. But we can go to the police and they'll help you."

She began wailing as, hand in hand, we picked our way over the uneven surface of broken stones, toys and other rubble covering the road.

Back at the space pod, we found Istvan looking uncertain.

"What's the plan, then?"

"We'll take her to the police, they can put her up for the night, give her a meal."

"We should help her. I haven't a clue about kids either."

Unfortunately, the police station turned out to be, quite literally, a shell of what it had once been. A shattered and drab husk, really, half of it missing, revealing sudden and unexpected vistas of desks and chairs that looked affronted by unexpected exposure to open air.

Assorted characters were digging around in the wreckage, turning over plaster, bricks, odd pieces of furniture. Looking for plunder, I guessed, at least they seemed like looters, out to mop up what they could.

"What do we do?"

"How about we ask these guys?" He nodded toward a couple of men sorting through the ruins. I'd thought they were scavengers, but, looking more closely, I saw they were in some kind of uniform.

"What should I say?" I hated myself when I felt helpless and lost, like I was betraying the woman I'd worked so hard to be for so many years.

"Ask how they process this kind of case."

I turned to one of the men. "Hello there, you part of the police force?" Embarrassed, I tried to arrange my features into what I imagined was a law-abiding demeanour.

"Us? No." The men laughed, finding my comment hilarious for reasons I didn't understand. "Keep trying, darling. Better luck next time."

It didn't feel like a good idea to ask where I might find some real policemen, so I trudged back to the space pod.

"No, no luck. Look, it's not ideal, but we may have to bring Oxie back with us. There's a camp bed in my room she could have."

Istvan shrugged. Whether to signal annoyed resignation, or good will, I couldn't tell.

"We'll try again with the police in the morning. They must have an emergency set-up somewhere."

Driving away from the remains of the station to our flat, I glanced at the devastation around us. This was more than a few skirmishes; more like annihilation of whole buildings. On the ground lay a broken flag pole, the green and yellow of Aballonia's natural colours stirring listlessly in the night air. It was difficult to imagine it flying proudly anywhere ever again.

Glancing over at Oxie, I saw she'd fallen asleep in the heat of the pod, her head tilting forward with her exhaustion. Falling out of her hand, though, and about to drop into a puddle on the pod floor was the toy I'd noticed when we first found her – a black mouse with shoe-lace whiskers and velvet-lined ears, looking as if he might have provided much comfort to his owner as a transition object to suck on and chew. Gently, I leant forward to pick up the mouse and place him in the little girl's lap again. She didn't stir, but the sleep talking stopped.

Four

IT WAS A gritty, pebble-covered path we were following that day as we tracked through waste land on the city's outskirts. Clouds crowded together into a miasma of dark blue and grey, layers of black percolating downwards through them.

"Let's get pictures," I began to Istvan. "I can do a piece to camera, if that works, and get those foxgloves. Famously poisonous, and all that?"

"Think we can sell footage of this?" As he spoke, his eyes were fixed on a squirrel scampering up one of the scrappy young sycamores.

The muddy, leaf-strewn path where we were walking was still squelchy from the previous night's rain.

"Hoping so. Not much point if we can't sell whatever we get."

Physically, he was in better shape than Ed, I thought, watching him lollop confidently ahead of me. But we worked together, I was the one paying him. He had to be nice to me, I shouldn't read too much into his attentions. It didn't mean he fancied me. And he was maybe married too . . .

"If I ever get you flowers, I'll be sure they aren't foxgloves." He smiled in a way that suggested I shouldn't start banking on any bouquets soon though.

"Very thoughtful. I'll look out some vases." I didn't want him to know I'd have loved him to bring me flowers, that I wished we did have that kind of relationship.

He wasn't blushing even slightly, though Ed would have been crimson by now. It still hurt to think about Ed, even after all these months, even at this distance.

As for Istvan, he was probably just buttering me up because I was his boss, so I made only a non-committal 'mmm-mmm' sound in response.

He responded with a peculiar, sideways look, straight-faced and searching.

"I'm joking!" He turned and smiled at me. "I don't have that kind of money."

"That's okay, relax, I don't expect flowers. Not on what I pay you." The patches of blue we'd seen earlier between strips of grey cloud were disappearing, the miasma and smog of greyness rubbing out the colour.

Grateful for the silence, I walked on, watching out for any of the adders said to hang about that part of the planet. They liked rainy ground, or so I'd heard.

A V-shaped formation of birds was flying across the sky, sweeping ahead with a purpose and direction underlying their noisy, disparate cawing and flapping.

"How'd it go at the university?"

"Not bad." Except for the small issue of the heavies throwing me out, but I wasn't telling him about that.

Quite suddenly, without warning, he leant over towards a hawthorn bush on my side of the path. Was he going to put his arm round me? Had he just grazed my left boob, or was I going mad? I hadn't time to work out how I felt, before he broke off a twig with an urgent, forceful nonchalance and put his arm back by his side again.

"Wha-aaa-aaa-ttt?"

What was happening?

He ignored my question.

"What do you think we should do? About this ban?" He didn't engage with the boob graze.

Glancing at the twig in his hands, he twirled it between his fingers a moment before putting it into his mouth and clenching it tight between chipped and tobacco-stained teeth. What would it be like to snog someone with teeth that bad? My body's treacherous response suggested the experience might have its compensations.

"Perhaps it's time to rethink." His face was oddly expressionless and set.

"What?" After coming all that way? And with so little waiting for me back 'home'? "Don't be ridiculous."

He shrugged, his shoulders rising and slumping down again, but not in the dismissive way he had when he disapproved of something – like me being taken into custody in mid-space or rescuing an orphan from smoking ruins.

The wind was in abeyance, so it was quiet enough to know Istvan was sparing me the theatrical sighs that could accompany this kind of thing.

"It didn't go well at the library today, did it?"

How did he know? And why so pleased about it?

He seemed to read my thoughts.

"I care about you, I can tell when you are upset. I feared the weather there might be stormy."

Something told me that when he spoke about the weather, he was thinking of more than just rainfall, hours of sunshine or humidity.

"How did you hear?"

"On the grapevine. We do talk to each other, us translators."

He nodded, silently, a doleful expression on his face.

For a moment, I thought he might even be crying.

"It wasn't good, at the library, but these things can happen."

Admittedly, they'd never happened to me before, but I wasn't about to tell him that. And I couldn't quit on something so important.

"I'm saying this to help you. Maybe the risks are too high, we should think again."

"What? Give up? You're joking."

"I'm trying to protect you."

"If we quit now, I say goodbye to my old job forever. Plus the money for this trip too."

A woodpecker was hammering at a tree, pecking with a noisy intensity that sounded like the bird wasn't planning on giving up either.

"I'd have to stop paying you too, if we cut this trip short. Isn't that a problem? I can pay you for some of the time I booked you but not the whole six months, I'm afraid."

He looked at the combes furrowing up and down through the far-away hillside, examining the interplay of light and shadow with an abstracted air.

"Your well-being and safety are more important to me than any contract."

Maybe he really liked me, and genuinely wasn't that motivated by money, perhaps he'd already earns enough to be relaxed about the fee. Maybe I was extremely naïve. He'd told me he normally worked for clients who spent more on their people than I did. My vanity wanted to believe he genuinely liked me; but snappers were a hard-nosed bunch, not given to sentiment. Maybe he'd already got a new financial set-up in response to the ban on journalism, he seemed like the kind of guy with contacts, know-how; not the type to go hungry.

Thinking about it, I realised I'd no real idea of how he was fixed for future work; strange, really, since we hadn't known each other long but he already practically knew my bank pin code and how many fillings I'd had (a lot). There'd just somehow never been a gap in the conversation to ask him many questions. Maybe I really just wasn't a very good journalist; the paper had been right to fire me.

"It's a beautiful autumn day; let's enjoy it." His face remained blank.

Without looking at me, he waved an arm at the trees covered with tentacled ivy and the bamboo growing in abundance there too, poles jutting out of rock and earth like a mid-air game of spillikins. "This land is beautiful, isn't it?"

Was it? Not on what I'd seen, no. And the country itself was in a bad way. Fighting for survival, facing twin threats of famine and war. Not blessed, not in my book.

"Yes, absolutely, it's beautiful."

I watched as he bent down and picked up a large, lichen-covered stick from the side of the path. Straightening up, he slammed it down hard on a nearby rock. Whatever his intention, something seemed to misfire, the stick shattering noisily. Frightened, I put my hands to my eyes, shielding them from splinters.

He glanced at what was left of the stick with what looked like disdain, but might have been curiosity, oddly unrattled by the splintering. "Let us think about what we'll have for dinner. Perhaps some good vegetable soup?"

I didn't understand Istvan, aware I was out of my depth with him. But I I needed an Earthen-speaking local as fixer, interpreter and middle-man. I'd no idea where I'd find a replacement, certainly not while I was also pretending to be an academic anthropologist. I needed a photographer for this to work. Without him I wouldn't have a sellable story, the trip would effectively be wasted.

It was just that I wasn't sure what he wanted from me.

"Istvan, I don't mean to be nosy, but why are you working as a fixer?"

After thinking for a moment, he turned to face me. He'd have been good on the stage, I found myself thinking.

"My mum is Aballonian, my dad was from Earthen. I studied languages at university. Translating, fixing was a natural choice, I guess."

I tried to look non-committal.

He began concentrating on the far ridge of mountains, crenellated into an undulating ridge carved out of rock by the volcanic scarring of millennia.

"We got enough pictures now of the countryside?" He gave me a questioning look, that might also have been him laughing at me, though I wasn't sure. Snappers were notorious for spats with writers, I'd known much worse than Istvan. "Time to head home?"

His words meant a slackening of the tension that had started as soon as we set out on this idiotic foray into the countryside. Was the tension sexual? Or professional? Both? Neither?

"Yes, okay, let's head back."

In the carpark, the sight of rivers of sleek black pods made things feel more under control. Only slightly, though.

Sitting down on a bench, I stretched out my legs, enjoying the tang of salt in the breeze, feeling as if it was flavouring my life. Seagulls were cawing overhead, turning with an almost imperceptible angling of a wing, proudly displaying their skill in aerial acrobatics.

After putting his pack on the ground, Istvan sat down next to me. After tugging at a strap on it, he turned to face me. He'd have been good on the stage, I was surprised to find myself thinking.

I kept my eyes fixed on the distant horizon, trying to assume a look of studied neutrality that would mimic a blend of acids and alkalis warring to reach that middle ground where colours settled to an equilibrium.

Leaning forward, looking as if the effort cost him physically, he put his head in his hands, perhaps hopeful the pose might help him gather his thoughts. When he turned back to me, his eyes appeared tear-stained; I felt awful for upsetting him, even worse for wondering if it was an act.

"Oh, dear, look, I don't want to upset you."

The wind was whipping in from the sea, bringing with it a foamy and metallic breeze scented with brine. Birds swooped overhead on the invisible motorways of the skies.

The day was darkening, a flock of birds squalling noisily as they passed overhead. Sunset came in fast for all three of Aballonia's suns at this time of year. I got to my feet.

"Talk more at home? Got to get back."

He zipped up his waterproof and pulled his hat a little lower on his head, obscuring his fair hair.

"Let's go?" He pulled his ethnic muffler in orange and red up higher onto his neck and offered me a hand to get up from the bench – an ironic gesture, I thought, and so one that I jokily declined - before we both turned towards our pod.

When we got home, I immediately wished we'd stayed away longer. Two men were standing outside the apartment block, blotting out the light, blotting out everything except a sense of their domineering presence.

Masks on their faces, goggles over their eyes. At last I understood what people meant when they talked about their blood dipping in temperature, not that I'd a thermometer handy to be sure.

"Cathy Prior? That you?" said one of the two figures through his mask.

"Me? No, I'm a friend of a friend of hers. She's not here. Said something about staying at a friend's tonight." I tried to make my face suggest that this Cathy was also a volatile tear-away who might not be following through on her plans.

The mask-and-goggle combo made them hard, no, impossible to read. I thought about a fake laugh but decided against it. You could tell these guys had come to the party prepared for trouble.

"Got this friend's coordinates? Where she's staying tonight?"

This was getting tricky, the 'friend' didn't exist outside my imagination, as they'd maybe already worked out. I didn't like them referring to me as 'she' either; I wasn't a criminal, after all, well, not officially.

Taking my crystal out, I pretended to scroll though some of its zones. "No, sorry."

One of the neighbours passed with a shopping trolley, giving me a kind smile as she pulled her load along.

"Got a number for Cathy herself?" asked the shorter of the two men.

A number? For myself? I thought they'd have already had that, from when I first entered their accursed orbit.

"Not sure." Why did my voice always sound so reedy, almost tortured whenever I was on divert from the broad super-astroway of the truth? "No, sorry. She's very private, doesn't give out her number much."

"Bit odd, that, in a journalist, isn't it?"

For a moment, I almost fell for their trick, my mind working slowly.

Almost.

A last-minute save rescued me, the neurons connecting up with each other just in time. "But she's not a journalist, of course. I don't think journalism's allowed here, is it?" I tried to make my features assume what I imagined was an air of honest confusion, creasing up my eyes to convey puzzlement.

The men turned to each other, speaking in Aballonian too fast for me to understand.

"We need that number. Give us your crystal."

"I can't do that," I began, my tongue struggling to form the words, the crystal's zones slick with my sweat. "I promised not to give anyone her number. Unless you've got a warrant."

"You hear from her, let us know. We'll be back with a warrant if necessary."

"How do I get in touch with you?" I was secretly hoping never to have any more dealings with them, but felt reluctant to share that with my visitors.

"We're not difficult to find."

"Okay." My mouth felt odd, dry. I couldn't imagine asking this lot for directions if I got lost.

It was the first sighting that was the worst.

The door to our flat was swinging loosely on its hinges, leaving entry free to any and all in the vicinity. Books, papers, pictures were scattered over the floor, along with broken glass. My stomach tight with fear, my throat hollow. I was a straw woman, insubstantial and light-weight, thinner and more weightless than a summer cloud.

Aware of Istvan's hand on my arm, I felt grateful for the reassurance of physical contact with another human.

"Not this. Oh, please, no." But it had happened, someone had broken into our flat.

Oxie was meant to be downstairs with Mrs Patcha, who'd agreed to watch her while we went out. Please God, she was safe and had missed our visitors.

Running downstairs two steps at a time to the Patchas, I held on lightly to the banister. At their flat, I began hammering on the door with both hands.

"What's wrong?" began Mrs Patcha, looking dismayed as she opened the heavy steel door.

"Is she okay? Is she okay?"

"Yes, she is fine. Look, you can see for yourself."

Oxie looked puzzled as I wrapped her in the tightest, longest hug I could remember giving her, and wriggled away, squirming like a fish desperate to be released back into the ocean from which she'd been plucked.

"Oh, no. You're crying." She sounded worried for me.

Clumsily, I tried to wipe the salty wetness away, poking myself in the eye as I did so, making more tears drip down.

"Silly me. I'm fine." I choked a little on all the snot and tears.

"What's wrong?"

"Nothing's wrong, my love." Fishing tissues out of my gilet pocket, I blew my nose more noisily than intended. But as long as she was okay, nothing else mattered, I understood that now, I wouldn't necessarily have been such a disaster as a mother, though I could have arguably done with some more support from my co-parent, but maybe everyone felt that way.

"It's all good. All good."

Together we walked back upstairs slowly to our flat.

Gingerly, I stepped over the threshold, frightened the thieves might still be inside. Maybe if I'd left an 'x' scratched into the lintel this wouldn't have happened, I thought; how strange our thoughts in moments of crisis could be.

"It's okay," said Istvan, looking tense, walking out of his room.

"No, it's not." I felt calmer after finding out that Oxie was okay, but wasn't prepared to accept everything was okay. Not when it was obvious things were far – very far indeed – from being even close to 'okay'. "It's not effing okay. I've got to go to the loo. Oxie, sweetheart, I'll get you some juice in a second."

She raised her head and smiled at me, in a hesitant way.

I didn't even notice it at first, my emotions too jangly and discordant.

It was only after I got off the toilet and was pulling up my knickers and leggings around my stomach that I spotted it.

The message was typed, making me think at first it was a bill of some sort, perhaps a reminder or final demand my landlady had helpfully stuck to the mirror.

"Stay away from our planet. Or you pay."

Grabbing the piece of paper, I unpeeled it from the mirror, where it was stuck on with blu-tack. I felt I needed to gag.

Hoping I'd misread it, I steeled myself to read it again. I swallowed, looked at it once more – no, no mistake. I couldn't afford to pretend I hadn't seen it. That wouldn't help us.

Not bothering to wash my hands, I unlocked the door, breathed in deeply, and ran down the stairs two at a time.

The hand holding the letter felt as if it were turning fiery red, contaminated forever by the hatred on the paper scrunched up in my fist. The note couldn't have been up there very long or it would have turned damp with the condensation in there. It might have come from those guys claiming to be coppers we'd seen outside.

"Istvan?"

The door to the sitting room was already half open. There could be no going back to the past, the illusory rose garden of joy and contentment.

"Istvan." For the first time since meeting him, I felt a genuinely whole-hearted relief at seeing him again.

"We need to get out of here." I held out the note to him, feeling lighter and happier as soon as I passed it over, though also disappointed that my hand was wobbling as I held it out. "Please. It's not safe here. We've got to leave."

He took the paper from me, unfolded it, straightened it, and scrutinised it through wire-framed glasses. At least he was taking it seriously, a good omen, I hoped, though in a back-to-front way I didn't entirely understand.

I sat down onto the sofa, oblivious to the doll underneath me, only realising it was there as I felt something sharp pushing into my bottom. Rearing up again, I pushed aside various cushions to unearth Alfreda.

Istvan tapped a communicator. "You're right. This isn't a safe place."

"Yes, but where is?" Almost anywhere else would be good.

Slight problem - I hadn't noticed any hotels operating there.

"I'll find somewhere for us."

I loved it when he spoke in that masterful, protective way. Even while also feeling uneasy about being even slightly subservient to him.

"Leave it to me." He scrolled through messages, not meeting my gaze.

"I'll start getting some things together. For me and Oxie. And you as well, if you like?" I wasn't sure I knew him well enough to start packing his things. Man things. Different, foreign to my own kit.

"Leave my stuff. I'll bring it myself." He sounded insistent, maybe embarrassed about me seeing his private things.

In my room, I opened the wardrobe and delved under a line of jangling coat hangers to get my case. I'd have to leave a lot of my stuff there, it hardly mattered.

Lifting the bag up onto the bed, I unzipped and opened it. There was a jumper in there I hadn't even bothered to unpack. It could stay behind; I'd never liked it much anyway.

Walking into the bathroom that led off our room, I spotted Oxie's skin cream for her eczema. We'd need that. Shampoo, toothpaste, toothbrushes, soap, flannels and medicines followed into the case's waterproof section.

Its weight made it difficult to lift down off the bed. Maybe Istvan could help pack it into the back of the pod, I wondered. I needed to stock up on some food for the journey, which wouldn't be easy, given the shortages.

Yet again, I wondered what I was doing there, when I could have stayed at home, in the land of plenty.

Too late to regret my decisions, there were no more flights off the planet.

"I've found somewhere for us," he announced, sheathing his crystal like an ancient warrior might his sword.

"That's good." How had he managed that? I'd tried a few places myself without success; the entire planet was in chaos, verging on civil war.

"Far away?" I felt like a tourist asking about the strength of sun factor needed.

He gave me a sharp look, the kind a parent might to a naughty child badgering them for sweeties.

"You do pay me to be your fixer. Just doing my job." He sounded peremptory. "The place is just around the corner."

"What d'you mean?"

"I mean that when we go out of the main door to this building we turn left, walk down the street and go into the entrance of another building, where we'll stay." He gazed at his fingernails.

"I've come across the idiom 'just round the corner' before. The thing is…" I gazed at him.

"Yes?"

"I've a feeling we might be able to put this story together if we head north, to Platignall. Zoltan had contacts there."

He blinked.

"To the mountains? No way."

"What's your problem with the north?"

"I don't have a problem with it. It'd just be safer to stay here for now."

I didn't want an argument with him about what we had or hadn't agreed. Instead, I turned to Oxie.

"Come on, we're leaving."

Hand in hand, Oxie and I walked out to my grubby and battered-looking pod. As I stowed the case in the boot, I noticed a gentle haze of mist clinging to the walls and roof of our block. It would evaporate as soon as the suns returned – due to happen in less than an hour. We could already see the first tentacles of dawn preparing to edge up over the hills as I moved the pod into forward flight. As we set off, gravel from the roadside spattered noisily against the pod's metallic blue undercarriage.

Five

OUT OF A paint-spattered radio on a table on the balcony came music that sounded vaguely classical, though I couldn't have named the composer, which bothered me. Glancing up, I watched the sky mellow and meld into the land, fusing together gases, liquids and earth. I could do with making some connections too, though admittedly of a more mundane kind; progress on this story wasn't going well; I wasn't happy about what had happened back in the capital either. Death threats on the bathroom mirror . . . Maybe I should have stayed with Istvan, he might have offered protection against whoever wrote the note.

Sighing, I walked up some stone steps leading onto more of the terrace, and walked over to Oxie, who was surrounded by large, terracotta pots of geraniums almost as big as her.

A housekeeper was carrying a pot of tea and a small loaf of bread out from the kitchen, the food peeping out from underneath an old-fashioned white dish cloth, decorated at the edges with woven green lines. She looked so tired, distractedly trying to wipe fly-away hair out of her eyes, that I didn't like to ask if we could have another tea bag.

"Don't worry, we'll share," I said quietly to Oxie.

The tea bore only the faintest relation to the stuff I'd known back home, it was more like how I imagined muddy pond water might taste, but I didn't like to complain. The poor woman looked so tired.

At least Oxie's pinafore was reasonably clean. I'd found a cake of dried-up hand soap in the hostel where we were staying and used it to do laundry in the toothpaste-coated wash-hand basin in our room.

The suns were all shining so brightly that at first I could hardly see who it was sauntering onto the terrace; it was only as I clocked the air of relaxed holidaymaker – an appearance too forced to be entirely convincing – that the new arrival gave himself away.

What was he doing there?

"Lovely morning, isn't it?" He flapped a hand casually in the air as he spoke, his other hand trailing through the bougainvillea trained up against the house. Wrap-around sunglasses hid most of his face.

"Cathy. Hello there."

I'd never understood why he liked to begin whatever he said by stating my name. Like I was a suspect in a criminal investigation or something. Did he expect me to confirm or deny my identity?

"Istvan, wow. Wasn't expecting to see you here."

"Couldn't leave you here to fend for yourselves."

"No, well. Suppose not. It's good of you to come here."

"Not at all, it's my job. Slept well?"

"Yes, thank you." I'd barely slept a wink, tormented by nightmares about events back on Earthen, missed deadlines and bogus information, dreams that had (unlike the information) felt all too real in the silent darkness. "How about you?" I felt mildly embarrassed, he'd appeared in quite a few of the dreams, in all of which I'd been aware of a strong and unfulfilled sexual longing. My hand shook as I poured out more of the liquid we were pretending was tea.

"How'd you find us?"

"Remembered you saying you wanted to come to this part of the planet. Made a judgment, put in a few calls . . ."

It was true only a handful of hotels were still operating in the area, he wouldn't have had to make many calls to track us down. Flattering, really, that he cared enough to follow us.

"Okay if Oxie and I go for a walk?" said the housekeeper.

I nodded. "Of course. Have a nice time. Be careful of the snakes."

After they set off, Istvan and I were left alone together. Alone. And together. There were a few questions to answer – how long we'd stay in hiding, what exactly had happened back in the capital. Was I alone in these sexual feelings or was he feeling them too? Should we act on them? Nothing important, just major, life-changing stuff.

"You're sad." Istvan gazed at the reddish hills slumbering under a duvet of suns. "Don't be. We can head home today or tomorrow."

Home? We'd only just left.

"You're also scared."

I wasn't liking the character indictments. They felt like criminal charges, but maybe I was being over-sensitive again.

Annoyingly, it was his kindness that made the tears began to well up, pricking at my eyes like tentative, slanty rays of morning sunlight across mountain tops. I didn't want him to see my weakness.

"Why so sad?" Still, he wouldn't meet my eyes, something in the fiery landscape taking all his interest.

We didn't know each other well enough for this kind of talk.

He stretched out, a big lion preparing to sun himself on the savannah.

"Not sad. Just upset about what happened and feeling like we're going round in circles on this story." I tried to smile. It felt as if we were going round in circles on much else besides.

It was difficult to know how jokey I could be; he'd the energy of a caged Jack-in-the-box; I didn't want him springing out and smacking me on the face.

All three suns were mounting higher, reminding me of other mornings, other places, other times. Other skies. A sudden pang of homesickness bowled across my heart.

As I spoke, I became aware of how little my words related to how I actually felt; no wonder they sounded hollow, damaged, off-key.

He harrumphed in seeming disapproval, giving me a glimpse of the man he might become when older. For a brief moment, I felt as if I'd met his father.

"I want to help you. We're a helpful people."

They hadn't come across as particularly helpful when I'd had to leave the capital in a hurry to avoid jail.

"Yes, you've all been very kind." A lie. I felt nervous even just thinking about being taken into custody back at the airport, a welcome that had set the tone for most of the subsequent events that followed. Okay, they hadn't clapped me in irons and made me wear an orange jumpsuit, but even I could see it hadn't been the friendliest of greetings.

"It was just a bad moment back in the capital."

"You're telling me." My mouth pursed involuntarily.

Shaking out my hair, I became aware of needing more deodorant. Whether I'd be able to find any was another question altogether.

"But we can go back now."

"Er, what?"

"To the capital. Get the flat cleared up, change the locks, talk to the police, explain we're doing nothing wrong. Get those bastards off our backs."

"You've become quite the optimist, haven't you."

"No, no. Maybe you just over-reacted? In the heat of the moment?"

"Over-reacted? Do you remember what happened?"

He shrugged, suggesting the memory remained conveniently elusive.

"Armed police officers broke into our home. Tried to arrest me."

He remained impassive and silent.

"Why aren't you saying anything? You were there, you know how bad it was. I know you do." Actually, I wasn't sure of his view. He was impossible to read as he pushed a packet of sugar around the table.

Glancing at the hills, the trees, the blueness, I saw all three suns slanting across the sky, carving out a horizon.

"It'll be safe there now."

"You can't know that. And I've research to do here. I haven't come thousands of miles to give up now. I've a lead from back home, I'm following it up this evening. Come with me, if you want." I paused, swallowed. "You're not the only fixer here, you know. If you really want to go back, I could find someone else?" There weren't any other fixers around there, or none I knew of. I was just praying he didn't know that.

I took another sip from the water we were all pretending was tea. If anything, the food situation here was even worse than back in the capital, which was odd, with so much farm land around. My stomach rumbled. Why had I ever come to this benighted planet?

Then I remembered...

"Cathy, ah, got a minute?"

Brief but meaningful looks between people in our constellation of desks, followed by a furtive attempt to pretend they were looking at something else.

When I got to his office, Barberton looked subdued, which didn't bode well.

"Sit down. Sit down."

"Thank you." I'd never known him so polite before.

"We're letting you go." He fixed me with a look that seemed to warn me not to protest at this news.

"Okay." A stabbing, wounding pain darted across my chest.

His eyes still fixed on me, he leant out a hand to a box of heal-all tissues and passed them to me.

"Why are you doing this?" It might hurt less if I just understood.

Baberton gave me what I think he imagined was a piercing stare. "You must already know why we're doing this. Surely?"

Of course I knew. He'd never much liked me, now he'd the ammunition he needed.

Rearranging his trousers, he turned back to the screen.

The humiliation and pain felt like arrows penetrating my flesh.

"It wasn't my fault the source did a runner."

Baberton rubbed a hand over his eyes. Stale alcohol wafted toward me.

"We're letting you go. Your story fell apart."

Wiping away the tears, I stumbled to the door.

"Pick up your cheque on the way out."

Dead leaves scuttled in muddy circles on the pavement as I walked back to the Tube and struggled to digest the news. Overhead, the condensation trail of a cigar-shaped plane wended across the sky. As I watched, I became aware of wanting to be going wherever it was, and carried on watching until the plane's smoke trail began to evaporate into the blue canvas of sky.

Six

AT FIRST, I thought the insects swarming over the spoil heap dominating our view of the landscape were bees but, in fairness, we were sitting some yards away. They weren't insects at all, it later turned out. Only when I stuck my head out the pod window to look more closely did I realise they were actually orchids. Orchids that had been designed to look like the little creatures, presumably in hopes of attracting pollinators. It was oddly comforting, in an admittedly strange way, to know it wasn't only me who sometimes got confused when it came to sexual relations.

As well as the 'bees', I could see the inevitable forest of bamboo making a mess everywhere. No containment method I'd ever come across could have tamed that growth.

I'd come there hoping to spot a potential target. So far, at least, the place looked dominated by nothing worse than the inevitable, striated lines of hollow and jointed grasses, their apparent delicacy belied by their profusion.

I was sitting with Istvan in this run-down area of desiccated countryside to follow up a lead given weeks earlier, but, like everything else on this story, nothing was going quite to plan.

"Give it another couple of hours, then head back? We're not getting anywhere. We could grab a meal while we're out?" He knew how much I loved eating out, though I couldn't often afford it.

"I can't, sorry. Not enough money left this month." I gazed out the window at the dirty beige boxes of mud-based buildings.

"Never mind. I'll make halloumi at home later."

Although Spoil Heap Central looked unpromising, it could be a step to clearing my name. Maybe . . . I'd to follow up every tip, check every detail, follow every instinct that told me something was wrong . . .

Reaching for a bottle of water, I wondered again if I was dressed right. The black outfit someone back at the lodge had lent me had more frills than I'd have ideally liked, and the fabric rustled every time I moved, making me think of when I tried to dress up like a gypsy as a child by tying old curtain rings to my ears. At least today I was wearing nice gold studs; some things really did get better, like that old therapist of mine was always trying to claim, not that I'd really believed her.

"I stick out, don't I."

He was peeling a peach with a penknife and doing so rather precisely, looking grateful that concentration on the task prevented him from talking much.

"No, you're okay." Istvan gave me a brief glance, turning away from the peach for a moment. In fairness, most of us hadn't even seen fresh fruit in more than a decade, it was only right he was paying proper attention to what he was doing.

"I'm wearing this to try and blend in," I said, as mildly as I could. "The black clothes, I mean." The get-up wasn't as obtrusive as my more obviously Earthen clothes. Sometimes birds changed colour to get through severe weather conditions, maybe changing my look would help me. "And I can smarten it up if need be."

The surrounding hillsides glistened like loaves slowly baking in the oven, a dense smokiness coming off them and evaporating as heat transformed and solidified them. Further down the hillside, an under-storey of heather, bilberry, oak and birch radiated heat, and, with it, aromas of inaccessible, hidden parts of the planet, now slowly bubbling to the surface.

It was a relief to clock some action. Through the dirty, splash-marked windows of the jeep, I spotted someone shuffle out of what looked like a disused factory next to the spoil heap.

Gently, I nudged Istvan with my elbow, doing so carefully for fear of startling him and making him say anything loud enough to attract our target's notice. We watched as a dapper, middle-aged man in a business suit walked briskly to a space pod, unlocked it and climbed inside. Heart racing, I began following him at a distance.

Luckily for us, our target seemed a sociable type; it was outside a roadside taverna he eventually pulled up, maybe hoping to impress the locals with his get-up.

"This is good," I said, as I pulled over.

"Is it? That place's a dive. I'm not eating there."

"Yes, it is good. Means we can engineer a conversation with

him. Easy."

"You sure about this?"

It wouldn't be easy, and, no, I wasn't sure, but I had to try. Or felt as if I did. So many years of work making me cancel on friends, who'd eventually given up and disappeared from my life. Of long, dirty, sweat-infused nights battling for space among the ruling egos of the newsroom, of seeing my stories posted no further than the spike. Years of guys who lost interest in me, because I'd no time to give them. Hanging around dingy, desolate bars in nowhere-land, places like this, reliant on whatever alcohol I could get to make the horror bearable. The loneliness and sordid despair. I couldn't abandon my career now, not after investing so much in it, no matter how much I hated it. No other news outlet would even consider me for work until I cleared my name, not after my recent misadventures had got me blacklisted across Earthen.

Istvan sighed and began concentrating on a sign advertising the bar's special offers that month. Something called 'Rootlings' featured big; whatever they were. Alcohol? Food? Turds? I felt an immediate distrust for them, a distrust worsened by the picture next to them of indeterminate animal parts.

The bar was annoyingly scarce in people, which would make it harder to strike up some sort of connection with our target, although I was surprised to find myself rather liking its grubby unpretentiousness, despite what Istvan said. Wooden chips covered the floor, rather like in the old butchers' shops back on Earthen. They'd stick to my suede pixie boots, but that was a small price to pay if this guy led to uncovering the story that some magical new food had been created on Aballonia. The furniture and fittings looked as if they were all made out of the same bendy yet tough wood – almost certainly bamboo – as the sawdust and chips, all of them bearing the dull, grubby patina of age. Some of the bar fittings were even shooting out their own bamboo tentacles.

As soon as I pushed open the surprisingly light door – one of the plant's later iterations, I guessed - I walked straight to the loos; only sensible to check my appearance before launching into battle mode. Standing in front of a speckled mirror lit by a single dirty light, I looked at my reflection. Tousled dark hair. Pale skin. Teeth that stuck out a tiny bit more than they should. Big eyes. I squirted more perfume behind both my ears. Got out my lipstick, a subtle pink I rather liked. Applied it to my lips, blotted them with a paper towel. Okay. Ready to go. A few deep breaths first, steady my nerves. No resorting to alcohol, however tempting, or I'd screw everything up. Again.

Out in the bar, the music was throbbing. Neolithic Bird Boys. If I hadn't been scared out of my wits, I might even have secretly enjoyed the ballad's sentimental melody, while of course pretending an ironic detachment from it. Only a handful of people were there, but a thick fug of smoke hung over the place, maybe left over from the previous crowd; Aballonia was the bad boy of the universe, they hadn't got around to outlawing stuff that felt mediaeval in more enlightened places. I was missing Earthen badly, missing the damp mistiness, its changeable weather, the sturdy yet affable determination of its people to make what they could of their lives, no matter the obstacles. I wanted to be among my own kind again. To go home.

Fluffing up my hair, I walked up to the bar. The place was designed in a not-entirely-successful attempt to conjure up an ambience of tropical ports, but was warm, lit shadily and offered access to my target.

He was standing propped up against the bar. Mid-height. Thinning hair. Stocky. A taut, shut-down, taciturn look on his face.

It should be easy enough to pull off a initial connection. Me as ditzy bohemian in need of a big strong man to protect me. Him as rescuer. Believe me, I thought of Ed as I perched on a bar stool near the wall, getting ready to play the routine – and missed him so much it hurt. But I needed to keep sentimental nonsense out of this.

I waited until the target tried to get more drink.

It wasn't clear why it was taking so long to serve the guy, they weren't exactly rushed off their feet. Maybe the bar man didn't like my new would-be friend, wanted to make him wait, maybe he knew something about him. Moving slowly, I walked towards the centre of the bar, my heart pounding with anxiety.

"What can I do you for?" The barman hadn't a problem taking

my order, I noted.

"A beemer, please." The drink wouldn't distract me, no association there with happier times, and it was non-alcoholic.

"You're in luck. Don't normally have much in stock, got a delivery just the other week."

"Good stuff." I sipped at the malty brew, aware of its impact on my tongue, mouth and throat. A final gulp, and I got up from my stool, pushing it back so I could stand up, get a better view of my target. Smoothing down my skirt, I breathed in and out deeply before walking over to the focus of my efforts.

"Hello there." I felt like a prostitute hooking a client in the back streets of a dirty port, but that was the fourth estate . . .

"Hello." He looked unsurprised to see me. "You took your time." Unlike him, I was surprised at him and his turn-out: the suit was surprisingly well-cut, his cuff links expensive and discreet, the shirt opened just enough – not too much, not too little. No jewellery, except a friendship bracelet threaded around his right wrist.

"What do you mean?"

He glanced at me. "You've had your eye on me since you walked in here."

"No, I haven't." In fairness, he was right. I obviously just hadn't been discreet enough.

I thought again of why I had to do this: prove myself to my world back on Earthen, prove I still deserved to be a journalist. That I was the ruthless, amoral huntress they wanted. Didn't feel much like one though . . .

Pushing my hair back, I rubbed my fingers behind my ears, hoping my perfume would waft towards him, though the air was thick with smoke.

I maybe overdid it with the ears because I felt an earring come loose and detach itself. Damn, but this could work to my advantage though it'd be messy. Falling to my knees, I started feeling for it with my hands. Lots of broken crisp fragments, wedges of used chewing gum, fag ash; I wanted to retch. Then I saw the earring, behind a leg of a bar stool, but pretended I hadn't. Best for him if I could make him think he was the big strong rescuer, finder of the earring.

"I simply can't see it anywhere," I began.

He placed his pint glass down on the zinc counter, then slid off his barstool and got down onto his hands and feet – a brave move, given the state of the floor.

"Here it is," he said, triumphantly handing me the earring, a glass rose.

"Very kind. Think I owe you a drink." I tried to twinkle.

"Let the champagne flow." He sounded sourly pleased.

"Champagne, what a great idea." I couldn't really afford anything that expensive, that'd take the rest of my dwindling pot of money, but I'd little choice. "I'm Tam, by the way." I wasn't, but never mind.

"A bottle of Pol Roger," he said to the bar man, making me wince again at the expense.

Glancing through the shuttered front windows, I could see seven moons dotted irregularly across the night's horizon, their haziness filtering into the darkness, looking as if a careless planetary God had thrown a handful of them against the sky and let them lie wherever they fell, their maker too busy with more important business to bother arranging lunaries and luminaries. They were doing their best against the encroaching darkness, but it still looked as if night would envelop them.

"What brings you to Aballonia, then?" He looked as if it was well-rehearsed patter.

"I'm an academic." I wasn't going to tell him what I was really doing. "We're trying to find out more about links between the Aballonian and Earthen cultures." Did I sound suitably serious?

"Fascinating." He took a measured gulp of champagne and gazed at my breasts. "Interesting work?"

"Sometimes." I didn't want him asking more about my job or other equally fictional attributes. "It can depend. Some years easier than others. I'm sure you have a far more interesting life than me." From under lowered eyelids, I watched to see how he was taking my flattery.

"Me? I'm an engineer."

"Wow. That sounds terribly important. You're just being

modest."

Even in the subdued bar lighting, the locket Ed had given me when we first met still glistened above my dress's neckline. I'd forgotten to take it off, I realised, a Freudian oversight probably.

"Too much flattery, Tam. You want more than my body."

Inwardly cringing, I forced out an unconvincing giggle.

Outside, the light was changing with the planet's tidal motions, a group of geese flocking across the sky, just visible in the waning light. A beacon of homing instinct driving them forward across unknown airways.

As he reached out for his glass, I spotted a wedding ring on his left hand – a plain, thick gold band without embellishment.

It was a shock when he put the same hand on my leg, complete with the ring. Even my metallic tights weren't enough to stop a tremor of revulsion shuddering through me at his touch. I wasn't quick enough to stop myself recoiling.

"Let's go somewhere we can be private. I can book a room for us at a place in town I use for this sort of thing." He took out his crystal, started calling a number on it.

I pretended to be interested in the fan revolving on the ceiling, while working out a response. Just how desperate would anyone have to be to go for this kind of move by Lover Boy? Insulting that he thought I'd stoop so low . . . The place felt sweltering, I could feel sweat trickling down my forehead. My treacherous body was beginning to betray me too, although the guy mostly just revolted me I could also feel a vague thrum of sexual interest stiffening my nipples. Between my legs, a hint of the old ache of desire and almost-painful longing, mixed with disgust at myself for feeling that way.

The bar felt pretty lawless, the couple of other women there were keeping their heads down. Maybe I ought to be more like them, but chaos and danger drew me in ineluctably, as if I were a piece of hair tangled in the air currents and machinery of a hairdryer.

"What about where you work? Out in the wilderness, is it? Why don't we go there?"

"What, out in the boonies?"

"Why not? You're not scared, are you?"

"Okay. Come on, I'll drive you out, give you a tour. Plenty of space in my office."

My heart galloping, I gave him a smile intended to be provocative, though it may have looked more like I'd stomach trouble.

"Great. I'm on for that." I picked up my handbag from the back of my chair. What the hell was I doing? This guy frightened me. "You sure you're safe to drive, though?"

He surprised me by taking a mouthful of water and suddenly seeming sober, his head and body straightening without the swerving of earlier.

"Maybe I'm not as drunk as you think," he said, looking absurdly proud of himself. "Come on, let's go."

"We haven't got to know each other yet." My armpits were soggy with sweat, despite the super-strength deodorant put on that morning. "I don't even know your name…"

"Alex."

"So." I cocked my head to one side. "I was promised a tour of this place." I paused, not wanting to sound too keen. "If the offer's still good?"

"Course it is. Let's chip."

The only other person left in the bar was a young boy with bucket and mop wiping down the floor with an air of resignation. He'd a pass key for the juke box and pressed a few buttons on it, making it light up. As I heard Chrissy Hynde's voice tell in plangent, hypnotic lyrics of love and hate, I walked toward the bar exit. Alex didn't bother to hold the door open for me, as I'd assumed he would; I felt myself recoil as the lignin swung back faster than I'd expected, tapping me hard on the side of the face. With my hand, I tried to stop the pain by patting at it. It didn't work. Although the door looked as if it was made from a lighter, newer version of bamboo, getting smacked on the face by it still hurt. Fair to say at that point my feelings toward him were an undiluted dislike, but the evening was yet young. If I could get a break on the story from him, that might make me change my mind, but I wasn't banking on it. The night air felt blessedly cool against my face as we walked away from the lights of the bar; then, somewhere in the darkness, a nightingale began to sing; loud, melodic, haunting, piercing and pure, sounding as if his notes were meant to encourage me to go forward. Pushing hair out of my eyes, I kept walking.

Seven

GRIMY WITH SAND, the dirt-spattered wooden hoarding in front of us bore traces of what might once have been a picture of a canine, but it was hard to be sure. Most of the paint had rubbed off a long time ago.

As I got out the pod, my body struggled to adjust to the cold. Some real dogs were howling, a few foxes prowling about, staring at us with a bullet-faced insolence as they sloped across the gravel.

Walking over to a featureless side door, I watched as Alex felt in his jacket pocket a moment before unearthing a bunch of keys.

"So retro." I laughed a moment too long to sound natural.

He didn't join me in my forced laughter, instead giving me a serious look and appearing to focus harder on fitting a key into the lock, trying different ones before succeeding. I got a feeling whatever lay on the other side of the door might not be entirely benevolent, and being near this guy was definitely making me anxious. I couldn't let that stop me now. If I gave up, the whole thing would be a waste of time, money, dreams and hopes. No turning back, not now. If I didn't manage to clear my name, almost as besmirched by now as the dog food sign, I'd be lucky to be writing badly-paid advertising copy for arseholes like this guy, if they'd even have me.

After finally opening the door, he turned back to me and smiled, his teeth white and almost vulpine in the light from the moons. "Not long now." Catching me unawares, he put out a hand and stroked my arm. To my horror, I felt myself respond to his touch.

"Steady there, tiger." I was struggling not to slap him. "Are we even meant to be here?" It was an effort to make my voice sound jokey. Nausea tugged at my stomach, the sickness fuelled by feelings of self-hatred and disgust.

"Course not," said Alex, not bothering to pull back his hand. "Wouldn't be much fun if it was allowed, would it?"

The interior wasn't what I'd been expecting: inside were white, pristine, antiseptic, steel surfaces. A smell of disinfectant. All rather different to the scruffy, unkempt exterior. My shoes squeaked on the floor; a frisson of unease passed through me. I was trained in self-defence, like every journalist I knew. One problem; I hadn't kept up my basic practice beyond the obligatory first few months.

Furtively, I looked around for anything I could use as a weapon; I'd maybe seen a broom propped up against the wall in the corridor. Yes, good. Trying to be insouciant, I picked it up, bouncing it in my hands, judging heft and weight, pretending a sudden interest in housekeeping.

"Going to use that on me, are you?"

"Don't be ridiculous. Of course not." I tried to make my features look as if this place was a dream come true. Which, in a weird way, it was, but not how he thought. "Just stretching after the journey. I get a bit stiff sometimes." As soon as the words left my mouth, I regretted them.

"Very interesting. It's quite an honour, you know, coming back here with me. I often get stiff. Hoping you can help me with that."

"And you're really allowed to have the keys to this whole space?" It must be a dump if they gave access to an idiot like him.

He smirked. "Perk of the job. Many people know you're here?"

Nobody else knew.

There hadn't been time to phone Istvan before leaving the bar, he wouldn't have been able to follow us.

"One or two."

He grunted.

I tried to keep my features neutral as we walked through yet more of the endless corridors, me battling my inner panic.

"Lots of people track me twenty-four/seven."

A lie.

I hadn't had time to tell anyone, meeting Alex had felt like a one-off opportunity to get into the factory, one that would disappear unless I acted on it fast. "What's this new stuff you're making here, then? Not dog food, is it?" I wasn't loving the unmistakable smell of human fear; a rancid odour that spoke of sweat, pain, faeces, terror.

"Might have to keep me sweet if you want to find out more about what's going on here." He turned to me in an abrupt, offended way that made me wonder if he was quite okay.

I nodded, though, despite feeling nauseous. Could any story be worth this sexual humiliation and attendant self-hatred? Even I was beginning to have my doubts.

"Come up and see my office." He rearranged his trousers.

Hoping my face didn't show what I really thought of this offer, I followed him toward an industrial-type staircase; its thick metallic steps fastened to the wall with heavy-duty fittings. His feet thumped, clanked and echoed as we walked up, making him seem slightly more human but also, counterintuitively, even less attractive than before.

His office was pretty much as I'd expected. A sterile yet seedy emptiness. The kind that went beyond meagre furnishings to something deeper, a soul sickness. The walls were painted an emetic beige, the furniture expensive, modern, charmless. A picture of a woman tennis player scratching her bottom. The window blinds were rattling, there must be a current of air somewhere making that happen, though I couldn't see how since we seemed to be deep inside the place's bowels, although I'd only a shaky grip on my bearings.

"Here, don't say I'm not good to you." Alex passed me something metallic, round and heavy.

A cannon ball?

I glanced more closely at it. Dog food? "You're very kind but I don't have a dog." Well, actually, I did. She was back on Earthen being looked after by neighbours, but I wouldn't dream of feeding her this crap. I loved her far too much to dream of doing that to her.

"Doesn't matter." He looked almost drunk on thoughts of his own grandiosity, bestowing tins of dog food on me like other men might trips to Paris or expensive jewellery. "Take it anyway. A memento."

A memento of what, though? Grisly research where I prostituted myself to get my story?

He looked genuinely baffled I wasn't keener. "It's highly nutritious, you know."

"For dogs? Yes. Lovely."

Maybe he wanted me to eat it. Or he was saying I was a dog myself, but in a roundabout way. "Thank you. Very kind." As I spoke, I put the tin into my handbag, squirming at the thought of it rubbing up against my things.

I watched as he sat down, lifted his feet and swung them onto the desk. He leant back, slinging one arm over the back of the chair and giving me a long look. It would have been easy to open my mouth, tell him what an arsehole he was; I'd to dig deep to remain focused. It was getting worrying, though, on my own in this antiseptic place, with this sour chemical smell – and a man whose fragile ego might mean an aversion to taking 'no' for an answer.

There was a sofa that looked, to my horror, like it might be leather, although I'd assumed he was vegan, like just about everyone else in the twenty-fifth century, including me. He surprised me by going over and lying down it.

He wasn't luring me onto that thing. I might never escape if I sat down on it.

"Tell me more about what you do in here all day."

"Why're you so interested, then? You an Earthen spy or something?"

"Don't be silly. I'm an academic, I work in a university." I paused, trying to think how to distract him. "What's all this clanking? You laid on a soundtrack for us?" I tried to keep my tone light; didn't want to annoy him, he looked the type who wouldn't hesitate to hit me, while at the same time blaming me for all his shoddy behaviour.

The clanking stopped. I turned to him, questioning.

"What's that?" A pause in dog food production, perhaps.

He shook his head, looking, for the first time since I'd met him, somewhat abashed.

"Nothing. Nothing."

Sitting on the sofa, he stretched out his legs again.

"Come here."

"No, really, I'm fine here." I was leaning against a high sideboard made out of mahogany.

My skin twitched as I breathed in more odd, medicinal smells.

"That's enough of you fannying about." He got up from the

sofa and stepped over to me, lunging toward me with his mouth half open.

"What the…." I recoiled, missing my step and almost falling as I veered backwards away from him.

"Oh, come on. This isn't your first Rodeo. You get me to drive you out here, show you the sights."

His hands were stroking my arms.

"Just get off me."

Panicked, I tried again to get away from him, hitting at his hands with my elbows; trying to unsucker him from my body. He was stronger than me, I realised with dismay.

I tried again to move away, scared and flustered, my palms sweating. Aware of losing my balance, I flailed and grabbed at the slats of some dirty, dusty blinds behind me. They offered little support, clattering as I clutched at them.

Stretching out to them again, I got a momentary, unexpected view through the window. Underneath us was a line of people in hospital beds, all of them looking ill. Very ill. With medical equipment, pulsing lights, numbers, symbols. Water vapour in the air had turned into tentacles of ice on the beds and equipment, glacial tentacles that were dripping down like old man's beards. In each of the hundred or so beds lay a person. All had bandaging, though some were in a worse way than others. Most were missing limbs, it was horrifying and distressing to see. Some lay flat on their backs, too sick to move. Others sat up in bed. Tubes linked them to liquids, medicines, unguents.

The shock of what I was seeing ricocheted through my body. My legs wouldn't hold me up, beginning to buckle under me like those of a new-born wildebeest struggling to stride out across the dusty savannah; I slumped down heavily onto the floor. Maybe I'd drunk too much, though I'd only had a few sips of wine, determined not to mess up again like in the past. Maybe he'd spiked my drink . . . He looked capable of that.

I couldn't believe what I was seeing, there had to be a sensible reason for it, because none of what I saw made sense.

As I registered being on the floor, I felt his hands on my legs, pulling down my tights, scrabbling at my knickers, his hands touching me in places I didn't want anyone except Ed to be touching me. I tried to lever his hands off me, but he was insistent.

"Get off me, just get off. I'm hurt."

"Come on. This is why you came here, isn't it?"

It wasn't, but I wasn't telling him that. He already looked like he wanted to hurt me, might even manage it.

"Come on, no, seriously."

And then, blessedly, a different voice.

"Cathy, are you there?"

Thank God.

The footsteps were heavy, tramping. Purposeful.

The door opened, it was exactly who I'd hoped.

"Get away from her."

"This your old man?" But he took his hands off me and moved away.

Relief scattered over me like grit from a snow plough machine making the roads drivable again.

"Istvan." My hands were shaking.

"Who the hell are you?" began Alex. The two were stags about to lock horns in a moor side stand-off. "You come to check on her takings?"

The last comment was a mistake. Istvan took three strides across the room, until he was close enough to lean down to where Alex was sprawled on the floor and grab him by his shirt collar.

"Leave it. Just fucking leave it."

I'd never heard Istvan so angry before, he was normally so buttoned-down, resolutely unflappable. He turned back to me.

"We're getting out of here."

"How'd you get in?" I kept my voice low.

"Lover boy left the door open. Had his mind on other things." Istvan looked at me sideways from under his eyebrows. I wasn't quite ready yet to laugh about any of this, but felt better hearing him belittle a man who'd frightened me.

"Something bad's happening here." I paused, breathing in deeply.

"No shit, that dog food smells disgusting."

"No, I'm serious."

"So am I."

"I've hardly had anything to drink, before you ask."

"Good-oh."

"Although I wouldn't mind one now."

"Fair enough." He didn't look receptive to the idea though. "You've had a night of it."

Istvan being nice to me . . . I didn't understand what was happening. The night was becoming more confused with every moment spent in its shadowy surroundings.

As we turned to go, Istvan turned back to Alex.

"You should be at home with your wife and kids. Not hurting and threatening somebody I care about."

I watched as Alex turned an unlovely shade of puce, giving him the appearance of what was once a popular root vegetable, before all the crops all failed.

"Don't tell my family about this."

Alex looked as if he might self-combust; spluttering like a sheaf of legal papers from a Dickens novel. He'd have fitted in well to Dickens, that sense of a life lived in the by-ways and castles of a nasty eccentricity, disconnected from others and himself. Too malevolent for one of the straightforwardly humorous characters.

In my confusion and distress, I made what would later come to feel like a huge error, and left the place without showing Istvan what I'd just glimpsed through the office window. Getting to safety felt too important to risk delaying; I wasn't thinking that rationally, too focused on escape.

As we began walking out of the factory, I felt prickles of disgust running up and down my spine. That man . . . Breathing cold night air in and out a couple of times, I began to feel better. Calmer. Steadier.

"How'd you know I needed help?" Good timing, turning up when he did, as Alex was getting difficult.

Istvan didn't reply, there was silence except for the sound of our feet scrunching against the gravel and a low, intermittent owl hooting. Instead, he tapped the side of his nose a couple of times with a finger of his black-gloved hand.

I'd no idea how to interpret this gesture, so gazed instead at the suns appearing over the hillside in front of us. Rosy-fingered dawn was stretching, yawning, getting ready for the day ahead. She hadn't quite woken up properly, but it wouldn't be long before she was spreading her watery beams across the valley.

"I just knew." He paused. "I care about you, you know. I was following you, at a distance."

"Thank you . . ." I felt my eyes begin to fill. "I thought I'd lost you, that we were separated. You stopped him . . ."

"It's okay. Just glad you're all right."

"Those invalids... The ones in the beds. They were in a really bad way. What was that?"

"Invalids? Beds? I missed all that."

Of course, Istvan appeared after I'd fallen over. He wouldn't have had a chance to see what I'd seen, though it was impossible to be sure how much would have still been visible when he arrived. Maybe the blinds were screening off the hospital again by then.

"It was bad, really bad. These poor, poor people."

When Istvan stretched out a hand to help me into the space pod I didn't decline like I would have normally, instead putting my bare hand into his black-gloved one, and climbing up into the passenger seat, my muscles relaxing, loosening, sinking and shifting in the relief of fleeing the accursed place. The gravel scrunched underneath us as we lifted off and began the flight to our temporary home.

"I need to go back, find out what's happening to those invalids. Help them."

"What invalids?"

For a moment, standing in the chill, I didn't understand him.

"Sorry, what did you say?"

"I don't know what you're talking about. Invalids. What invalids?"

I felt myself blinking.

"You sure you're not imagining things?"

It felt odd, hearing him tell me I was just imagining what I knew I'd seen.

Self-doubt was an insidious beast, like the grot that grew unwanted in the cracks between floor and wall, hope and achievement, choking healthy growth, scoffing energy and nutrients for itself.

"But I saw..." My voice trailed off. Maybe I really was going mad. "I saw these people." I couldn't bring myself to say much more about the state they were in, it was traumatising even to think about it. I could hardly bear to think about what was happening for the people in those beds.

"You sure?"

"Yes, yes, I am."

"You had a lot to drink back at the bar? I don't blame you, you've been under a lot of pressure."

"I wouldn't screw up a job this important by getting pissed."

"People say you like a drink."

Did they, indeed. Who were these people, I wondered.

"I wasn't drunk." I wasn't.

The shadows of overhanging rock were retreating with the ascent of the suns, darkness receding almost visibly back to its more natural home in the crevices, where it could usually survive all but the most piercing sunlight.

"I didn't see any invalids there. That's the simple truth. And you were under a lot of pressure. It's okay if things got confused in your mind. I'm not judging." He looked censorious.

Had I been imagining those beds and their occupants? It wasn't impossible.

I'd go back again tomorrow and find out more about what was happening to those injured people. As I reflected, I noticed the rays of the planet's third sun peep above the escarpment of rock and sediment, edging out the darkness of the night.

Eight

GRAVEL RICOCHETED UP against the pod, spattering noisily against its hull like gun fire. The numerous toadstools looked as if they were making the most of the morning too, absorbing all the nutrients and energy they could from the sunshine.

Walking back to the house, I noticed dandelion filaments in the sunshine performing an aerial dance, unable to stay still or sit the dance out. As I got closer, I noticed that Oxie was already awake and standing at the window. A weariness in her face suggested she'd maybe been there a while.

She opened the door looking a little out of breath, (I could imagine the sound of her slippers would have scuffed against the tiled floor as she ran), and buried her head against my jacket.

"Hey, we're home. It's okay."

I couldn't see her face because she was nuzzling so deeply against me. Unconvinced by my words, she wouldn't let go, clinging on like water attaching itself as ice to grass on a cold winter night.

"It's all okay. Nothing to worry about. We're home now." Not true, there was still rather a lot worrying me, but we were at least home again. That bit was true.

Minuted passed before she let go of me.

"Did you bring me a present?" She looked hopeful.

"Oh, sweetheart, I'm so sorry."

She plunged her hands into the pockets of her blue-and-white checked pinafore, looking reluctant to show her disappointment.

"There might be some pencils in my bag. Let me have a look."

Gingerly, I took out a couple of lipsticks, their smooth metallic surfaces dotted with hairs and crumbs. And then there was that strange gift Alex had insisted on bestowing on me. I picked the tin up, wiped down the surface and put it on the table.

"No!" Oxie was suddenly screaming, bawling. "No, not that."

"My love, what's the matter?"

Her hand was shaking as she stretched it out. And pointed, tears flooding down her face, at the tin of dog food sitting on the table. I held out my hands, hoping to comfort her. But she veered away, as if frightened I might contaminate her.

"They took my parents," she said, wiping her eyes and nose. At her feet, tears were falling onto the polished stone floor, forming circles of shiny, iridescent wetness. "They are the people who took my mummy and daddy."

We reconvened later that morning, after I'd had some breakfast with Oxie and then a few hours' sleep and tried to scrub myself clean of Alex in the chilly dribble of a shower.

"Where are you going?" Oxie looked as if she hoped some fun might be in the offing.

"Nowhere special. Just drive about, get a change of scene. Clear my head a bit." I didn't want to tell her I was going back to the suspected nexus of evil, not now I knew how she felt about the place and its products.

Istvan walked over to me.

"Enjoy yourselves."

I picked up my bag, lifted it up onto my shoulder and walked to the door, where I paused and turned back.

"We'll have lunch together, all right, Oxie?"

She nodded.

The weather was balmy, the three suns cooperating on the tasks of lighting and heating the planet. Wind was ruffling the dried and withered crops in the fields, underscoring the desiccation and loss brought about by the famine. I saw a few farmers standing in their now useless fields, looking bereft, purposeless, heartbroken.

I was so preoccupied with planning out possible interviews, it was a shock when I heard the blankets on the back seat move and stir. A rustling sound as sweet wrappers landed on the pod floor.

"Hello?" I tried to keep the greeting neutral, unsure who or what I was addressing, though I already had my suspicions.

No answer.

I stretched out a hand, touched the blanket, a grimy affair blotched with greasy stains. Something – or somebody was there.

"Oxie?"

More rustling.

"She's not here." It was Oxie's voice speaking, though.

What was she doing here? That tin had frightened her, maybe she didn't know I was going to the Aballonian equivalent of its mothership.

"Come out then." Life with her was like looking after a young and headstrong filly, not yet accustomed to her own strength.

She wriggled out of the travel rug and leapt at me.

"Cathy."

Luckily the pod was on autopilot or I'd have crashed.

Wondering what was going on, I gave her a hug. She'd dried mud on her face, probably from the blanket.

"What are you doing here?"

"You're not angry at me?"

Confused, I shook my head. I was angry, but didn't want her to know.

"Of course not." I'd try not to be.

"I can't lose you too," she said. "Not after Mummy and Daddy."

My heart felt tight enough to burst, my eyes oddly prickly.

"Oh, Oxie."

We hugged.

"We're going to try and find them. Meantime, I'm here to look after you." Poor child.

I needed to get her back to the farmhouse as fast as possible, because I didn't want her seeing the injured, although I was privately beginning to doubt myself about what I thought I'd seen the previous night at the "factory". Despite my doubts, I wasn't putting Oxie at any risk. It'd be simple enough to take her home, then come back again later on my own.

"We have to get you home."

"Not without you, no."

She began wailing and shouting, it was frightening to hear.

"It's not safe for you here." I paused, hoping for inspiration. "I have to do the next stage alone."

The expression on her face suggested nothing could persuade her to change her mind.

"Seriously. We've got to get you home."

The screaming resumed, pushing the decibel count even higher.

Even her pigtails were damp with tears.

I gazed at her face, reddened by emotion. I couldn't take her back to the cottage where we were staying, not with her feeling like this. The factory felt equally difficult. What had happened with the dog food to make her so anxious?

She crossed her arms around herself, hunkering deeper into her pink-quilted anorak.

"I can help you," she said, sounding serious. "I can . . . how do you say, make the words for you."

"You mean, translate for me?"

She nodded.

"Oh, sweetheart, that's kind of you, but no need."

Seeing her face fall, I dug more tissues out of a box and handed them to her, grabbing a few for myself too.

Pulling into the pod park, I noticed the paint on the walls peeling off in great, curly flakes.

"You know how we're going to have a look at the factory?"

She nodded, looking as if I'd suggested nothing more frightening than a visit to inter-planetary soft play.

"If I say we're going home, you must do as I say."

"Okay." She looked mutinous.

Our feet scrunched across the pod park to a reception area I hadn't even noticed the night before.

A woman behind the desk looked at us as we walked over to her.

"Yes? Can I help you?" She looked pale, to the point of being unwell.

"Alex there?"

"What's the surname?"

"Foley."

She swept her gaze back and forth across the screen, drilling into it.

"Nobody here of that name."

My heart felt as if it had left the building. I'd been there in the factory with him, less than twelve hours earlier, he'd opened it up for us. Before trying to rape me.

"You sure? Must be some mistake."

She leaned forward and fixed me with her gaze. I felt like a fish finger left on its own in the freezer for years: abject and unwanted.

"Don't worry." When she smiled the effect was like looking at pictures of a fake fireplace insert in a magazine – way too far removed from the real thing for any happy feelings of imagined warmth.

"What d'you mean?" I managed. Don't worry? I knew the guy existed, they'd a nerve to say otherwise. I'd been fighting him off in a room in that same building only hours earlier, breathing in that revolting aftershave of his.

"We have tours."

"Tours? Oh..." My voice trailed off. Tours indeed. But I wanted to check the place out, this could be my only opportunity. "That would be lovely, how kind of you." It sounded utterly grim. "Is it, is it, ahem, suitable for children?" Going by what I'd seen, the only possible answer to that was no, it wasn't. It most definitely wasn't.

The receptionist got up from her chair and leant even closer to us; she'd a smear of pearlescent lipstick on her teeth and I felt awkward for her, as well as unsure over whether I should say anything or not. I touched at my own teeth with my hand, hoping she might take the hint. She didn't.

"Suitable? Absolutely. We're a very child–friendly organisation. Pride ourselves on it." She fixed me with the talons of her smile again.

I forced myself to smile back.

"What time does the tour start?" It was looking like it might be the only way I could access the place.

"One's setting off in half an hour."

"If you don't mind putting our names down..." My voice trailed off as I imagined what might be in store. "Are you sure this is suitable for children?"

"Totally sure. You'll both love it."

We waited half an hour in a holding pen at reception, spinning out a game of Guess the Animal as long as we could. Antelope? Anteater? Aballonian werewolf? Abalarder? Aardvark? Eventually, a different woman came through some industrial-type doors and walked over to us.

"Joining today's tour?" She hugged the metal breastplate of her clipboard close, looking confident it could deflect most missiles thrown her way.

"Yes, we're on the tour." The words sounded like code for something else, I realised. On the tour . . . Leaning down, I spoke to Oxie in a whisper. "And remember, if it's unsuitable, we leave." It felt worth repeating, though I'd still the feeling Oxie'd go her own way on this, as on much else beside. "You're remembering that, aren't you?"

She nodded in the same perfunctory and dismissive way that had already made me uneasy.

There weren't many people on the tour. Me, Oxie, an elderly couple.

As our guide held open the door into the main factory, I remembered the previous evening, my flirtation with Alex, the sight of those people I'd come back to try and help. The ones lying prone and helpless, linked up to tubes.

Walking across the metallic floor, I listened as our boots reverberated and echoed. Remembering the night before, I looked down with dismay to where I'd seen the line of beds, bracing myself for what I'd see.

No beds. No patients. No medics. Nothing suggesting illness or disease.

Instead, a large, fenced enclosure with a few young dogs yapping and playing with a carefree abandon.

"As you can see," said our guide, gesturing with manicured hand towards the dogs. "We are love our dogs." Lowering her clipboard, she continued: "Yes, we love and care for them. That isn't a problem for you, is it?" The expression on her face was triumphant, her mouth curled into a cruel smirk so pronounced it made me wish an aardvark would break into the place and savage her. She had even managed to clean the lipstick smudge off her teeth, I noticed sourly.

Nine

THE FLIER LOOKED innocent enough; sans serif font lettering scribbled over colourful images of children in plastic aprons, all showing an admittedly improbable fascination with the palm-sized lumps of clay in their hands.

"Can we go? Please?"

I hadn't noticed Oxie standing behind me.

"Please?" She'd the same neediness on her face when supplicating for hot chocolate.

Maybe it'd give Oxie a chance to be with other kids, and I could ask any parents or carers there if they'd seen or heard anything going on at the factory.

We walked back to the sitting room, where Istvan was sitting on the sofa watching the local news on his crystal.

"Look what we found." I held out the flier to him.

"Another lead? Great." He looked discomfited though, probably annoyed at the idea it was me making headway, not him.

"No, nothing like that. Just an outing. A bit of fun, really. Pottery classes for kids. In town. With coffee for grown-ups."

"Sounds fun. Be sure and show me whatever you make."

I glanced at the wooden stairs leading up to Oxie's room, the banisters and treads now covered with jackets, scarves and colourful hoodies.

"We're going to go to the pottery," I called up to her. "Get dressed in clothes you don't mind getting dirty."

Oxie walked out of her room, looking as if she'd stumbled on the pot of gold at the end of the rainbow after long years of being unsure it even existed.

Picking up the flier from the coffee table where Istvan had left it, I folded it up roughly and pushed it into my handbag. Sunlight filtered through the cottage windows.

The pottery place had a shabby, well-loved air; there was a tidiness about the stacks of plates, mugs, pots, egg cups, baby feet imprints and similar artefacts. Whoever was running the place must have had a love of their craft that went well beyond fleecing sentimental families of their money.

Outside a spider's web decorated with water droplets glistened in the sunshine; a woman sitting on a three-legged wooden stool was painting the yellowish gold of the planet's suns onto a plate with the tender concentration of a parent caring for their child. The smell of wet clay and dusty earth soothed and calmed, humbling as it healed.

There were only a couple of other people there; the potter herself and a mum drinking her coffee like it was intravenous life support taken orally. The place didn't look promising in terms of new leads, but I'd enjoy a coffee there while I waited for Oxie.

Predictably, Oxie took to pottery with relish, moulding clay into a variety of shapes: pot, coaster, elfin princess, frog. She looked enraptured, I felt happy to be able to give her even a couple of short hours of fun.

It happened just as I was finishing my tea and thinking I'd need to give up on proving my story was right and go home. My money was almost all gone, disappearing on Istvan's wages, rent, food bills and other necessities. The story was going nowhere. I might as well see about taking Oxie home with me to Earthen, if we really couldn't find her parents.

I'd just about decided to stay on the place only long enough to see if we could track Oxie's parents down. I wasn't really the maternal kind, as recent experiences had underlined, but I wasn't going to leave her on her own on a planet facing civil war and chronic food shortages.

She walked over from where she'd been looping coils of clay around each other.

"Is it okay if we stay longer? I'm loving it here."

"Course it is. Enjoy yourself." It was a nice feeling, this sensation of helping someone else, putting their needs before mine. I could get quite used to it, if I didn't screw it all up – or 'self-sabotage', as the therapist was so fond of calling it. Maybe I wouldn't have been such a disaster as a parent after all, though a bit late to be worrying about that now.

Sighing, I took a slurp of my coffee, scalding hot against my tongue, and put it down again too fast, making it slop over the rim onto my hands. Embarrassed, I wiped at my mouth with the back of my hand.

Before I officially called it quits I'd maybe put in a couple more calls, thank people for their earlier help. But if I didn't have at least two people to back up what I'd seen at the dog food lab, the place's supremos could - and would - blow me out of their orbit.

"Going outside?"

It was a middle-aged man clearing tables. Straggly hair, untended by barber or hairdresser for months, if not years. Clothes that hung off him, as if they were desperate to flee the sinking vessel of his body.

"Yes, I might. That okay?"

"You don't need to ask my permission." The man laughed, as if the idea of anyone checking anything with him was incomprehensible.

I couldn't work him out, he'd an understanding of irony and subtle humour and there he was, clearing tables. Maybe, like so many, he'd fallen on hard times in the impending civil war.

"There is evil in the world," he said, conversationally, appearing to concentrate on his mopping and not looking me in the eye. Yet again, that old, uncomfortable feeling of not understanding.

"What do you mean?"

He shrugged, and swept the sodden mop left and right with a loud swishing sound. Clearly, he'd decided against saying anything more, instead watching the mop as he swished it from side to side. The studio felt calm, industrious, a haven, however temporary and fragile, of honest labour.

What the hell was this guy on about? Funny, gnomic utterances about evil . . .

A dishevelled chorus line of insects was swerving through the air.

Lowering my voice, I tried again.

"What kind of evil are you talking about?" I wasn't even sure myself whether I meant the question rhetorically or not. I kept my gaze averted from him, avoiding eye contact might make him feel freer to talk, although I suspected this guy might actually be a pretty slick operator – assuming he wasn't completely off his head, in which case I was wasting my time. Or he could be some kind of trouble-maker, wheeled out to sow confusion and panic – also possible.

At last, he stopped the mopping and straightened up, came over to my table and pulled out a chair, its metal frame scraping against the newly-mopped stone floor, before sitting down. Despite myself, I glanced at my bag, picked it up and slung it over the back of my chair. It was hard not to feel wary of him, although I liked him, too. There was a perfume of cleaning smells to him, of attempts to blot out the darkness.

He reminded me of someone, too, although I couldn't remember them.

Of course. Zoltan.

The man who'd started me on this insanity. The man I'd come to this forsaken planet to find.

I didn't want to be the one to introduce his name, though. Better my guest steered things.

Some of the lighter branches on the trees outside were bowing and curtsying gently in the breeze, I noticed, athletes warming up at the track in readiness for the big event of springtime. Above them clouds trailed lazily across the sky, inexpert yet beautiful streaks of white paint.

Not for the first time, I felt out of my depth as I watched rain drops reflecting and magnifying sunlight, their new-found roundness curtailed by the surface where they'd landed.

The man at my table surprised me by his clipped and business-like manner. He put both elbows on the wooden table, placing his hands together in the confident, professional manner of a soldier or priest. I looked to check on Oxie. Yes, stuck on a decision between cobalt or petrol blue for the princess's turret-shaped hat.

"I want to tell you what happened at the factory." He remained oddly detached from his words.

I felt a fascinated horror.

"Go on."

"The convoy left early that same morning, less than an hour after you saw what you did. The vehicles had northern number plates."

"Northern? What do you mean?" There was a sub-text to this I couldn't understand.

"Isn't it obvious?" He looked and sounded pained I hadn't cottoned onto what he meant, though also a tiny bit pleased with himself.

"I'm not from Aballonia, I don't know it well."

"They've gone to Platignall. Yes, Platignall."

Platignall. Even I'd heard of that. A byword for some of the nastiest and most dangerous drug warfare in the galaxy. It'd make a horrible kind of sense if the Aballonians were hiding their secrets in a place already so crime-ridden that more atrocities wouldn't exactly stand out.

"How'd you know this?"

He shrugged. "It's my job."

"What is your job?"

He made brief eye contact.

"I can't tell you. But I know people, I have connections."

"You're not really a cleaner, are you?"

He tilted his head to one side, saying nothing.

I wanted to find out more about him, but instinct made me wary.

"When was this?"

"Early that morning. An hour after you left."

"They must have moved fast, packing all those people into airbuses."

"It's probably fair to say they aren't people who mess about." He looked sad, as if he wished they were.

"What about your escort? Where's he?"

"Istvan's a translator and fixer. Not an escort." He wasn't a prostitute, I felt like saying, but I needed this man's information.

"Where is he then, your fixer?"

"At home. Having a rest. It was a long night."

My new-found friend gave me what might have been a look.

"No, not like that."

"Could you tell me your name?" I was timid, afraid of scaring him off by asking too many questions.

"No, I can't." He didn't look bothered by his unwillingness to co-operate, his features barely moving. As if the need for secrecy had been drilled into him.

"If I don't have any evidence, I can't run a story." Getting anyone to let me write for them was going to be difficult enough anyway, with my track record. No-one was going to touch a story written by me unless I'd several sources, none of which vanished on us.

"If you need evidence, follow my suggestion."

Platignall was a dump. But never mind.

I glanced over at Oxie, now concentrating on painting the hat of an elfin princess. She looked cross when her hand slipped and some of the blue paint smudged over the face.

Moments later, she came over to me with the figurine in her hands.

"Cathy! Cathy! The paint is going wrong."

"Oh, sweetheart, don't worry. I can fix this."

Using a napkin, I dabbed at the princess's face.

I held the statuette up to the sunshine filtering through the windows.

"She's fine again now."

My heart sank when I put the figurine on the table and turned to look back at my new acquaintance.

Damn.

Gone. Nowhere to be seen. Only shelves of clammy and unfired clay shapes, with a line of shiny glazed pots above them.

Maybe he'd finished his shift, gone home, taking his leads with him, and I'd find him again the next day, though that felt unlikely. There wasn't much of an incentive for anyone to talk, everyone knew the Aballonians acted ruthlessly when it came to food supplies. Their planetary flag even had a picture on it of something that looked suspiciously close to a butcher's hatchet.

I began to think through different options. If I went to Platignall, Oxie would have to too.

There was a nervous happiness in my boot-clad step as we walked back to the pod.

Oxie was in ebullient mood as we walked. Pine trees stretched out their branches, foliage fluttering, as if they were waking up only slowly after a long and deep sleep. The spattering of wind on the pod roof was like the sound a handful of dry spaghetti might make on the canvas surface of a drum.

"You're back."

He turned to face me.

"How was your trip?"

"I've got news." His face didn't look as happy as I'd expected, which I didn't understand; anything that kept me on the planet should be good news for him; I was the one employing him after all, as well as paying for his food and keep.

"Aren't you pleased?"

"Go on." He was playing with a biro with a sea centre logo on it, clicking and unclicking it.

"I've made headway on the story." I tried to keep excitement out of my voice.

"Great." He didn't sound very happy.

"You not interested in what I've found?" My pride was hurt.

"Please, tell me more."

"You know how Zoltan asked me to come here? Ages back."

"Yes, of course." He leant back into his chair. "Why do you ask?"

A loose flap of carpet next to the skirting board was exerting an almost magnetic attraction on him.

"How flexible can you be for the next few weeks?"

He looked non-committal. Again, the lackadaisical charm contrasted with the energy burning inside him. Maybe he was short of cash, worried I might find a different fixer. It was hard to be sure. Maybe all Aballonian men were like this, and I should have spent more time reading up on the place and its fiery-tempered people.

"So..." I paused, cleared my throat. Where had my voice gone? "I need to go to Platignall. I'm taking Oxie and I'd like to bring you too." I'd have preferred to find a new translator once we got there but didn't rate my chances.

"What a wonderful idea. You are a brave woman."

"I'm not that brave, you know." Why was he making such a big deal about being brave?

"I disagree. You're very brave."

"I don't know about that." Why was he flattering me so much? It felt uncomfortable.

"It's good, you'll need that for Platignall."

Stirring my coffee again, I wondered just how bad the place could really be as I watched different shades of froth and milkiness merge together in the cup. I wasn't brave, I was frightened of spiders and rats. And of ending up on own, unloved and alone. No, not brave at all. And I was gripped by a paralysing horror when I thought of my lost pregnancy and all that blood, not that I could bear to do that very often.

"I just think I might be able to follow up on the story there, that's all." I wasn't going to acknowledge Platignall's criminality.

"Somebody's telling you lies." He didn't look at me.

"This is the first lead I've had." I turned my head, trying to unknot the tension in it.

"Since the dog food place? That turned out to be . . . a dog food place?"

It was my turn to gaze at the floor carpeting. Really, that fraying edge needed fixing.

"You want to go thousands of miles on this guy's say-so and you don't even know his name?"

Put like that, the plan did seem ambitious. Fingering the pendant around my neck, I reflected. "It does sound crazy. But this is one of the few concrete leads we've had."

For a moment, a brief moment, I thought he was being supportive. I felt doubly idiotic when he continued.

"You're right, the idea does sound crazy. How can you drag us there after one, short conversation with a guy in a cafe? You don't even know his name." He gave a half-laugh. "I'm always happy to support you. I'm just trying to protect you."

"You don't need to come with me, There's a stable of interpreters and fixers up in Platignall. I got details before I left, I'll find someone when we get there." None of that was true, the paper wouldn't trust me with their precious contact lists. Even if they had, I'd have been surprised to find anything on the Platignall entry, but he didn't need to know that. I tried not to blink like my eyes seemed to want.

"Maybe you'll find an interpreter, but nobody high-calibre." Or not as high-calibre as him, he seemed to be hinting.

"I'll manage." It was annoying, my voice kept disappearing. "Maybe I won't be able to find anyone as good as you..." I watched him carefully, he looked inscrutable. "But I'll cope."

"Don't do it. It's a waste of time."

"I know it's risky, but I'm doing this."

"At least sleep on it? Decide tomorrow?"

Where had I left that rucksack, I wondered. I'd use it for Oxie's stuff and mine. We should be able to get away early the next morning. With Istvan, or, more probably, without him.

"Don't go. It's not safe."

Nice to feel he cared about our safety.

Normally, I'd have been opening the fridge then, looking for alcohol. Glancing at it, I admired how Oxie had decorated it with drawings held in place by magnets. Then I'd have spent the next few hours drinking and crying over life's cruelty. Tonight I didn't even feel thirsty.

Too much work to do.

I needed to wash Oxie's much-loved pink and hooded onesie before packing it.

Through the window I could see trees thrashing their branches, pop fans at a live gig.

"I'm only thinking of you and Oxie when I suggest holding off on Platignall."

"I know, it's good of you. But we have to do this. We'll see you when we get back."

I felt a tremor of anxiety as I noticed the last of the planet's moons sinking under the reddish horizon of far hills.

Ten

"IS IT MUCH FURTHER?" Oxie sounded like she was preparing for a long trek.

I watched with dismay as she half-slipped in the snow we were navigating together, righting herself without actually falling over and then straightening up again.

"You okay?" I called over to her.

"Fine, yes. Are we close now?" She wasn't letting this lie.

"Not far, promise." I hadn't a clue where we were; Oxie didn't need to know that though.

Phrases such as 'bleak midwinter' and 'frosty earth made iron' kept coming to mind as we trudged along in the early morning, only the tips of shrubs visible as they poked through the snow covering them. I was having no trouble relating to that Wenceslas bloke and his travel issues with snow.

She gulped.

"Where's List-van?" Her mittens swung from her coat sleeves, as she spoke, dancing on crocheted lengths of yarn attaching them to each other. Why she wasn't wearing them I didn't understand . . . Oh, she had her gloves on today.

She didn't seem bothered about his absence, just curious.

"At home. Didn't fancy the trip. Are your hands not cold like that?"

"No, they're good. Got my gloves on." Oxie was a child, but a hunkering-down in her expression reminded me of photos of Sherpa Tenzing and the doughty mountaineers of old. "Couldn't we stay at home too?"

"No, I have to do this, sweetheart. It's why I came here." How to explain that work was my identity? Being a journalist was about more than making money for me, it was more a vocation than a job. The source of what little self-esteem I had.

"You'll understand when you're older." I cringed in recognition of words my mother used to say to me. "I'm sorry, it's not much fun for you, I do see that."

She didn't reply, but her expression of grim stoicism made me feel even worse for putting her through this. Together, we began singing a jingle I'd taught her. She'll be coming round the mountain when she comes . . . Our spirits lifted as we watched the suns climb higher.

Once arrived at the space port, we queued up at the counter after stamping on the floor to get the snow off our boots.

"It's a lovely morning." Oxie was determined to remain cheerful, but winds were pounding at the station roof, howling, swooping, circling, lifting up loose slates and dropping them again.

"Will we find my parents in this new place?" Hope and fear battled it out with each other on her face.

"We'll try. Sweetheart, whatever happens, you're stuck with me." Worse luck for her.

Hearing my words, she turned and hugged me tight, nearly knocking me over as she did so.

Through the station's windows I noticed a jagged sharpness on the crests of the surrounding hills, light and shadow jostling with one another for space and power. The pine trees were looking quietly pleased – smug, even – at their appearance, ready now for all the carnival and fun of the party. Only looking more closely did I see the hooded heaviness of a crow standing perched on the branches of a nearby tree.

Once in our seats, I found myself relaxing, shoulders dropping with the warmth blasting out of heating flues.

"Mum." Oxie had fallen asleep, I realised, and didn't know she was mumbling. Her eyelashes fluttered. She must mean her real mum, not me, I didn't know how to be a mum, wasn't any good at it, as recent events had proved. At least the bleeding had – finally and thankfully – stopped so I was spared that reminder.

Across the blue, two birds were allowing air currents to support them, swooping without discernible effort on the invisible conveyor belts of the sky. How I envied them their freedom.

I turned back to Oxie, who was gazing around, bleary-eyed.

"Hello, sleepy head." I smiled at her. "You had a long nap. Was it nice?"

"Yes, very nice. And now I'll be rested for when I see them again."

I sighed, sad for Oxie, because she might never see her parents again, and, selfishly, sad for myself too, because, if she did, that would mean me losing her, like I'd lost that pregnancy. We needed to have a chat, to prepare her for what she might be facing with her parents.

"Very sensible of you." For a moment, I gazed out the pod window again; a pinky-golden hue had settled on the horizon, melting hills and sky into one another, making it unclear where one ended and another began, layers overlapping into layers and other layers. "Sweetheart, about that . . ."

A solitary peak stood out; one side in deepening shadow, the other in sun-facing light. A place of extremes all right.

"Yes?" Her innocence and hopefulness were making this even more difficult. I couldn't let her carry on believing something that might very well be untrue.

I'd have to say something. But what? I could hardly burden the poor girl with my own fears over what might – or, in fairness, might not – have happened, but I needed to warn her, prepare her for what might be to come.

"Oxie . . ."

She turned to look at me.

"Darling, the thing is…" My voice was disappearing on me faster than frost melting in early morning sunshine. I swallowed. "Oxie, love, we might not be able to find your mummy and daddy."

"At this new place, you mean? Where we're going now?"

"It's possible, I'm afraid, that we won't find them anywhere."

The smile disappeared from her face. I took her hand, clammy, unresponsive and cold. She wouldn't meet my gaze or hold my hand. Pain rolled off her, a tidal sweep dragging itself onto the shoreline.

"You said we were going to find them. You did. You said so."

"No, not exactly." The previous night felt shadowy, its exact meaning dissipating like early-morning mist in the higher and fuller sunshine of mid-morning. "I mean, it's not what I meant."

An attendant was starting her tour of duty with the food, you could see people struggling not to grab the proffered snacks from her gloved hands. One small wheaten biscuit in a plastic wrapper was all we were each allowed, provided we could afford it, but even that was a treat for us.

"Sweetheart, we're going to do our best to . . ."

She cut me off before I could finish.

"I am NOT your sweetheart. Stop calling me that." She crossed her arms, her forehead knitting into angry music lines; fear and pain hidden under her anger.

"It's going to be okay."

But she wouldn't respond, crossing her arms and looking away.

The space pod was slowing down, then came the announcement.

"We are making an emergency stop to pick up supplies and other cargo. Fasten your seat belts, brace for landing."

People began looking at each other in confusion. The woman sitting across the aisle put the two parts of her seat belt together with a resolution that suggested she was expecting turbulence of some kind.

Half an hour later we stumbled off the space pod, the tiredness in my back and legs a stultifying ache. Maybe I was simply too old for this kind of job, being in my mid thirties. As Oxie grabbed at my hand, we saw what might have been the reason for our stop; leaking out from underneath a tarpaulin was a pool of crimson-red blood, thick and oily, staining and destroying the snow's whiteness. I put a gloved hand over Oxie's eyes. Then, worrying she might trip over, I lifted her up and held her close to me.

"It's all right. It's all right. Just don't look at it."

Oxie didn't protest, for once, allowing me to carry her past the tarpaulin and whatever it was trying to hide.

Even without the blood, it wasn't the most prepossessing spot for a stop-over. A shack of corrugated iron was sloping downwards at an angle. The air smelt of cordite and acrid, stale food. It was difficult not to start fearing we might be in for a repetition of the dog food experience; I found myself peering around, hoping to spy out escape routes. The only lights seemed to come from the shack.

"Don't worry, it'll be okay." I wasn't a good liar, though this trip seemed to be giving me plenty of practice in that department, even if it wasn't turning into quite the redemption I'd hoped. "They're probably just filling up the tank. Nothing to worry about." Except we were in half-light in the middle of nowhere, with a sprawl of blood on the ground the size of several small rooms, maybe big enough to allow for patio extensions too. A mere detail . . .

We were wiping our feet on the ridged-back plastic mat on the cabin floor when I saw him. That by-now-familiar lurch and shock in my stomach coupled with an inability to imagine things ever being any other way.

"Istvan." I tried to keep my voice calm. He turned to me, his look suggesting he considered it only natural to stumble across a friend in this desolate spot.

"Hello, there."

"What are you doing here?" Heat spread across my face; my forehead and cheeks reddening at the bluntness of my own question.

He flapped his hands, looking embarrassed.

"Trying to help you, of course."

Oxie was whispering. "My tummy is hungry."

Glancing at other tables and behind the bar, I couldn't see anything edible.

"I'll ask the bar man." Who'd probably tell me to get lost, and not very politely, either.

Pushing back my chair, I walked over to the bar, where a youngish guy was drying glasses with a towel. It was just possible to hear the squeak of fabric against glass as I leaned over the bar top.

"Serving lunch?"

He didn't answer, instead giving me a look that I took as a negative. The entire planet was struggling with famine, nobody had a clue where the shortages had started, or how to get rid of them. So, no, there wasn't any food on offer, the look seemed to be saying.

On the menu board was a diagonal chalk line. And the words 'Mañana, mañana', probably written by someone young wit trying to cheer everyone up.

"Crisps? Or peanuts?"

He appeared satisfied with the beer glass, placing it on a shelf with the others.

"No, love, no." He half–laughed to himself.

My heart thumping fast, I decided to risk it. "It's just I have to get something for that little girl to eat." Awkwardly I scuffed at the wooden bar with my foot.

Agitated, I glanced around the room. Through the window was a tiny, distant seagull, though it was far from any shoreline, flapping its wings to gain traction. With the wind so strong, the poor creature must have had its work cut out.

Walking back to the table, I put down the glasses of orange juice on cardboard coasters soaked with a brownish liquid. Probably beer.

"One for each of you."

"What about you?"

"Drank mine earlier." There hadn't been enough to go round, I'd cope with water. "Very tasty it was, too."

Remembering about them, I put our one crisp pack out of the pocket of my hand-knitted cardigan and put it on the table too.

"Is that all? Just one packet?" At Oxie's wailing, people turned their heads.

No, we weren't abusing her, I wanted to say. We loved her and were looking after her. It seemed wise, though, to say as little as possible.

He who guards his mouth and tongue protects himself from trouble, and all that.

Looking disappointed there wasn't going to be a fight, the other customers turned back to their drinks.

It was an older woman with white hair tied up in a simple ponytail who was the one to help us out. Watching us even after the others at her table had turned back to their match, she walked over, the expression on her face conveying that she too knew the struggle to look after one's young.

Standing beside us, she reached into a pocket of her fleece jacket, took something out of it and tentatively held it out to me.

"For the wee one. If that's okay with you?"

The sight of a crumpled-looking packet of salt-and-vinegar crisps brought tears to my eyes and I dabbed at my face with the tips of my index fingers.

I turned back to our benefactor.

"Thank you," I managed. "Thank you."

"It's hardest on the kids, these shortages."

"You're very kind. Can I get you a drink? To thank you?"

She shook her head, smiled at us again and went back to her table.

I passed the packet of crisps to Oxie.

"Look what the kind lady has given us."

Oxie was keen to open the bag. Maybe too keen. When she finally managed to tear open the gummy silver covering, she fumbled and dropped the bag. It fell with a quiet and muffled thud onto the floor. Her face became pink and flushed, tears making her eyes glassy and round.

"My love, I'm so sorry." Sorrier than I could really express.

Looking down at the crisps, I could see most were now on the dirty, waterlogged floor. Beyond hope. Oxie and I both eyed them intensely, and I knew, in that way where you just know, that we were both wondering if we could eat them anyway, even after them landing on the dirty floor.

I'd have made a terrible mother. Who fed dirty crisps to their child? It didn't feel like I was measuring up well as a journalist either. A failure on every front, that was me.

The bar man came out from behind the counter, in his hands was a long metal stick that looked like it might unfurl awnings or feature in modern-day iterations of jousting.

"I can maybe help you."

"Go on." I hoped he wasn't going to try and sell me hard drugs.

He laughed.

"Sorry, I don't understand." He'd probably laugh at me again for admitting that.

He put his hand in one of the pockets of his snow-proof jacket. When he took it out, I spotted a silvery foil wrapper covered in cartoon characters. Oxie must have seen it too, because I could hear her whimpering in delight. If the next lot fell on the floor, I might feel a tiny bit annoyed, though duty-bound to be tolerant; I'd be opening these for her myself, I decided.

"Would your daughter like these crisps?"

"Yes, please!" Oxie got up from her chair and snatched the packet from him.

"Don't forget to say thank you," I started.

His eyes open, Istvan was staring at me with an expression I couldn't understand.

"Want me to open those?" I asked Oxie.

Maybe remembering the fate of the last packet, now being devoured by a dog, she acquiesced.

"Okay." Just because she was letting me open them didn't mean she had to like the arrangement but nobody wanted any more crisp-related disasters.

The packet safely opened, I felt happy seeing her sitting there, eating the crisps, drinking her juice. Less good was the thought of the conversation I'd soon need to have with Istvan, which I didn't want her hearing.

"There are some toys over there. Why don't you go and play with them while Istvan and I chat?" And I could try to find out why the guy was borderline stalking me.

Although I was expecting her to protest, Oxie proved biddable about playing on her own. With her ensconced in the play area, I turned back to Istvan.

"So, what brings you here?" I tried to affect a light-heartedness I didn't feel. Maybe he was an axe-murderer who lured vulnerable women into his snares by pretending to be helping them . . .

"Me?"

He was play acting too, something about the surprise he was affecting felt very fake.

"Couldn't let you go on your own."

It wasn't immediately clear to me why not, but I stayed quiet.

On the other hand, I was only too well aware of the dangers facing us, which were horribly clear. Civil insurrection, famine. Extremism.

"I knew you'd be on the Fast service, so you'd be near Platignall around now."

But how could he have known the pod would stop here?

He was so eccentric and weird, it was annoying.

"How'd you know we'd be getting off here? It's not a scheduled stop."

"I'm a native, remember. Grew up here."

"I know what a native is." Maybe they'd a scheduled rest stop there.

"Even men can be sensitive, you know." He was laughing at me.

"Yes, of course, I already know that." Though after breaking up with Ed, I'd had my doubts.

"I couldn't let you and Oxie go into danger without me." He crossed his arms.

Some rogue, self-destructive part of my character gnawed away at me, unable to let things go.

"Bit of a coincidence, isn't it, though? You turning up here when we've been forced to land."

"We're on the front line here, we're a war-like people. And I have contacts in the transport industry."

I glanced over at Oxie, who was now working on a drawing of what looked like an ogre. In his arm was a stick that could have been a druidical wand or a spear. Or both.

"Nice picture. We'll get that framed." I called out to her, at the same time giving her a thumbs-up signal.

"Why so committed to following this story?" He picked up one of the damp beer mats and played with it, turning it round and round. "Never tempted to give up? Go home?"

Home? A frightening idea.

"No, I enjoy travelling."

I watched as he gazed around the bar, where a cluster of depressed-looking travellers were making up for the shortage of food with whatever alcohol they could find.

"Seriously? Even to somewhere like this?" He looked as if the bar didn't measure up to his standards, but I got the impression practically nowhere could. "Do you not want to settle down, have a family of your own?"

Of course I wanted a family of my own. But it was none of his business and things weren't really working out like that, something not even a juggernaut of alcohol would allow me to forget. Still . . . He'd followed us all this way north, he must care about me a bit to travel so far to find me. Maybe I could speak more honestly with him about Ed and the whole horrible, humiliating mess back home.

"You forgot something, you know." He passed me a bottle opener I remembered from when we'd lived together in the capital in those first few weeks.

Not like me to be lax about drinking equipment.

"Okay, thank you." I slipped it into my bag.

On the other side of the room, Oxie didn't look aware of what we were saying. We'd started talking in Earthen again, which she couldn't understand, and she was colouring in a flower with a purple felt tip.

"Look, I know we've never really talked much about this. But I don't feel as if I have much choice."

"What do you mean?"

"This is my only chance of getting my career back." My voice faltered. "After that mistake. The one that led to me losing my job. Contacts tell me my source, a guy called Zoltan, is somewhere on Aballonia."

He said nothing, although I couldn't help feeling we'd reached a point where he should have done.

For just a moment or two, it was tricky to tell who'd buckle first and break the silence. Perhaps inevitably, it was me.

"I don't have a choice. Not if I'm ever going to get a decent job in journalism again."

He remained calm and unmoved.

"So we're going on this trip to Platignall."

"You don't have to come with us, you know. You could go back tonight. Skip all this."

"No, no, I couldn't." He shook his head. "I'm an honourable man. I'll stay with you."

"I'm serious. You don't need to come with us. You've already helped us so much. I'll give a good report of you and your work to the papers back home." Privately, I didn't think anyone back home would listen to a word I said, I was a bad joke to former colleagues, but I'd do what I could.

"Very kind of you."

"Not at all. You've helped me so much." The formality felt awkward, almost cloying.

He put his upper and lower lips together, as if signalling both self-deprecation and agreement with my statement.

It was a relief when one of the staff members appeared at the door.

"Passengers for Platignall," he shouted into the room, now warm from the crush of people in it. "Passengers for Platignall."

We hurried to our feet and gathered our things together. In a corner of the bar was the same dog from earlier, bits of crisp smeared over his friendly, hairy face. At least the crisps were not going to waste.

Eleven

I WAS MEANT to be clearing away the dirty breakfast plates littered with crumbs, marmalade and smears of jam. But the view out the kitchen window was impossible to ignore.

Looking out past cobwebs and smeary panes, I could see acres of what would once have been fertile farmland. It was just about possible to make out traces of their old boundaries, though there were no crops any more.

Looking down from the hillside, it was difficult to imagine anything except bamboo ever growing there. The fields were empty, nothing much growing in them except of course the inevitable lanceolate leaves of our old friend.

Even before the crop failures, it couldn't have been easy to farm there with those gradients. Ironically enough, one of the few survivors was indeed bamboo, fastest-growing grass on this planet, same as just about everywhere else in the universe.

Our home for the next few days was a cottage just outside Platignall itself. On a hillier part of the planet than its other "beauty" spots.

"They should have made those offerings to the dead," said the cleaning lady, who was sweeping a mop back and forth with cheerful resignation across the black-tiled floor. "Might have all gone better."

I got the impression she wasn't entirely unhappy that events were vindicating her gloomy world view.

Offerings to the dead, though?

I gave her only a cautious half-smile.

Through the window, two birch trees were dancing in the breeze. They'd a look of embarrassed hesitancy about them, like dancers who find themselves unexpectedly alone on the dance floor and aren't sure whether to scuttle away or tough it out.

We'd been so relieved to find a place, we hadn't worried about there not being an indoor toilet.

You had to scuttle outside, feeling like a woodlouse exposed involuntarily to sunshine, then clamber down a rocky slope using a faded orange rope attached to steel struts welded into the rock.

My bottom felt cold as I perched on top of a rough circle carved into the large, dark, chiselled rock. I wasn't confident at all the Aballonians were following the latest waste disposal guidelines since, as far as I could see, our waste was simply hurtling hundreds of feet down the hillside.

Pulling up my leggings, I couldn't help thinking that vindicating myself professionally was turning into quite a thing, though it no longer seemed as important as it had before, probably because I was now looking after Oxie.

It was all a bit of a shock to be realising how self-centred I'd been in my old life. I was only aware of that now I was thinking of someone else – Oxie – as well as myself and even putting her needs ahead of my own.

There was no chance to think any more as I trudged back up the hill. Bamboo covered most of the slope, perhaps after being originally installed there as a firebreak, and last season's foliage lay on top of older growth, creating nature's own version of a luxurious, thick-pile floor covering.

The market wasn't exactly bustling that morning, there were some stalls balancing on rickety legs, a couple of them actually displaying a few food items for sale. And there was the odd person out shopping too, dour looks on their sun-burnt faces. Sun cream was probably yet another shortage, a real problem on triple-sunned Aballonia.

After our mid-flight stop–over the day before, I'd stopped taking even limited food availability as a given. Or anything else either.

Whatever was causing this latest food crisis, nobody seemed to be sure, theories ranged from mutant bacteria to sabotage by mysterious enemy forces from a rogue planet. After yesterday, though, I couldn't believe the whole thing was exaggerated nonsense.

Somebody must have brought a family of goats with them to market. Their bah-hing and bells made for an attractive, though plaintive backdrop.

"Why have we come here?" Oxie liked to get straight to the

point with her questioning.

"To get food," I told her. "Potatoes, pasta." She already knew that, though . . .

"No." She paused, perhaps measuring how safe it was to continue. "I mean, why have we come to this town?"

"To look for someone." I scratched at the side of my neck. "Who might be able to help us."

We were standing by a stall when I became aware of arms grabbing at me around my waist. I was terrified, they took us by surprise. My stomach went liquid, evaporated.

"What... What... Put me down."

I tried to swing my arms free, to get away. It didn't work. The man pinned both my arms to my sides.

"Leave us alone." In my panic, I was screeching.

They ignored me, continuing to half-pull, half-push me.

I wanted to kick but was too scared. They looked like they wouldn't hesitate to hurt us. I screamed, screamed again. Kept screaming. My throat ached, and I kept making noise.

When I saw a different guy - someone I hadn't even noticed before – grab Oxie and lift her up, I began to respond physically, pushing at him. It didn't have much impact, it was like he was made of steel. He pushed me away from him, like I was an annoying fly, pushing me so hard I staggered against the stall behind me and fell.

Winded, I put my hands on the cobbles to push myself up. That hurt, it really hurt. My arm was throbbing so intensely I couldn't tell where the pain was exactly, somewhere in my right arm. A throbbing pain so bad I was crying.

"Put her down."

None of the people standing around would meet my gaze.

Where my legs used to be, there was now a dizzy, vertigo-inducing absence of feeling. I could feel the vomit rising up my throat; I wanted to be sick – and was. Puke spattered everywhere. Using the back of my hand, I wiped it away from my mouth as best I could.

The man hustled me past other shoppers, who turned to gawp.

"Put us down." I tried to elbow him but couldn't reach his body. "Put us down." He ignored me.

He opened the side door of a biggish pod van, shoving us inside. The door slammed shut, the engine started and off we went, I'd no idea where, our take-off even faster and bumpier than usual.

I reached out as best I could to comfort Ox.

"It's okay," she whispered, taking hold of my good hand. "I know you're doing your best." We both knew my best wasn't much good, but neither of us said anything.

Holding hands, we clung onto some netting attached to the sides. In it were buoyancy aids. A sudden lurch downward meant we couldn't hold on any longer, my fingers hurt too much. Hurtling down, we let go of the netting. Reeling backward, I fell onto the floor, landing on a pile of old rags. They were dirty, smelly and there weren't enough of them to cushion the fall.

Just as I was recovering breath and balance, the pod dipped sharply again, veering like a yo-yo suspended from a piece of string that turned out to be more tightly wound than suspected, and turned fast as it sought a new equilibrium. My arm was so sore I could hardly bear it, pain eddying in waves through my stomach and upper body.

I wanted to try the breathing exercise a yoga teacher had taught me, but the pod was shaking and vibrating too much, loud clanging and clanking sounds reverberating through the ship from engines underneath the cabin. I couldn't focus on anything, the pain was too bad.

It was impossible not to scream, though I wanted to be strong for Oxie. Tears were splashing down my face, I yelled and yelled. Maybe whoever was doing this would relent if they heard me.

Next to me, Oxie was shrieking. A piercing wail, then guttural sobbing.

It was no good, I had to be sick again. I didn't want anyone else to see this, but I'd no choice.

I vomited up my breakfast onto a pile of life jackets stowed away at the side, too sick to care about the mess I was making.

The life jackets gave me an idea.

"It's going to be okay."

I took off my cashmere scarf, wrapped it around Oxie's wrist and used it to attach her to the large, cobweb-covered pipe running down past different nets and storage units.

The jolting happened again.

"Hold on tight."

She was screaming, but the scarf appeared to be helping.

"It'll be okay."

"How do you know?"

"I'm a journalist. We're trained to cope with tough places, tough people." Though only with words . . .

The ship began to slow down. Preparation for landing, I guessed. My heart rate sped up again.

"I'll do the talking"

She nodded.

Landing with a thud, we sat on the floor, dazed and nauseous. My arm hurt more than anything had ever hurt me before. Maybe childbirth was like this, but much worse, all across your body. I wouldn't know, not after losing that pregnancy, miscarrying when I wanted that child so much. My only hope of clinging onto Ed, and a pregnancy that felt like it might have been my last chance to become a mother.

The door opened automatically.

Unsure what to expect, we staggered off the pod and down the gangway.

Around us, we could see ruined remains of stone houses. The rubble looked as if it hadn't been actual houses for many years. Ivy sprawled over stone masonry that might once have been a doorway. Solitary disjointed wooden beams looked odd out of their usual context. Like oversized spillikins in a children's game. A thick covering of evergreen tendrils and heart-shaped leaves was claiming the space for itself, winning the battle for space, nutrients, light.

The wind was lifting up the sheet of corrugated iron used as a roof for one of the dilapidated dwellings. The metal banged back down again onto the stones with a loud clattering.

The sky was dotted with the residue of clouds trailing lazily through the vista.

An assortment of oddly coloured rocks was scattered over the ground, I could also see a few fruit trees.

It was so cold even they were shivering.

The pod jerked back into life again, breathing out fire like an aged and petulant dragon who knows he'll have to return to the fray, regardless of being too clapped out to stand much of a chance against his enemy.

My hand was shielding me from the suns, the fretwork made by tree limbs helping.

There was a kind of compound in front of us. Half military? With all the communication masts I'd expect from a military place, certainly. It had an oddly medical feel to it, as well, with people in germ-proof scrubs. A place for the latest instalment in the endless war between germs and cleanliness.

No signage, everything temporary, rootless. As if it could be dismantled and moved at only a few hours' notice. A leaden heaviness overlaying everything, despite the purposeful medics.

It wasn't clear what kind of hospital the place was, or what we were doing there.

I was gazing at the tents when I saw him. Yes, him. The man I'd come all this way to find.

A moment of doubt. Was it really him? Terrified of seeing a mirage summoned up out of my febrile longings, I gazed at him a few moments to be sure it really was him, I had to avoid the wishful thinking that had got me there in the first place.

Sandy hair greying at the temples. Wire-framed glasses. Faded chinos. A blue shirt striped with white. Bearded. An air of anxious determination. Someone more comfortable with action and things than with words? Not a man given to chatting.

"I'm sorry, we'd no choice." He held out his hands, large and well-formed, I noted with approval. "That must have been frightening, I apologise. Especially with your daughter here."

"No, she isn't . . ." Glancing at her face, my voice dried up. Trying with one arm to pull her closer, I gave Zoltan a defiant look. The other arm was really hurting.

The suns were lining up against the brow of the hill.

Trails of feathery condensation criss-crossed the sky.

"But where are my manners?" Zoltan smiled at me in a shy and self-deprecating way that helped me relax a little. "You are our guests. Please, let us offer you refreshments."

"You haven't been treating us much like guests." I didn't want to anger him, or even just risk alienating him, although the manner of our meeting wasn't promising, so I tried to sound jokey. But his people had just kidnapped us, and it hadn't felt friendly the way they'd bundled us into that Rat Trapper pod of theirs. "Funny way of treating anyone." He couldn't expect us to pretend that had never happened. Could he?

Or maybe he could. That inscrutable quality of his, I remembered it now.

"I gave the men orders to escort you safely. If I find they have disobeyed me I will discipline them."

"Your idea of escorting someone safely is different to mine. Also, you left me high and dry on that story. I lost my job because of you." I wasn't meant to be strident, but couldn't hide my anger, even while also aware I must sound self-righteous.

"Yes, I was sorry about that."

But not very sorry, I noted, annoyed at his perfunctory tone.

"Were you? You didn't answer any of my calls."

Without my source - him - my story was discredited. Doomed. Like me. Tears of vengeful self-pity were forming in my eyes. I brushed them away.

I'd been waiting for this meeting a long time. A long time. Couldn't ruin it now by collapsing in tears.

"I lost my job because of you," I repeated. I was longing to add more colour and detail but also aware of Oxie watching me.

"Yes, you already said. Most regrettable."

Most regrettable. Huh.

"That all you've got to say?" I wanted to growl and attack him, though the three minders he'd got in tow made me think that probably wasn't such a good idea. "Most regrettable? That job meant everything to me."

He looked awkward.

"Everything. Since I was a kid, I've wanted to be a journalist."

I let my good arm fall to my side, but didn't dare move the one that was hurt. Too painful. It was never just a job, it was everything. A vocation. A calling. Something that allowed me to escape my life and myself, to transcend the shittiness and self-hatred. All the scars

– emotional and physical.

"It was everything to me."

"I know it was important to you." He looked at the gently undulating hills as if he expected them to thank him for his insight too. "But not as important as your real priority."

"What's that then?"

"Isn't that obvious? You really need me to spell it out?"

At his words, I knew what he meant, the understanding hitting me in the stomach.

"Just because I like the odd ..."

He wouldn't meet my eyes, gazing instead at his feet. He was the one who'd destroyed my career by baling on me. He should be apologising to me, not criticising me for my alcohol intake.

"Right now I really need a medic to look at my arm."

He began looking through his crystal until a rustling sound of papery leaves dancing across the forecourt seemed to interrupt his thinking.

"This young girl is caught up in the crisis, yes?"

"Yes. I'm trying to help her find out what's happened to her real mum and her dad."

"I'm so sorry." The contrition in his voice sounded oddly genuine. "But my life – and the lives of my family – were in danger. After you named me as your source I had to leave Earthen . . . But, come, I'm a poor host."

Maybe the kidnapping was him getting his own back on me, revenge for the mix-up in the story, though that was nothing to do with me.

If so, he must have begun to relent towards me, because he followed up the drinking comments with a different note.

"You know, though, for now I would say you are her real mother, in the most important sense of the word."

It was odd, tears at unexpected kindness. For so long since the pregnancy ended, I'd tried to hide behind anger. It wasn't getting me good results.

"You've more or less kidnapped us, you know. It's not recommended in any of the etiquette guides." Watching him, I saw his features remain blank, his ego too fragile, I suspected, for him to admit to not understanding the reference to etiquette.

With my foot, I scuffed at the dust and pebbles of the path.

"Come." Zoltan held out an arm as if he were a shepherd and I was the lost sheep being welcomed back to the flock.

Oxie started following him.

"No, Ox, don't."

"He said he'd help." She looked obstinate.

"We don't know if we can trust him. Better to stay out here." I glanced around the reddish earth, devoid of vegetation and shelter, except for barbed spears of bamboo spiking up from the earth. Always deceptive-looking, even now so many people still expected fragility when they heard the susurrating movement of the stems in the breeze.

"You're not afraid of me, are you?" Zoltan stretched out his hands, as if to protest at how ridiculous I was being. It was hard to tell if the question was rhetorical or not.

"Actually, yes I am." My voice was betraying my fear, cracking and disappearing on me. My stupid pride meant I didn't want to admit to being scared. "I am afraid of you, And with good reason. Your men kidnapped us. When you disappeared on me you cost me my job. So, no, I don't trust you. Why should I?"

"You've been through a lot. I'm sorry. But you broke your promise to me."

"Is that why you're doing this? To punish me?"

He said nothing, but shrugged and held his hands up to the heavens in a gesture that suggested he was inclined to blame a forces of the universe whose will he wouldn't dream of trying to oppose.

"We'll stay out here." We walked over to a rocky outcrop in the shade.

It was a hot day, the land itself appearing to evaporate under the intensity of the suns.

I began rummaging in my bag.

"Why'd you do this? Make us feel you're kidnapping us?"

Glancing at Zoltan's sandal-shod feet, I noticed that his big toes were discoloured, somehow that made him seem more human.

"Haven't you worked that out yet?"

"No, I haven't."

"We had to get you away from your, er, escort."

Escort? What was he on about now? The term sounded like a range of car or an elderly roué who rented himself out by the night. Or hour. Never mind, we'd come back to that later.

Oxie must have picked up on my ambivalence.

"Are you the people who took away my mummy-daddy cuddles?"

"It's all right, Oxie." It probably wasn't, though.

"No, it is NOT okay," she shouted, agreeing with my private assessment, her tears falling onto the parched earth. Maybe we'd see miracles of new growth sprouting up where the tears fell, but then I remembered the high salt content. Putting an arm around Ox, I could feel her shaking with the strength of her emotions. After some moments, she relaxed against me.

"You've got me, Oxie. Bad luck, I know, but there it is."

Hearing her giggle, even for a half-hearted moment, was wonderful.

"Come," said Zoltan, surprising me by the kindness in his voice. "We might be able to help."

As we followed him out of the tent, our exodus was enough to make the wind chime tinkle out a couple of brief notes, tuneless and tinny but still just about musical.

Twelve

WALKING TO THE mess tent to meet Zoltan, cradling my arm, I was aware of smelling grass – not the pharmaceutical kind, its gardening homophone – and was reminded of times when, if not exactly happier, I'd at least been more carefree.

Stumbling over the interlinked spears of bamboo was trickier than I'd thought with my arm hanging painfully at my side.

It hurt even more if I tried to move it, so I didn't. The grass was pushing up through the ground faster than it could be trimmed back. As usual, the slender, almost fragile appearance belied its underground hinterland and strength.

The root system might have been shallow, but I still managed to catch my foot in it, lurching forward and almost falling over. The pain eddied and sharpened, my arm in greater agony than before. I couldn't move it or use it, so let it hang, my left arm touching it gently out of a desire for protection. I needed a doctor but didn't feel especially optimistic about finding one. I also needed pain killers but wasn't sure whether or not to ask for any; we were facing a global shortage of analgesics. My arm hurt, aching and stabbing me so much I couldn't think.

As soon as I got my balance back, I looked around for Zoltan. Still no sign. Fear bubbled up in me, stronger than ever.

We'd agreed to meet at two. It was already ten past.

Those scratches on the watch glass were new, it must have got damaged when we were being flung about earlier on the journey.

Another grievance to add to my ever-lengthening list of resentments against him, though of course he would see things differently.

We'd a history of missed assignations, me and him. The kind involving broken promises, betrayal and life-changing hurt. Unimportant stuff like that.

Could I manage the meeting with my arm so bad?

"Oh, dear. You all right?"

Thank goodness. Finally. It was him, Zoltan, looking more God-like than ever. I smiled as cheerfully as I could.

I needed him to help me with this story, it'd go much better if I could establish rapport with him.

The pain was so bad, I couldn't stop myself being sick, bending over and clutching at my mouth, trying (and, of course, failing) to keep my hair away from the vomit.

"I'm fine, thank you." I winced in pain." How are you?"

Swaying and rustling in the breeze, the bamboo was higher than the tents, I noticed. Whatever lateral space they were liberating through their root systems, they were clearly determined to make up for vertically

"You don't look fine." He looked more curious than concerned. "My people take their loyalty to me seriously. I do hope they didn't cause this damage to your arm?"

"Not directly, no." Unless you counted them kidnapping me and forcing me to travel at light speeds in a broken – down old banger unfit to take to the air.

"We could always talk later? Or another day?"

"No, don't be silly, don't worry about me, I'll be fine." It was hard to imagine ever being pain-free or fine, but I'd come several million miles in search of this man. No way was I giving up now.

A complex interplay of emotions on his face made me think he maybe felt guilty for having any role in me getting hurt. Even after so long spent blaming him for our fraught and unsatisfactory connection, I felt sorry for him.

It was as if he read my thoughts; he launched into an explanation of his thinking.

"The only reason I'm suggesting we meet here is it'll be easier for us to talk privately," he said, before blinking rapidly several times in succession. It was like the projector at the cinema breaking down for a moment, before resuming transmission.

Together, we walked a short distance towards some boulders.

"Want to sit down?" He pointed at some scruffy-looking stones big enough to perch on and sufficiently low to the ground to use as temporary benches.

"Do you want to? Sit down, I mean?" As I spoke, I realised the question hadn't been asked in hopes of an answer. Polite formalities could still confuse me, something I suspected Zoltan and I had in common.

This was feeling uncomfortably close to the first awkward steps in a relationship, but I knew he was married. Maybe I was still a little light-headed after hurting my arm. Was it broken? I'd no idea, I needed a professional to tell me. Shame I'd no time to see one.

We managed to sit down. A sharp rock was digging into my thigh, so I got up again and rearranged myself.

My arm was tormenting me, I wasn't sure how long I could last. I didn't have even ordinary painkillers with me, they were back at the house, probably still in my case, not even unpacked.

Sooner or later I'd surrender and limp off to the hospital tent, which seemed dark and hidden.

"What happened to those people you're looking after?" I kept my voice low. I hadn't seen more than a distant glimpse of them back in the 'dog food' factory.

Even with the trio of suns high in the cloudy sky, I shivered. "How come they're here now?"

"We seized them a few days back, freed them, gave them what antibiotics we could, brought them here." Zoltan stared at his feet, clad in fibres of Phyllostachys. He looked sad. Might even have been crying, I wasn't sure. "We do what we can for them. It's not much, but we keep them comfortable. We use old-fashioned pain relief whenever we can, since it's so hard to get hold of the modern equivalents. Some may recover, we don't know yet."

"Who are you working with?"

"Anyone opposed to the cartel. We're only small, just pockets of individuals, really. Someone suggested we call ourselves Resistance, but it's such a cliché." He laughed to himself in an embarrassed way.

"Who are the others working with you, though?"

"Scientists, like myself. People who've seen first-hand what's happening. Medics. Teachers. The odd underground journalist. Anyone who's lost loved ones."

"And who's behind all this?" This had so far remained vague, at least as far as I was aware.

"The cartel and government, of course, as you hinted in your piece. You got a lot further on the story than any other journalist I know. You've managed to make quite a few enemies. You're an honest person. The paper didn't manage to take you over to the dark side." He shuffled, moving his position so he was angled slightly away from me. "Not entirely, anyway."

"What's in this food, then?" I decided not to say anything about his 'dark side' comments, despite feeling annoyed at them. In fairness, I wasn't the one who'd masterminded an evil death food. Feeling self-righteous, I gazed at the line of hills stretching across the horizon.

"Bamboo, mostly. And bacteria."

Lovely.

"You're joking."

He shook his head and gazed at his toenails, as if personally responsible for what was happening.

"There can't be much about bamboo we don't already know."

The plant must surely have long ago exhausted its potential uses . . . It'd been a mainstream crop for centuries, tricky to imagine anything new coming from its jointed and hollow stems.

"No, I'm not joking. The plant remains of interest to many scientists. Myself included." He wouldn't meet my eyes, gazing at some stitching along a seam in his walking trousers that was coming loose.

"And what about the bacteria? Where's that coming from?"

In fairness to the guy, he looked upset at the question, shuffling his feet again and clicking at a pen he'd found in a trouser pocket.

When he eventually spoke, he did so quietly and while clicking his pen so fast that, at first, I'd trouble hearing what he was saying.

"Sorry, what?

"Toadstools." He spoke angrily, presumably out of guilt. "We used toadstools. They're typically produced above ground. Unlike the rhizomes of the bamboo, of course. The spore-bearing, fruiting body of a fungus. We thought there might be synergetic potential there."

He'd the grace to look ashamed.

"You were involved in these . . ." I hesitated to call them trials. "In these experiments?" Torture would have been a more accurate description of what was involved.

"I'm ashamed to admit it, but, yes, initially I was. I'd bills to pay, the work was honourable." He paused. "At least, at first."

I didn't have to pretend to be incredulous.

"You did this for money?"

He nodded, face crimson.

Although I liked Zoltan, even respected him, he appeared to operate in a moral zone inaccessible to the rest of us. Today he'd the grace to look more closely at the ground.

"It might have worked. When I discovered the problems, I left. Literally that same day. I got out. I couldn't be involved in it."

In fairness, I couldn't imagine him setting out to hurt anyone deliberately. But he seemed to be hinting at stuff I didn't know about...

"Problems? What do you mean?"

"We'll let you see for yourself. It's best that way." He gazed at his hands, as if suddenly uncertain about the length of his neatly clipped fingernails. "I'm not going to hurt anyone. Not knowingly."

"I know you're not, but you didn't say anything back when we met about people getting hurt in the trials." Neither of us had been exactly straightforward with the other, we were paying for our dishonesty.

"I was afraid for my family." He exploded a moment, spit spattering onto the dusty earth, guilt over his behaviour no doubt fuelling his anger towards me. His rage didn't prevent a stab of jealousy darting across my heart when he mentioned his family, no matter how much I knew rationally I was being silly, his words reminded me of how I felt doomed to be on my own forever, no boyfriend, no baby, no nothing. Just me and my self-pity. "You don't know what these people are like. It wasn't safe to tell you. They'd have hurt my family. And you didn't say you were going to give the paper all my details, come to that."

"You don't understand what these people are like. I couldn't refuse them your name, your details."

"Sounds to me as if the cartel has influence over the paper. Ring any bells? Know anything about that?"

I shook my hair, enjoying the feeling of it lifting and billowing in the wind.

"You were my only source, and you vanished on me." I tried to keep my voice matter-of-fact. "Vanished after we'd gone to press and there was no taking the piece out of the public domain."

"And you're sensitive to men who vanish on you, of course."

How did he know about Ed?

How much did he know about what had happened? He must have heard about me and my old lover to be making pointed comments like that. Maybe he'd been making his own enquiries, while I was trailing across the universe in pursuit of him, and the illusion of redemption he'd once represented.

"You used my name in that piece, I said everything was off the record. You didn't respect that. I'm a wanted man now, thanks to you. The cartel are after me. If they find me, they'll use me in the trials. I know you haven't seen the state those guys back there are in, but believe me, it's not good what they're going through."

"I told the paper about the story, said I'd agreed not to name you. They demanded your details, used your name without telling me."

Saying nothing, he growled.

He wasn't exactly straightforward, I realised, thinking again of how he'd bailed on me back home, hidden away for months.

"Why didn't you get in touch with me sooner? You could have let me know what was happening?"

"We're fugitives. You know what that means? On the run. From the police. From authority. We've managed to stay one step ahead so far, but we often have to move on, sometimes without notice. If they catch us, they'll use us in the trials."

The suns were getting in my eyes. I knew it was selfish, but I felt like crying.

"I lost my job over this, you know. Jobs like that don't just come along, you have to graft for them. Suck up to people you despise. And now I'm blacklisted. Untouchable. Thanks to you."

"I hadn't forgotten any of that." He subsided, looking as if I were cruel and perfidious for stating – admittedly a little selectively – the facts of our involvement. "You won't let me. Maybe you are getting what you deserve, have you considered that?

Of course I had.

"What about you kidnapping me and Oxie? She was terrified." And I didn't enjoy it much either, I thought silently, remembering lurching into the steel. "My arm, I think it's broken."

"We'll get you medical attention."

He gazed at the undulating hills, heat evaporating from the land like steam on a figgy pudding. "I didn't want anyone to get hurt.

He shuffled closer to me, until he was close enough for me to smell the creepy whiff of antiseptic I remembered from our handful of meetings on Earthen.

"You had me and Oxie kidnapped."

He held his hands up in a display of pretend indignation. "A fake kidnapping. Not a real one. It was to protect you."

"Felt pretty real to me." I hated how sullen and broken I felt. "We didn't know it was fake. Kidnapping a child? Was that really necessary?" I paused. "And protect me from what, anyway?"

With my foot I tried tracing a line in the sand, but only managed to kick up sand.

"I was helping you!"

"Pretty weird protection, isn't it."

"You can't talk. Look at you, always drunk."

"I've hardly touched a drop today. I'm sober. Anyway, drunk or not, I'm your only hope of getting this story out."

It was odd, such a sunny place. And yet, amidst the glistening light, these strange bacteria. Taking food and energy from other organic matter.

Underneath a slender birch, I could see a few toadstools, maybe escaped from the labs. Flattish, rounded, smooth, red, like miniature granite outcrops.

"Why'd you want to work for people who treat you badly?"

"Because I'm an alcoholic." People kept telling me I was, anyway. "I like it when people treat me badly."

"What about Oxie, though? That's a kind thing you're doing, looking after her, helping find her parents."

"Least I can do. I'm wondering if they might even be here now." I paused. "Or were in the past..."

Giant hogweed umbrellas gloomed over us. Next to them hovered the delicate filigree of a spider's web, preparing to trap whatever the night might bring its way.

A handful of trees tall enough to stand out against the bamboo were bowing to each other like elderly gentlemen at a social; trunks stolid and rigid with the stiffness of old age. Their thinner branches were essaying the first pas de deux of the afternoon.

It was still early in the year, large gaps of sky visible in the fabric of air, lignin and water. By mid-summer, leaves would have colonised every gap they could.

"Is it possible that Oxie's parents are here?"

"We don't know yet. We'll find out what we can about them?"

We arranged to meet again at the hospital tent, the project's dark underbelly.

"Don't wear anything you don't want getting dirty." Zoltan called back over his shoulder to me, not bothering to turn round and look at me as he spoke.

Thirteen

ON THE BELL-SHAPED tent a large 'H' was in wobbly green letters. It didn't seem like the letter had anything to do with helicopters, medicine felt the more likely option, though the place didn't look even vaguely antiseptic, and the horizontal stroke of the 'H' was streaked with bird poo; presumably staff being too busy saving lives to wash it off. I was standing there waiting to meet Zoltan, the guy I'd crossed the universe to track down. My arm hurt so much it was impossible to ignore, but I was so scared about what this meeting might reveal that I seemed to have lost sensation in my knees.

Despite the signage, the place didn't look like any hospital I'd ever seen before. Nobody loitering in a wheelchair with a fag. No anxious visitors. No gritty but exhausted medics. No instructions on notices about leading healthier lives.

Instead, edges of dirty canvas were flapping noisily in the breeze despite the aged, grey tie-backs wrapped around them.

As I leant back against a eucalyptus tree to wait for Zoltan, familiar hospital smells of antiseptic and pain drifted out. I thought I might even be sick, although at first it was hard to be sure. The stink was bad enough to make me forget for a second about my arm, which was clamouring with pain.

After a few moments, there was no room left for doubt about my dodgy tummy. I'd have to lean over to be sick. And so I did so, pushing hair behind my ears to avoid getting puke on it. A shock to remember I couldn't use my bad arm to steady myself, my balance so off-kilter I nearly fell over while retching up beige-coloured gloop dotted with oddly familiar bits of food in it. Peas? Beans? Chocolate?

Breath back, stomach settled, I straightened up, noticing ivy enmeshing the spindly branches of some nearby elderflower trees. There wasn't much tree left, the ivy had pretty much turned the original set-up into nothing more than scaffolding to support the colonising newcomer, so the effect was a hill of ivy; long tendrils of the stuff hanging down like coiffured locks in a fancy wedding hairdo.

Using my left arm, I wiped stray bits of hair and vomit off my face, unsure how Zoltan'd react to my appearance; he'd probably assume I'd sunk a few too many while waiting for him, if past experience was any guide. He could be very judgemental but then, so could I, though I was in no place to judge anyone about alcohol intake. I didn't like admitting to being high-handed and superior, not even if it was just to myself, it felt so wrong to me, but I was addicted to that way of thinking. For some reason, I seemed to keep meeting people like Zoltan, people who just couldn't understand that my lifestyle involved liberal quantities of booze. Unimaginative, dull; that was their problem. Clearly.

Since we'd arrived, I'd been wondering about asking the medics to take a look at my arm – but I'd hesitated, unable to stop worrying that maybe I'd lose the interview with Zoltan if I went off to see a quack. I'd get my arm fixed after speaking to him, if he ever bothered to show up, that was. Something told me this place might not even be there any more in a few hours; I knew from experience they could pack up and disappear in virtually no time at all. No need to get too dramatic, but impossible to escape a 'now or never' feeling about this meeting. Now wasn't the time to be getting cold feet.

Thinking of feet, I glanced down at my chipped red toenails and heavily tanned feet peeping out of my walking sandals. Part of me didn't want him to turn up, I realised. Didn't want to face whatever lay inside the 'hospital'. Or Zoltan and his ego. Another part of me saw him as, well, it was embarrassing to admit it, but a form of personal salvation. Vindicating me.

With a no-show, I could run far, far away from this khaki-coloured empire of pain. I wasn't seriously expecting him to bale, though, it felt more like him enjoying the chance to remind me who was in charge via a small power play. He'd gone to a lot of trouble getting me there; it'd be odd if he dropped me now.

Sure enough, he did finally arrive, though more than twenty minutes after we'd arranged. When I noticed him trudging toward me, I was gazing at some discarded grass foliage scattered on the sandy ground, the leaves striated, dry and wind-cracked. As soon as

I noticed him, I straightened up as best I could to greet him, sucking in my stomach.

"You're here," he said, sounding a little surprised I'd bothered to wait, as if he couldn't believe I hadn't got a better offer.

"Yes, of course." I forced myself to smile. Wasn't going to tell him I'd been secretly hoping he wouldn't show; no need to share my tendency to self-sabotage, my problem in believing things were finally working out for me. "Where else was I going to go?" I let my good arm turn so the palm was facing skyward, and, with my head, gestured lopsidedly at the vista of sand, cliffs, ravines and rocks. The gesture was meant to be ironic; I couldn't help wondering if it simply came across as bitter, which was probably closer to how I actually felt. "It's been quite a hike to get here."

We didn't say anything as we walked the few metres over to the hospital entrance together. I thought about a light-hearted joke to improve the mood but was too scared of saying the wrong thing; as for Zoltan, he looked too wrapped up in his own thoughts to say anything at all.

Yet more desiccated plant matter lay ahead of us, heaped up at the side of the entrance. Depressing.

We disinfected our hands, throats, noses. Walked further inside. Shards of living bamboo were already poking up through the canvas flooring, though staff probably cleared the stuff away daily. I couldn't have said which genera we were looking at, much less the species. I'd never have made it as a botanist, no matter how much I loved plants.

Be nice to have bamboo's stamina, though. I'd come a long way on this story, knew logically I couldn't give up now, not after all those weeks with dwindling supplies of vodka to keep me going, but, boy, was I feeling tempted to call it quits . . .

His next words surprised me.

"I heard about how the paper treated you. I'm very sorry."

"It's a tough world." Inter-planetary journalism wasn't exactly famed for its soft and cuddly ways.

I was fearful he could hear my heart, it was pounding so fast.

Nervously, I followed him deeper into the inner tented space, wondering if I was going to hold up to this.

Only as I focused more closely did I begin to understand the secrecy surrounding these people.

I'd rather be dead than left half-alive in the kind of state they were in.

None of the four of them had the full complement of limbs. One woman lying hunched on her side had no arms, her eyes staring blankly at the canvas. The patient nearest the door had only one leg.

"What happened to them?" I kept my voice low, my heart threatening to seize in horror.

"The food experiments happened to them," replied Zoltan with a softness that somehow only underlined the evil we were discussing. "These are the ones who survived. The lucky ones. We've buried the rest."

These food tests sounded chaotic and evil, not exactly the randomised and double-blind trials conducted by a reputable university, by the sound of things, that you'd ideally see in experiments on new ingredients. But that hardly did justice to the scale and depth of the evil we were seeing. On a selfish note, I'd at least finally found the proof I needed for my story, though that was feeling less and less important by the moment. But it was true about the republics coming up with an amazing new foodstuff, just like I'd said in the story so many had rushed to deny. Vindication. It was awful, though, seeing the price so many men and women were paying for this new food. Even I couldn't feel triumphant about my story being right, not when confronted with so much suffering.

"We want you to write this story. When I heard you'd made the effort to come to Aballonia I thought I owed it to you to let you have all the facts I do. Slight problem, there's a news blackout. Emails and internet are jammed shut, no traffic in or out of here. Distribution's going to be an issue. We're working on it, but don't have an immediate solution." Zoltan looked exhausted as he spoke, rubbing the backs of his fingers against first one eye then the other. "We'd have done the story ourselves if we'd a way of releasing it.

I'd at least got more on the story, most importantly I now knew why they were so suspiciously keen to keep it all quiet. This stuff was mutilating people, taking their legs, their arms, leaving them deformed, cripples. None of it looked good, of course they'd want to hush it up.

All I could do to help them was write this up as soon as I got enough material together, then worry about how to send it back to a paper on Earthen. True, communications were compromised; one of the main receivers was said to be down. Nobody could send or receive messages outside Aballonia itself. I'd cross that bridge later, though. First, I had to get the material together and write my piece.

I looked again at the two men and two women huddled in the beds.

Were the survivors the 'lucky' ones, I wondered?

In the first section of beds were four patients, two of them on one side, two on the other. All of them lying flat, silent. Bandaged. As if they'd gone to a place from which they knew they weren't returning.

Medical equipment, bleeping lights, monitors. Lines ferrying liquids curling downward from the 'ceiling'. Medics with forcedly impersonal expressions looked unable to hide their horror. One of them had already admitted defeat and was leaning against a stack of heart monitors, tuned out, eyes shut. Intermittent beeping sounded that might - or might not – be presaging further loss, finality, emptiness. Even here, in the inner sanctum, new culms of the grass were all too visible under the beds, tiny fronds acting the foot soldiers of an invading army.

Keen to avoid betraying my fear, I forced my facial muscles to relax, then turned to look again at the invalids – presumably some had been among the people glimpsed back in the so-called dog food factory, though I'd been unable to do more than glance at them back then.

No wonder the authorities were desperate to hide this. Insurrection was already underway on planets across the universe over shortages. If news of these atrocities got out, every planet in the universe would go up in a bonfire of rage, pain, horror.

"You know who's behind all this?" My voice rose loud enough for a nurse to turn and give me a nasty look as I spoke to Zoltan.

"Sorry." I glanced at her apologetically. Her look didn't soften.

"Businesses, planetary governments."

The usual suspects, no surprises.

"Which planets? Which businesses? Can you give me names?"

"Later, not now."

"Tell me now? Please?" I knew as I spoke he wouldn't; I'd forgotten how difficult he could be, or, put another way, how impervious.

My heart tightened as I looked again at the patients lying on truckle beds. The four I could see looked close to death. Going by their appearances, even if they survived, they'd be living a tiny fraction of their old lives.

And they were going through this rollercoaster without even the balm of adequate pain relief, (or so I suspected), and without loved ones to comfort them.

No doubt they were convicts, rebels, troublemakers. The vulnerable, the outsiders. The tactless and naïve. People soft enough to care about others. Convenient victims.

A nurse stuck her head around the canvas.

"Excuse me, Commander Zoltan? We've an update on those morphobinia supplies. A quick word?"

"Of course." He turned apologetically to me. "I'll only be a few minutes." His expression of doubt mixed with resolution returned.

I smiled gently at one of the patients who had their eyes open and sat down beside them. Grabbed some paper towels from a plastic dispenser on the wall, picked up a jug of water from the table stretching across the bed, poured a little onto some of the towels. Picking up the dampened paper, I felt its soothing coolness on my fingers.

"Would it be okay . . ." I looked at the paper towels in my hands. "For the heat?"

The man managed to move his head a fraction.

Praying that whatever was wrong with him hadn't mutated into anything contagious, cursing myself for being so self-centred, I sat down on a three-legged wooden stool by the bed. Afraid of making a mess, I squeezed out excess water onto the ground before unfolding the paper and gently laying it on the man's pitted forehead. I could feel his body relax, some of the sore tension unwind and dissolve, and we sat there together quietly for half an hour or so, no sound except the occasional beeping from one of the monitors.

Later, when Zoltan returned, I asked again about Oxie's parents; he said nothing, instead letting a brief shake of his head do the talking.

I managed to stop myself asking how thorough he'd been in his questions. Sadly, body language must have given me away.

"Yes, before you ask, I checked thoroughly. We'll let you know if anything changes." He tried to sound gruff, but his voice betrayed him, softening with the kind of sympathetic decency that must have got him involved with resistance in the first place. Abruptly, he turned away, muttering something about the high pollen count irritating his eyes.

My first priority was filing copy. Even allowing for communication trouble, there might be other hacks sniffing around, maybe I just hadn't bumped into them yet. Probably paranoia, but I wouldn't have wanted anyone else beating me to it with news of these trials, we were measured for speed with the type of attention normally reserved for racehorses and athletes, not that anyone could mistake a boozy, rheumy old hack for a sports star.

I wouldn't be winning any prizes for speed, but it didn't matter since there weren't any other reporters on the planet, or none that I knew of, anyway. Getting round the network blockades was another matter altogether, but I'd at least get the story together first, then worry about getting it out.

I sat down and began bashing out the story.

It was as I paused to do yet another of my myriad word counts that I first noticed the blur of a dark figure moving at speed toward us. Nobody was supposed to know we were even here, that this place existed. The rider was too far away to identify, but there was a strength, a verve and determination to their stance, visible even at a distance of several kilometres that felt oddly familiar. The sight made me anxious, my stomach plummeting. Were they planning on screwing with me? And my story?

Thinking the rider might be out to stop me from doing my job,

I picked up a communication chip, spoke into it. Waited to be put through to my old paper.

Contacting them awakened the old ghosts; inferiority, shame and horror. I couldn't let that stop me, I had to do this. It was why I'd come to Aballonia in the first place, I couldn't give up now, not when I'd come so far, no matter how tempted I felt to quit at the thought of launching back into such a murky world.

Fourteen

STANDING IN THE central courtyard, I squinted into the sunshine. Tramping feet, shouts and cries, stained bandages, stretchers. Groaning. Foreign, unpleasant smells. Medical-sounding orders featuring phrases such as 'stat', 'bleeding out' and 'fluids', all an attempt to depersonalise what remained deeply personal. At the centre of the melee dozens of unimposing, shrunken figures.

I'd risked just about everything on this trip, I had to make it work. Praying no-one would stop me, I slipped into the hospital tent.

One of Zoltan's lieutenants was standing at reception. I was close enough to hear his words. Not the bluster I'd have expected from him.

"Anyone seen Cathy? We need her to tell that kid we've found the parents." He spoke in a subdued, bluster-free way. His voice dropped lower. "They're in this latest intake."

At last. We'd been looking for them since getting there. This didn't feel like the breakthrough we'd been hoping, though. More like a bell was tolling somewhere, tolling for all of us and bloody loudly too.

I'd find Oxie, tell her. She might have only minutes to spend with them.

Thoughts of possible misunderstandings filled my brain with a powdery, cloudy confusion.

Thinking things through, I realised I'd better go and check these patients really were her parents before I involved her with them.

Cautiously, reluctant to draw attention to myself, I walked over to the nurses' station and began searching through an index of patient names and rooms. Yes. The surnames matched up. Oxie was an Ilyanovich, same as the new arrivals.

When I got there, the scene in their cubicle made me want to run and be sick. The looks of bleak, hopeless annihilation on their faces. The fact they'd both so obviously given up hoping things could ever be any better. Faces turned to the wall. Eyes open but turned off.

"Betrayed by another partisan," said the medic looking after them. "And forced to take part in the earliest trials. Toxicity was at its worst then."

"I'm so sorry." That hardly did justice to how horrified I felt. "So very sorry."

Something in my reply must have struck a duff chord, maybe a note of detachment.

"You're not family, are you?" He sounded as if he'd a few theories as to what I might be, none of them particularly nice.

"No, no. Just helping with identities." God help me. Not a complete lie, though. I glanced at the patient's face. Yes, she looked like Oxie. The same eyes, nose, prominent cheekbones. And the surnames matched. This had to be her mother, with her father in the bed next to her.

The medic shrugged, as if to say he didn't believe me but had more important things to do than waste time on me.

"Zoltan brought me here."

The medic looked slightly reassured.

"Did he?"

I nodded, and the medic visibly relaxed.

"How long for them?" I had to know, for Oxie's sake.

If he started discussing pieces of string, I wouldn't be happy.

"Who can say?"

"Yes, okay, but please, you're a senior doctor in palliative care, I need your best guess."

"A few hours, maybe." He paused. "If they're lucky."

Hell. I had to find her now.

My heart beating heavily, I ran around the compound looking for her. Some orderlies were burning off bamboo, a daily ritual. Smoke was wafting through the sky, streaking and besmirching the atmosphere. Clouds of gaseous carbon danced further and yet further away, diffusing into the sky.

Unsure where she might be, I stopped for a moment to think. With my feet I scuffed at a clump of bamboo at the side of the path.

Horrible plant. If people hadn't seized on it as the answer to climate change a few hundred years ago, it wouldn't now be taking over entire planets. But where was Oxie? She was fond of playing with her soft toys, I knew. Maybe she'd decided to invent some new games for them.

Looping hair behind my ears, I hurried to our tent. One of my silver earrings was missing, but that wasn't important. It was outside our tent that I finally found her, sitting on the ground with her beloved collection of pinecones and feathers, odd little bits of fabric and soft toys, too. I sat down on the dry and dusty earth next to her, trying not to cry, telling myself to be strong for her.

"Hello," she said, matter-of-factly, picking up one of the sticks and moving it so it was horizontal to the others.

"My love." I had to pause, breathe, clear my throat. "That looks nice. Is it the hills? And the valley too, maybe?"

"No. It is a picture of Mr Bear." Mr Bear was one of the best-loved creatures in Oxie's menagerie.

"It's beautiful. Well done, you."

"Are you okay?" She looked genuinely worried.

"Sweetheart, something's happened. Now, don't get too excited, but we think we've maybe found them."

Hurriedly, she got to her feet.

"My mummy and daddy? You've found them?"

"We're pretty sure, yes."

Her face blushed with happiness.

"They haven't been very well, I'm afraid … Sweetheart …" Her face drooped, I took her hand. I wasn't going to resort to the euphemism of 'very poorly', she deserved better and, anyway, might not understand, poor child.

"What do you mean?" She looked as if she knew all too well what I meant.

"Mummy and Daddy are in the hospital. They got hurt. Pretty badly, I'm afraid."

"But they'll get better again, won't they? They will eat their apples and get strong?"

"I'm sorry, my love, but they're not at all well."

Tears falling down both our faces, I held out my arms to her.

Wordlessly, she shuffled closer and put her head on my chest. I wrapped both arms around her, feeling even more determined to protect and love her than ever.

"But they will know it is me, won't they?"

"I don't know, my love. I hope so, but they're not really awake."

"Not awake? What do you mean?"

"Sometimes, when people are very sick, they sleep all day and all night."

"Will they give me a mummy-daddy cuddle?"

"I'm not sure, my love. I know they'd love to cuddle you and maybe even tickle you as well . . ." My attempt at levity was a mistake, she looked even more distressed. "I said the wrong thing, I'm sorry. I know they'd love nothing better than to hug you."

"Will they talk to me?"

"Maybe, I don't know."

She sat quietly a moment or two.

"Should I take this bit of the tree or the feather for them?" She held up both the pinecone and the feather for me to inspect them.

"Why not take them both, then decide when we get there? Your mummy will be so happy to see you, she won't mind what you bring with you."

"Are you sure? Because I'm making this for them." Her eyes glistened. "I knew I'd see them again. I just knew it."

"Seriously, my love, it's you they want to see. They don't mind about presents."

"How can you know that?"

I faced her.

"I just do."

"But how?"

"From experience. From life." From the sort of experiences she was going through, might even face again in the future. "This is how love works. Come on, we'd better go."

Clutching pinecone and feather in one hand, Oxie slipped her other hand into mine. Together, we turned toward the tents.

As we got closer to the main compound, she began to look uncertain, her palm sweaty in mine. "Will they still love me, my mummy and daddy?"

A relief to feel sure of something at last.

"Yes, no need to worry about that. They'll always love you." I paused, scanning her face to see if she was taking in my words. She looked marginally less anguished, so maybe I was managing to help, even just a little bit.

"You can't turn love off, it's not like electricity, or running water." Here, though, I began to feel less certain. What did I know of lasting love? It became interesting to look at the lichen clinging like thick cobwebs to the path.

As soon as we got to the tent, I spoke with the team looking after the latest intake and explained Oxie's connection.

They responded with the restrained, professional sympathy medics are trained to show in the face of impending doom and life-changing calamity. One of the nurses gave Oxie a lollipop.

"They're very poorly," she whispered to me, when Oxie was out of earshot. An understatement that was usually code for 'close to death'. It was what doctors had said when my grandfather was in his last days. It still hurt to remember those days, but I was an adult when I lost him. Oxie was too young for facing a loss on this kind of scale.

Taking her hand in mine again, we walked over to the numbered beds as instructed.

"Try not to worry, my love." I wished I'd something less vacuous to say but that was the best I could manage.

Who wouldn't be worried at a time like this? There'd be something wrong if she wasn't freaking out. Nobody could go through what Oxie was without struggling to keep going, and Oxie was still only a child.

She was already crying, so was I.

Pushing aside the tarpaulin shielding them from other incumbents, I looked at the two figures lying on stretchers in front of us. They were gaunt, their energy stripped away along with the life force itself, like shells in a hinterland between life and death. A barrage of medical equipment fortified their beds, much of it out-dated and grubby.

"Mummy! Daddy!" She hurled herself at them as soon as she saw them. For a foolish moment, I wondered if I should say to be careful not to hurt their poor, damaged bodies, but thankfully I had the sense to say nothing.

It was hard to tell how much Oxie's mother was able to take in; I liked to imagine a mystical connection between mother and child that transcended earthly constraints, but both her mum and her dad had their eyes closed.

"Mummy," she said again, pushing with her hand at her mother's arm, her heavily chipped nail varnish reminding me again of how young she was. Her mother didn't stir, instead breathing rapidly and shallowly.

Despite the difficulties, a look that suggested contentment seemed to spread across her mother's face, though, relaxing her frown.

Perhaps the three of them didn't need words to re-establish their connection. They looked so alike, too, the same snub noses. Magda and Oxie both had the same billowing, curly waves of cloudy, dark hair. Madonna and Child, almost, the effect spoilt only by the scuffling sounds of rats brushing past bamboo shoots as they scurried over the canvas, although the stable in Bethlehem must have had a few rats kicking around it too.

A nurse bustled into the room carrying a metal bowl with syringes and medicines. When I'd dealt with her before, she'd looked disgruntled. When she saw Oxie draped over Magda and her dad, her body pressed up close to her mother, she paused, though, and reversed out of the room again. People could surprise you with their kindness, even the most difficult of them could be unexpectedly kind.

It felt important to let Oxie have this special time with her parents without anyone else around, so I whispered that I'd be outside in the central atrium and quietly tiptoed away, my heart feeling like it was breaking at the thought of all that was happening.

I spent the time Oxie was sitting with her parents giving sips of water to a patient in the next section. After a few failed attempts, I eventually managed to persuade him to take some water from a sponge I held to his mouth while kneeling at the side of his fold-up truckle bed, then I moisturised what was left of his lips, too.

It was a nurse, not Oxie herself, who told me of their passing, her head bowed.

"Oh. Oh. Oh, no, my poor Oxie." My heart felt cold and heavy.

"Is she in there now?"

"Yes, saying her final goodbyes. We'll only prepare them for the next stage when Oxie's spent as long with them as she'd like."

"Should I go in to her?"

"Maybe let her have this time with them on her own? Up to you, though."

"Of course, whatever you think best. Will you tell her I'm here to help her? Whenever she wants."

"Of course, I'll tell her now."

I'd no idea how long Oxie'd need to spend with her parents and didn't like to ask. Something so precious and heart-felt surely couldn't really be measured in half-hour chunks logged on a spreadsheet held in a crystal.

But the time passed faster than I was expecting. After an hour or so, I went hunting for the same nurse again.

"Is she okay?"

The nurse looked puzzled.

"Who do you mean?"

"Oxie, of course."

"But I thought she was with you. She went out a while back. Very upset."

"Hell. She didn't come to me." Oh no.

"Let's get outside, start looking." We turned, made for the exit.

"She can't have gone far." I was trying to convince myself as much as the nurse.

Through the tent flap, rain was blurring and altering the colours of the landscape, melding blue into a medley of pensive, muted greys with odd, discordant, crashing chords of flashy purples and reds. The sky and land looked unending, the places for Oxie to hide countless.

Shouting out her name, I hurried around the camp as fast as I could, searching behind water tank, septic tank, air cooling units, spare hospital beds.

Looking under tarpaulins, ferreting about on rock piles in case Oxie had left a glove or a scarf there, even checking strangers' tents after explaining I was looking for a missing child – my missing child – worry engulfed me.

The hunt wasn't helped by the bamboo everywhere, new shoots were emerging that hadn't been there hours earlier, reminding us who – or what – was really in charge around there. I felt a jolt of anxiety when the mess tent clock rang ten o'clock at night.

As the wind subsided, the elm trees that had colonised much of the area looked as if they were reaching up their arms in supplication to the sky. When branches and leaves shifted position, I caught a glimpse of a red jumper I recognised.

"Oxie?"

Scuffling sounds from behind a large rhododendron, all jagged branching arms and legs, confirmed someone's presence.

"It's me." I didn't want to frighten her.

"Go away. Go away."

I wept with relief that she was at least safe. Physically, anyway.

"Please come out, my love. I want to help you."

"No, I don't want to come out. I want to stay here."

"All night?" Maybe she was thinking of sleeping out there, I could hardly blame her. To lose both her parents so young . . . When the nurses had offered to let me spend private time alone with my father's corpse after his death I'd refused; even in death his waxy body still scaring me.

"I will stay here always."

"Sweetheart, this is a terrible time for you. I'm so, so sorry about your mummy and daddy."

"This has nothing to do with you." In her distress, she was shouting. "They are my mummy and daddy, not yours."

Were her parents, I thought silently. Although maybe some relationships could never dissolve, transcending mere mortality. But that was hardly much comfort to a young child so recently and cruelly bereaved. The wind seemed to be howling in sympathy with Oxie.

"I know, darling, I know." I didn't know what she was going through, though. "This is hurting you." Even I could see that, though I wasn't at all sure I understood her pain. "If you come out, I can help you. Look after you. Maybe even make some hot chocolate."

There was a sound of branches bending, breaking, the shushing of leaves being pushed aside, a rustling and crackling.

She'd never looked more forlorn than she did that evening under her paper-thin veneer of angry defiance, and my heart was breaking for her. Bits of rhododendron were attached to both her hair and jumper, her socks were down by her ankles, her legs covered in crisscross scratches.

"You poor, poor thing."

Released from the predations of the rhododendron, Oxie buckled under the weight of her grief. Trying to support her, I wrapped my arms around her.

Even as she reluctantly hugged me back, she muttered again about me not being her mother.

"I know I'm not your mum, really I do." Damn, I was crying too now, even though this wasn't about me. "But I love you and I will care for you for the rest of my life, if you'll let me." Tears were running down her face, too, leaving parallel pathways through the powder of the day's dust and muck.

I hugged her anyway, scared she might otherwise evaporate in the chilly half-light of daytime suns unless I anchored her to the earth.

"Dear Oxie. I'm so sorry."

After a moment, I felt her relax against me, great heaving sobs filtering out toxins of loss and unhappiness, leaving in their place a renewed calm.

"It's going to be all right," I said, aware things could be far from even vaguely 'right', let alone completely so but desperate to offer what comfort I could. The words calmed her, though, and she seemed to feel safer with my arms wrapped around her.

Hand-in-hand we walked back to the main camp, where we sat for a couple of hours, drinking hot chocolate and saying little, but relaxing with the reassurance of each other's presence. Eventually, I managed to persuade her to lie down in our tent and sleep, her face still puffy and reddened from crying.

Tip-toeing out, I looked back a few times to check she was okay. Yes, good, sucking her thumb, Big Horse snuggled next to her. A chance now for me to think through our next step. I gazed at the moths noisily mobbing the torch light outside, their darkness juxtaposed with what little illumination we could offer them. I was so tired that for some moments I couldn't even drag my gaze away from the little circus being performed there by torchlight, my exhaustion making the performance so compelling that it was some moments later before I could begin to summon the energy needed to brush my teeth and get ready for bed.

Fifteen

AT FIRST, I thought the figure on a dirty trike heading noisily toward us must be Zoltan returning from some expedition or other, probably foraging for odd-looking herbs with curious medicinal properties and so I felt pretty relaxed. But when I looked up again from my typing to see someone on a vehicle flying fast towards us, blowing out clouds of brownish-black air like an annoyed dragon I knew it probably couldn't be Zoltan; he'd never have driven that fast, not even in a planetary emergency.

So, who'd tracked us down to this hideaway? What did they want with us? Without even thinking about it, I picked up my stunner, preparing for trouble.

The guy's arrival was all very Meat Loaf, although minus any rock music. Almost fun enough to make me forget for a moment the pain in my arm.

Almost.

Typing left-handedly meant progress on the story was slow, but I'd decided that only once I got my story written would I see about getting my arm fixed. I didn't want to have come all this way and endured months of crappy food, fear and danger for nothing.

Craning my neck, I tried to get a better view of the new arrival. Something – maybe the intensity of how the rider was crouched over the handlebars – didn't match with how I thought of Zoltan, who was dusty, academic, fussy and pained, more a man for Schubert than hard rock, I'd have guessed; this rider was going fast enough to flatten the bamboo plants in the fields with their slipstream. In their wake was a trail of flattened, yellow-gold foliage.

My good hand shaking, I managed to close the laptop and watched apprehensively as the figure drew closer. Nobody was supposed to know we were here, though if it was Zoltan that was okay . . . Then I remembered seeing him twenty minutes earlier outside the tents, attempting to propagate some recalcitrant Solanum; he couldn't be Bike Rider. Somebody must have betrayed us, tipped off the authorities to our co-ordinates. I felt sick at the thought, and started putting on my shoes so I could run over to the garden, where Zoltan would normally be working at that time of day, coaxing his much-loved cuttings along.

I'd a chance to think things through more as I gingerly pulled on my boots and began to relax. Glancing in my mirror, I felt stupidly pleased that all these weeks with three suns shining down on us all had left my hair lighter than before, like a dose of instant highlights but cheaper and without all the bits of foil and the mess normally involved in changing hair colour back home.

The Aballonians would never have sent out just one officer on their own; there'd have been at least two of them, possibly, no, certainly more, if their goons had properly scoped out the refuge. One guy on his own couldn't exactly overpower us all, though he could grass us up to his mates back home. Might have already done so. I needed to find Zoltan, tell him about our visitor, who was getting closer and closer to us.

Even worse, the new arrival might be another journalist, planning to steal my story. I pulled tight the knots on my boots, got up and hurried out of the tent. Outside, to my dismay, I could see the visitor parking their trike.

Damn.

Still unrecognisable under their helmet, they climbed down off their steed. Their dirty, dust-marked leathers had various cases attached to them; making the figure look like a rather unusual kind of Christmas tree, decked out with baubles, except, in this case, I'd an uneasy feeling the decorations probably held firearms . . .

I watched as the driver finally took off their helmet and goggles, arched their back, stretched and looked around. The suns were shining straight at them.

Screwing up my eyes against the light, I managed to look at the new arrival more closely.

Oh, hell.

Hadn't been expecting to see him there.

Praying I'd got it wrong, aware I almost certainly hadn't, I looked again.

Yes, it was him all right. Or all wrong, depending on how you saw it.

I'd no trouble recognising that crop of sandy-coloured hair

sticking out at odd angles. An expression hinting at being lost and confused, while failing to disguise an adamant strength of will.

We were meant to be hidden from the rest of civilisation.

Including him.

Typical, really, him acting as if the rules applied to other people. Never him.

He knew damn fine he wasn't meant to be here.

How'd he track us down? I'd a sneaking admiration for him finding us, but it was all very puzzling. No fixer or photographer I'd worked with before had ever shown this much determination to stay close to me.

Stumbling toward him, I nursed my arm, trying not to jolt it. In my confusion, my footing went and I lurched forward, almost falling. Though I braced for him to laugh at me, he surprised me by darting forward and grabbing hold of my arm (the good one, thankfully) to steady me.

"You okay?"

"I'm fine." That wasn't true. Not only was I in agony with my arm, I was also worried about what he was doing there.

I could have stayed with him holding onto me a lot longer but, reluctantly, I moved away. I thought he was maybe sad at letting go, too, but wasn't sure. I couldn't believe someone as decent, as attractive, as together as him would want to be close to me. Unless they'd an ulterior motive; either sexual or professional. Probably both, if experience was any guide.

"What took you so long?" I wasn't expecting an answer involving delays on the Northern Line.

"I'd half the planet to search. It took a while."

We both smiled, but it remained impossible to tell what he was thinking as we stood there under the trio of suns. Winds zipped back and forth, making hair flap in my face.

His eyes were kind, and the shy smile didn't quite fit with his Hell's Angel apparel. His lack of confidence reflected my own, and he certainly wasn't vain – that dark blue jumper he was wearing had worn away altogether in places; both elbows were holed, strange bits of bobbly fluff clinging to every inch of it.

"Are you okay?"

"Yes, apart from my arm." Grimacing, I glanced down at the site of throbbing pain. Under my grey jumper, the limb seemed to have doubled in size. "But I'm fine. And getting my arm fixed in just a few minutes."

"So you're fine?" He looked quizzical, teasing.

"Yes. Thank you for asking." Only after I stopped speaking did I realise his comment was meant as a joke. "More to the point, what are you doing here? How'd you find us?"

"I've been looking for you since you disappeared."

"That's good of you." Also slightly creepy? Couldn't he give me some space? "How'd you find us?"

"Rented this trike, trawled across the more likely parts of the world."

"How'd you even know where to start looking?"

"Someone in the market saw the van lift off, noted the direction. So I just began with places out this way." He gestured at the summits wrapped in mist spooling out in fractal repetitions, lining up in a protective formation. "Here, in the Northern mountains."

"Got to say, I'm flattered." I tried to make my words sound ironic, uncomfortably aware they weren't. "That's quite a journey, a quest, really."

"Don't go getting any ideas, now." He sounded only mock-serious, but might have meant to make a point.

"Of course not, wouldn't dream of it." I tried to sound light-hearted, but my mood dipped as sharply as scree tumbling down a mountainside.

"I'm here because we're colleagues. I know you'd do the same for me." His voice was gruff, perhaps a sign that he did have feelings for me? Oh dear. Mad, crazed stalkers probably got started like this. "You'd do the same for me, wouldn't you?"

"Yes, of course." Would I, though? I wasn't sure . . .

"Now I'm here, I'd like to see more of what's happening, if that's okay. We could get some great visuals. All right?"

Great visuals? Of the sick and suffering? No . . .

"We'll need to check. They wouldn't like just anyone wandering around." It seemed only right to check with Zoltan first before letting Istvan hang around in the compound.

"I'm not just anyone, though, am I?"

Wasn't he? I'd not seen this more confident side to him, although, in fairness, he'd tried to sound ironic; maybe it just hadn't quite worked.

He was coming across as more focused and driven than I could remember him ever being before. I was also vaguely aware of not understanding yet what exactly was driving him. Maybe wanting to reconnect with me? That didn't quite make sense, though.

"Of course you're not just anyone. You're a fixer, an interpreter." I swallowed, oddly unable to meet his eyes. "You're my fixer. My interpreter." Privately, though, I didn't think Zoltan would see things that way. As far as he was concerned, an uninvited fixer would be just another potential threat. He wouldn't be making an exception for this latest arrival.

Perhaps aware his words were falling flat, Istvan fixed me with a hopeful smile.

"I'm a media professional." He sounded as if he was struggling to remain professional, though. "This is what I do. I've every right to explore a new setting. No, more than that, it's my duty to explored it. Tell me, what is this place?"

"It's not for me to say." I was awkwardly aware of sounding prim; his arrival had caught me off guard.

"Doing publicity for them now, are you? Got a project on the side?"

"Don't be ridiculous. You should just talk to the boss, check it's okay with him first."

"Since when did you get so keen on asking permission?"

In vain, I tried to remain impervious to his taunt. The truth was Istvan's arrival could rebound on me – badly. "Come on, this isn't my thing. It's down to the guy in charge. He'll have to say if he's okay with you seeing the hospital tent." I paused. "Or not." As the words 'hospital tent' left my mouth, I cursed myself for saying too much. "I need to go there anyway, for my arm."

"Hospital tent? That's what's happening here? A place for the sick? The wounded? You joking? Are they contagious?" He recoiled, veering back from me in a mock-dramatic swerve that I suspected he maybe meant seriously.

Dumbly, I shook my head. What had I done? "No, no, no. I wouldn't joke about something so important. But I'm not meant to talk about it. If they find out…." If they found out, Zoltan and I might start yet another phase of no-speakers. This one lasting decades. I might never get to leave Aballonia. And I'd never get back into mainstream journalism, though maybe I'd just have to make my peace with that. The whole trip would be another dead-end waste of time and money. One involving yet more wasted hopes.

"Who're the patients in this 'hospital' of theirs, then?" He'd a way of getting physically close to me as he asked, I felt I'd no choice but to reply.

I could also hear a suspicion, a contempt to his voice. For me? Or the rebels? A hardness to his voice that made me want to justify myself. He didn't seem remotely worried about my arm, though he'd just ridden thousands of miles to find me. Wherever I went, it was always difficult to understand what was happening there. Whatever was wrong, it must have been my fault.

"Just people." Although the patients weren't just anything, they were human beings, real people. Sick people, too. And they deserved kindness. Not that they'd received much so far.

In dismay, I watched for a moment as he squared his shoulders and began walking towards the big tent, his usual determination still evident even as his figure began receding. He'd forgotten he was still wearing a day pack on his back and, when he tried to enter the tent, he became caught up in the guy ropes mooring it to the ground.

Alarmed, I began to follow.

"No, please. Come back . . . It's not allowed." I didn't like breaking the rules, was always too frightened of authority figures to be comfortable with infractions.

Catching up with him, I saw the tent itself trembling and shaking with the force of his attempts to free himself from it. He was going to huff and puff and blow the house down if he wasn't careful. A couple of doctors directed meaningful looks our way.

"Everything all right?" The doctor speaking sounded doubtful things were even close to being okay.

I wanted to scream that no, nothing was okay, but my politeness chip, installed and downloaded many years before, refused to eject.

"Yes, absolutely fine, thank you."

I turned back to Istvan. "Okay, stay still while I try and disentangle you."

The balance of power shifted as I battled to separate guy ropes, day pack and Istvan from each other, me enjoying for once having more control over the situation than him. He seemed resentful, either about that or something else, since he didn't bother to thank me for freeing him, just muttering angrily to himself in Aballonian.

Satisfied we weren't pulling down their hospital, the medics no longer looked bothered by me being there with a strange man they'd never met before, which seemed odd, but I'd probably spent too long as a journalist, suspicious of everyone and everything, baffled by anyone with priorities beside word counts, news leads and by-lines.

"Look, please, will you stay here while I try and find the medic who's going to help with my arm?" I gave him a hopeful look, but he didn't smile. "Don't wander around without me."

Not meeting my eyes, he nodded in a perfunctory way.

I walked over to a nurse sitting behind one of the hastily erected desks. Dark shadows underlined her eyes, she looked as if she couldn't have slept in weeks. "Please, I've arranged to see a doctor. It's my arm. It's broken."

"And you are?"

For a moment, I began worrying they might refuse to treat me.

"Cathy Prior. Zoltan brought me here."

The mention of their leader's name was enough to trigger action; she began talking into a crystal.

Two medics appeared, ushered me into a sticky-looking wheelchair and pushed me towards a curtained-off section.

In the room, they injected me with something that spelt blessed relief, scanned my arm, gave me a temporary sling and explained about having to operate on me. Ideally, the sooner the better.

"There's a child I'm looking after, I need to tell her what's happening."

"Be quick. The sooner we operate, the better."

Leaving the doctors, I was wheeled back into reception. It was a surprise to see Istvan still sitting on the grubby beige plastic chair where I'd left him, playing games on his crystal. It didn't look like he'd ever left, but I couldn't ignore niggling suspicions he might have. Suspicions that obstinately refused to leave me, not unlike Istvan himself.

I also felt stupidly surprised the world had continued to function despite me being hors de combat in the medical side-room. It felt shameful to be still so self-centred at twenty-seven.

"What'd they say?" He got up, walked over and knelt down at my side.

"They want to operate. Ay-sap."

"Christ. Must be bad."

"Yeah, well, the morphine helps. Nothing's hurting now, in fact."

"Want to go and rest? You must be wrecked."

The thought of a sit-down and cup of tea had an almost hypnotic effect on me. Who cared if they didn't make tea properly on Aballonia? It was at least still tea. After a fashion.

"I need to find Oxie first, tell her I won't be around while they operate. I don't think they let you eat or drink before an op."

When I saw the tall, stooped figure I'd been half-dreading, my heart bounced around my chest like a football kicked into touch. He was standing in the corridor talking with a couple of doctors. Even with morphine dulling my responses, I could see the situation was far from ideal, given Zoltan's feelings towards the new arrival.

"Why don't you come and say hello to Commander Zoltan?" Turning round to where I thought Istvan was standing, I saw only a trolley of bed pans and catheters. Where the hell was he now? Hiding from Zoltan? That would only made him look even dodgier.

"Istvan?" Glancing around, I tried not to raise my voice too much, worried about waking other patients.

He materialised at my shoulder. "Yes, you were saying? I was in the toilet."

"Would you like to meet the guy in charge here."

"Maybe later? We need to get you into surgery first, don't we?"

Was he deliberately stalling? Afraid Zoltan'd kick him out – or worse?

"I've got to talk to Oxie first."

I got up out of the wheelchair – an unlovely contraption with debilitation writ large. Walking over to our tent, I found Oxie, told her what was happening.

"It'll be fine," I told her, my voice mounting higher with each word. "Absolutely fine. Come and wait in the hospital tent, if you like, while they do their worst." I laughed, trying to tell her that everything would be okay.

She nodded guardedly and followed me back to the tent. Istvan was lounging around in a side room opening out of the surgical area.

"All okay?" He looked as if he might even genuinely care about me; I'd never understand him.

"Yes. Should be out in about an hour." I paused, embarrassed. "Wait for me?"

"Of course I'll bloody wait for you. Go and get your arm fixed."

"See you when I get out."

"Yes and enjoy all that morphine. Top-grade medical-quality opiates."

It was certainly bliss not to be in pain any more, I wanted to remember how it felt, never take it for granted ever again. But in a few minutes I'd have forgotten ever having trouble with my arm, except for the fabroplast fabric moulded onto it.

It wasn't until I was lying in recovery that I saw him again.

"Nice look, must say." His attitude was gentler than normal, though, and when he sat down on the side of my rickety wooden bed it was only with great care.

He'd maybe only waited for me because I was his entrée to the compound, but still . . .

It wasn't only my arm that was broken, I was feeling pretty shaky more generally. So much so, I could've sunk into his arms and stayed there forever, hamming up the "damsel in distress" angle. Except that wouldn't have been professional. Or cool. And might also have hurt my arm.

My relief evaporated when I saw Zoltan's face in the canvas window. Walking into the room, he looked as hunched and peevish as the Oxford don he might once have been, in a different lifetime.

"Cathy! Got that arm of yours fixed up then?"

"These guys have been great, sticking me back together."

"They good to you?"

"Very much so. Thank you all."

I was buttering up Zoltan to encourage friendliness toward the new guest. It didn't work. As soon as he noticed Istvan emerge from behind a blanket at the side of the room, Zoltan's attitude changed. I watched in dismay as he reached out a hand to an emergency button dangling from the tent's canvas, pressing it several times in rapid succession, all without taking his eyes off Istvan, who looked oddly unphased by the turn of events. He even stayed calm while Zoltan grabbed a dirty broom covered with bits of hair and indeterminate grit, wielding it in his hands like a sword for performing martial arts.

"How do you do." Istvan stuck out his arm. He couldn't have been expecting the handshake to be returned; Zoltan had no hands free, for one thing. Possibly even more important, I wasn't feeling any trust or connection between them.

Men I'd never met before crowded into the space and grabbed hold of Istvan, one pulling his arms behind him, the other cuffing him. He was oddly passive throughout; maybe thinking there was no point wasting energy trying to resist, since he was outnumbered. Or maybe he didn't want to risk angering the guards.

"What would you like us to do with him, sir?" asked one man.

"Search him. Every last inch of him. Anything you find on him – trackers, monitors, skin plants, ghost devices – bring them here."

I felt revolted at the thought of where they must be planning to search. Poor Istvan, it sounded like they were going to put on the rubber gloves. Oddly, though, Istvan himself still looked unphased by this turn of events, the same zoned-out serenity playing across his features.

"When that's done, bring him back here. I've questions for him."

"You didn't get this rank in the Aballonian navy, did you?" said Istvan, with some bravado.

What did he know about career prospects in the navy? An odd thing to say.

"None of your business, though, is it, Mr Istvan?" Zoltan knew perfectly well that Istvan was a given name, not a surname. The honorific was sarcastic. "How'd you find us? Cathy give you our co-ordinates?"

"No, I most certainly didn't." I tried not to sound self-righteous, though with what I feared was only limited success.

"I didn't ask you, I asked your friend here." Zoltan spoke with a scientist's precision.

"Following my nose, that was all."

Zoltan looked sceptical at Istvan's words, nodding to the guards to continue their work.

Two of the men put their arms through Istvan's and dragged him off, his feet pushing through the bamboo spokes decorating the flooring.

"Did you betray us?" Zoltan looked as if my betrayal wouldn't have surprised him in the slightest.

"No! No, I didn't. I really didn't." Had I unwittingly done or said anything to betray us? I racked my brains, rifling back through the memories of the last few days. Then remembered, sighing with the relief. "You took all my devices. I couldn't have contacted him. Or anyone else."

"Maybe you've a device we don't know about . . . that you've managed to hide." He looked as if no treachery would have surprised him, he'd seen it all. "You've got the laptop. Maybe there's secret functionality that allows messaging." He looked angry. "I convinced people we could trust you, even after you allowed information to slip out on that first story. You didn't understand then what we were up against, maybe still don't. I'll tell you this, Cathy. I can't be answerable for what those men will do if they find out you've betrayed us."

Fear cold as ice cubes tinkling in a glass of vodka ran through my blood.

"Please, no. No, I haven't done anything."

"Say what you like." Zoltan waved in an imperious way, as if the situation now bored him. "The men are administering truth drugs to your gentleman friend now. We'll soon find out how he tracked us down. If you led him to us there will be consequences. And we'll certainly be making sure he can't spread the word about our location." He inspected his fingernails, which, as ever, were clean. "You Eartheners are fond of betrayal, aren't you?"

I ducked my head, reluctant to say anything for fear of angering him.

When Istvan returned, he could barely walk. Two men, one on either side, dragged him in. His head was lolling forward, as if his neck was no longer strong enough to support his skull and brain. Drool was slicked over his face.

I started getting out of bed to go and comfort him.

"No, don't," said Zoltan, in the pained manner that was making me hate him even more than before.

"Istvan, love." I was crying. What had they done to him? "We'll get you okay again."

Slumped into a chair, Istvan managed to give me a wink with the eye that wasn't blackened.

I felt increasingly fed up; I'd already broken my arm being carted around in that death trap of theirs, now they'd hurt Istvan, who was only there because of me. And it was clear their leader distrusted me too.

"Did she tell you our details?" Zoltan looked supercilious.

"No, she didn't," mumbled Istvan. "Somebody in the market saw the direction your ship took, I started hunting on this side of the planet."

I'd worked with plenty of handlers, snappers and fixers over the years; none had ever shown anything like this dogged interest in me. I'd wondered a few times if he fancied me, sexual passion making him follow me to the ends of the earth. But he'd never got even remotely close to making a pass. It was strange . . .

"Can we speak privately again, please?" Zoltan looked as if this might be about more than chipping into the office Secret Santa.

"Of course."

He wheeled me to the room next door.

"Who is this Istvan? What's he doing here?"

"He's my fixer, like I said. When you took me and Oxie, he came looking for us."

"He tracked you all this way using nothing more than instinct? Come on. You can't expect me to believe this nonsense."

"It happens to be true." I felt a tiny bit smug, while also aware of being totally out of my depth and potentially in a lot of danger.

"You trust him?"

A good question. Yet I was aware, at a deep level, that I did. Without necessarily understanding him, though.

"Yes, he's a good man."

"I don't want him betraying our whereabouts; it may be too late, he may have already got word back. I've already told the guards to double down on decoys and defence."

"He's just a fixer. They're desperate for work, these guys. Food prices are going through the roof. I'm probably the only source of money he's had in years and that's why he's come after me. I can vouch for him." Could I, though? Unbidden, the voice of doubt insisted on filling my thoughts. "He deserves danger money for this."

"You don't understand, do you? You're from a different background to us, life here's a struggle. You can't trust anyone."

Feeling like I'd just had a lecture from my dad, I allowed Zoltan to wheel me back to the hospital room, where Istvan was lying slumped over on some old crates.

"Okay, haven't found any devices," announced one of the guards. "Far as we can see, he's clean. We're getting him out of here on the first transit tomorrow."

"Can I look after him until then?"

Zoltan nodded in a grudging way.

"No more trouble from either of you, mind."

"Of course not." Istvan was in no kind of state to be breaking any more rules, even if he'd felt so inclined. Blood was coming out his nostrils; we'd be lying low.

We limped out of the tent together. I sought his hand, took it in mine, gently squeezed it, smiled at him.

"It'll be okay," I whispered, privately wondering how 'okay' could even be possible and unsure what it might look like.

I was clear on some things, though. It was Zoltan, not him, who'd kidnapped me and Oxie, breaking my arm in the process. The only reason Istvan was even on this wretched planet was because of me, I'd hired him to come here from Earthen with me because I needed an Aballonian fixer for my story. At the very least, I owed him a duty of care. Leaving him to the tender mercies of Aballonian rebels wasn't exactly a caring way to behave; he deserved better.

He was more subdued than I'd ever seen him before, slumping brokenly in blood-stained and mud-marked trousers as we staggered to the tent, his eye large as a football.

"Thank you, Cathy, thank you."

Together we stumbled off, Istvan stumbling and limping.

"Where are we going?" He sounded confident I must have a plan of some sort that would set out our next move.

"To my tent. I've some gear to protect us, and a bit of food and drink."

"This is good of you."

"Guess I owe you. By the way, how did you find us without a tracker? We'd have been a needle in the proverbial haystack."

"I'd a tracker all right. Dropped it a few miles from camp, so I'd look clean."

I was quietly impressed by his cunning.

"And you didn't spill the beans? Not even after they gave you the truth drugs?"

"Built up an immunity to those drugs. Took a couple of years, but I can handle hefty doses now."

I found myself doing a double-take.

"You did all that for your work as a fixer?" Normally their work didn't involve anything more taxing than organising travel arrangements.

He looked awkward, but given how swollen his eye was, I might have been misreading his expression. Since when did fixers do programmes aimed at fostering resilience to the latest truth drugs?

"How's the eye?"

"Fine."

It didn't look fine; it was red, pulsating and about five times its normal size.

"Some rest might help," I suggested.

His response made me begin to feel less anxious for him.

"No, don't be silly. I'm fine." He struggled across the tent towards a camp bed, holding onto a succession of chairs and tables and allowing them to take his weight, until he made it as far as the metal-framed bed and collapsed heavily onto it. "Absolutely fine."

Even if he was a long way from "fine", at least he was on the mend.

Sixteen

"WHO ARE THESE PEOPLE?" He sounded concerned more than curious, which was unlike the response of any other fixers I'd ever met or had the dubious pleasure of working alongside.

"They were . . ." I kept my voice low, awkward at talking about anyone in front of them. "They were in the trials."

"Trials? What trials?"

"The food trials, of course." Was he trying to get information by pretending to know less than he did? "You must've heard about them? We've just never had evidence before. Now we can prove the story was right – and then some."

I couldn't feel elated about the discovery though, not with it coming at this cost. Maybe I was going soft, no longer the heartless predator I'd tried to be in the past.

After staring at the bandaged stumps of the man in bed in front of us, Istvan turned around abruptly to face me. Something about the speed and precision of his movements was disquieting, oddly out of keeping with how I thought of him – eccentric, hippyish, obsessive – in a harmless, benign way. Part of me had maybe known about this other side to him all along, but hadn't been able to accept it.

Until now.

"The food trials did this?" He was struggling to keep his voice to a whisper. "That can't be, it's not possible."

"Yes, the trials. All too possible, I'm afraid."

"Sure?"

"Yes. Quite sure."

"You verified this?"

"Yes, with Zoltan."

"Zoltan? The guy who got you fired. Who got me beaten up? How can you trust anything he says?"

"Because it all adds up." Anger at his disbelief lent an edge of self-righteous indignation to my words. "How else d'you explain what's happened? They're the people I saw that night."

"Don't talk crap." He became more emphatic. "There was no-one else there that night."

Not this again.

"We've been over this." And would do so again, judging by my lack of progress in winning him over to my way of seeing things. "There were invalids there that night, some of these guys must have been there." I nodded as discreetly as I could towards the patients. "The Resistance freed them and brought them here. What exactly is your problem in believing what I say?"

It was odd, seeing someone normally so sure of himself falter, his bad eye making everything seem worse. I felt panicked, less sure of myself at discovering his uncertainty, suddenly aware of how much I delegated responsibility to him for taking the big decisions, steering our lives.

"But I was told it was . . ." It was strange, becoming aware of hearing him sounding genuine for the first time since I'd met him. His new-found authenticity was putting all his previous words in doubt, though, I realised queasily as I began to wonder how much of our time together had been an act, a performance staged for reasons I didn't yet understand - and quite possibly never would.

"Told what?" And, possibly even more to the point, by whom?

"Nothing, nothing." He shook his head with an agitation that suggested something was indeed very much the matter.

"Look, it'd be easier to talk outside." Where we wouldn't disturb the sick and dying.

"Got a couple of things to do first." He looked inscrutable as he spoke.

"Under orders to report back to your real boss, are you?" I meant the comment as a joke, he didn't take it that way.

"What are you talking about now?" Specks of spit flew through the air towards me.

I'd never seen him this angry. Normally the emotional, volatile one was me, while he got to be jokey and calm. Or to play that part. It'd be good to swap roles, although I couldn't help feeling sceptical as to how well it'd work.

"It was a joke." I wished I didn't sound so apologetic; why the hell shouldn't I attempt a clumsy pleasantry?

For a stupid moment, I thought he might actually be going to apologise. I watched his shoulders relax, warrior-priest pose shifting to something more peaceful. Yet again, of course – why was it even a surprise? – I was wrong.

He shook himself, as if physically clearing away some kind of mental detritus, pushing back his shoulders and resuming the mask of affability that had kept me and the rest of the world at a distance.

"How many are here?" he asked.

"In the hospital?" I wasn't sure why I needed to confirm what he was asking, it was pretty obvious what he meant. Maybe I was just nervous.

"Yes, of course."

"No idea. Couldn't say. Dozens?"

"I'll ask around, get stats, I'll have to anyway."

"No, no, I'll do it." He'd his buttoned-down, enigmatic face back on.

Why so keen to do the dull leg-work, I wondered . . .

"You sure?"

"Very."

He frightened me in that fixed, determined mindset, as if he'd gone to a place out of bounds to the rest of us. Something about dragons being found breathing fire there . . .

I'd worked with various fixers over the years, but none of them had been as driven, as dedicated, as determined as Istvan. He was much more than a fixer and translator, I began to realise with horrified fear.

Episodes from the past insisted on me revisiting them. Things that had puzzled me at the time but I'd later dropped or put to one side – they were clamouring for me to think about them again, as if my brain had always known things didn't really add up with Istvan but I'd not had the confidence to listen to my doubts. I'd forgotten how he was so mysterious in how he rescued me from that spaceport cell on our first day on Aballonia, now it was coming back to me.

It had been odd, too, his ability to access help from the supposedly evil authorities. How he'd always been able to source food for us, when the rest of the planet was close to starving. How he'd moved around in the slipstream of my travels, always appearing to be at the back, in the shadows, while maybe he'd really been the one in the driving seat all along. The memories were falling into place like a house of cards propped up, one against the other, that all toppled over as soon as one of them went.

My faithful companion. But where did his fidelity lie? Not with me, I suspected. Feeling uncertain, I watched his back as he headed off to find out more about the tent's occupants. He didn't bother turning back to look at me as he left.

He was back about a hour later, looking even more tired and gaunt.

"What'd you find?"

"There's more than two hundred people here."

"What, in just these tents? You're joking." Yet I knew, even as I spoke, that he wasn't.

"No, 'fraid not."

He was the most emotional I'd ever seen him, disturbed in a way I hadn't expected.

"Let's take a break, get some fresh air."

Silently I followed him to the front of the tents, where he held back the canvas sheeting to allow me to pass. There was none of the ironic banter I'd have expected; maybe he just thought it would have been inappropriate. But I knew his manner that afternoon would stay with me a long time, knew without necessarily being able to articulate why, or at least not at that point.

Outside a light breeze crossed the improvised courtyard, lifting leaves that rustled against the stone paving as they set off on flights that would close their life cycle. Eventually they'd again become food for the trees they'd so recently adorned. For now, though, as the wind quieted, they flopped down again with relief onto the stone squares.

A few people – medics? soldiers? – were sitting on some newish wooden crates with the labels still attached to them, playing cards and drinking beer. A local brand, not one I'd tried myself. One of them looked so traumatised his features had taken on a waxy, frozen quality. The rest were matter-of-fact, stoical, though you could see in their taut, stretched features the effort it was costing them to pretend to be fine.

And that was when it came to me, watching the men and women opening their beer bottles, lifting them to their mouths, swigging from them. I finally worked out how Istvan must have managed to track me. The crafty bastard. He'd exploited my fondness for a beer and used it to keep tabs on me. He must have weighed up my character flaws very carefully, no wonder he'd been so interested in me but never made a pass. And what kind of fixer went to all this trouble of tracking their client to the ends of a planet?

I'd often wondered at his interest in me, the kind of interest that sent him thousands of miles across dusty plains, over icy mountains, following wherever I went, no matter the personal danger. Fixers didn't normally go to all that bother for a client, it wasn't worth the hassle and effort for them. Yes, work was scarce and money tight. But this level of effort couldn't be cost-effective; no matter how much he was making from me, that couldn't come close to covering his costs. However I could think of a group of people who wouldn't hesitate to track their targets, though. Who'd see surveillance as the bread-and-butter of their working lives. My blood pressure was rising as I began – belatedly – to wake up to just what Istvan was really doing as my shadow.

He'd been spying on me. The sneaky bastard.

"Can't have been easy, tracking us all the way over here," I ventured, feeling my brain close to exploding as I plotted out this new understanding of my faithful co-pilot.

"No, it wasn't. But I care about you. And Oxie too, of course."

"And I care about you too." Actually, I was angrier with him than I could ever remember being with anyone in my entire life. I didn't want to give away my discovery too soon, though, so made my face look how I imagined 'caring' might be. "But you must have had help to track me all this way. You couldn't have done it on your own, unaided."

He'd the grace to blush, surprising me again. I thought he'd been trained – although I'd no idea by whom, probably the Aballonians – to the point where he no longer felt ordinary human emotions like embarrassment.

The skies were clear again, their thick bands of black giving way to a sunny blue. I hadn't yet had a chance to smash the bottle opener apart and confirm my suspicions about Istvan and what he was really doing there. I thought I'd try forcing his hand first, see if he'd admit what he'd done without me having to go to the trouble of taking apart my drinking aid.

"Clever, though, exploiting my weakness for a beer after work. And I was so touched you'd got me a present, too." He'd used it to track me.

"How'd you find it? Take it apart after I pitched up here?"

He'd fallen for it. Confirmed my suspicions without me having to ask him a direct question. Now I knew what he'd done, I knew my suspicion was correct, and I hadn't needed to shatter the wretched bottle opener to find out the truth.

Take it apart after he pitched up there. I shook my head, a deep sadness mixed with anger washing over me as I mentally replayed his words. Yet another person betraying me. It felt like that was what people did, or maybe just what they did to me. Ever the victim, that was me, or maybe I should grow up, accept the world was a tough and nasty place, be more responsible for myself, stop expecting it to be any different. I shook myself – self-pity was a destructive emotion.

"You did guess it's in the beer opener, didn't you?"

"Just thought it might be there, that's the only 'gift' you've ever given me. Now you've just confirmed it. Thank you very much. Why exactly are you doing this to me?" I probably already half-knew why, but wanted to hear it from him.

"I'm sorry. I'd no choice."

"You did have a choice." I felt close to shouting, but didn't want Zoltan hauling us into custody, so instead whispered angrily; we'd never spoken to each other like this before. "Of course you had a choice, nobody made you do this."

"You don't understand, you don't know what that world is like."

"What world? I've worked as a journalist for more than ten years. I'm not a complete ingénue."

"I know." He sounded regretful.

Photographers didn't normally go round planting bugs on

people; they relied on complex chains of tip-offs for picture opportunities and could be among a newsroom's most unsavoury characters, but I hadn't heard of them being into illicit espionage. Or not when the spying would have involved huge personal expense and effort, anyway.

"You're not just a photographer, are you? Snappers don't plant bugging devices on people."

"What do you mean, not 'just' a photographer? It's an honourable trade." He wasn't meeting my eyes, though, instead playing with a piece of young bamboo, bending up the narrow leaf with a pent-up energy into a concertina shape before releasing it again. "I'm serious about my work."

"Yes, you're serious about your work. But your work doesn't really involve photography and fixing, does it? Or not as anything more than a sideline." My mouth tightened. "If you're a photographer, why aren't you taking more pictures, then?"

He shrugged, putting a little too much vigour into the move to suggest the insouciance he might have wanted.

"You're not a snapper, are you? You're a fucking spy." There were tears in my eyes. I

He looked at me, really looked at me. For a moment I thought he might act huffy and aggrieved. But then he shook himself, as if dispelling one spirit from his body and summoning the ghost of a long-forgotten stranger in its place.

"Okay." He shook himself again. "Yes, I do that kind of work. I'm attached to the ministry of defence, as you say."

I felt my eyes widen, found myself doing an almost a literal double-take, my head turning back to check I'd heard correctly.

A spy. A spy. In my life, in my dreams, in my home, in my heart. And I hadn't known. Suspected, yes. But not known.

His words made me feel my world narrowing and closing in on me, making me struggle for balance. It was one thing to wonder, privately, if he'd other roles besides photographer. Another to hear him confirm it.

"You've betrayed me completely."

My eyes felt like they were out on stalks, like the characters in Top Cat who lived lives of such emotional extremes that only acrobatic cartoon drawings could hope to convey their heightened realities.

"I can't pretend any more, not after seeing what's going on in there. I do work for the Aballonian government, as you suggest, yes, I admit it. I can't just sit back and pretend what's happening in there isn't happening, though. These people, the people in the tents, they're Aballonians. I got into this kind of work to protect people like them."

There were still rather a lot of questions, though.

"Be honest with me." At the words left my mouth, I couldn't help feeling pessimistic about the chances of honesty manifesting anywhere in my life, least of all in connection with Istvan. "Why's the Aballonian government paying you to track me all over this planet?"

Looking at him, I noticed his hair was beginning to resemble the irrepressible spears of bamboo sprouting up from the land wherever they could get purchase on it. He looked at me as if his life depended on me forgiving him, or at least me agreeing to making some kind of peace deal with him. I gazed off for a moment at the crest of hills snaking along above the tree line, streams bisecting the land where it rolled down between the hills, the land moulding and adapting like a wedge of plasticine.

The sight made me a little calmer and I sat down on a nearby boulder.

"This has been a set-up from the start, hasn't it?"

Credit to the guy, at least he didn't smirk as he nodded a silent agreement.

"Kolya is quite unharmed," he added, sounding as if he expected praise from me for not harming the guy originally meant to be my fixer.

I wanted to reply by saying, "So I should bloody think." But I didn't want to make him any angrier than he was already. So instead I tried to look meek and accepting. Given how I really felt about the situation it was all quite a strain, my face muscles were hurting with the effort.

Seventeen

TIME SLOWED DOWN and hurried up again in that annoying concertina way it often had, usually when you most wanted it to stop moving.

Istvan working for the Aballonians? He was meant to be a fixer and photographer. Wrong, again.

"Is this true?" I felt like a hungry beggar asking for money, not expecting to achieve much except a pitying look. I looked him in the eye as I spoke.

He'd the grace to nod in an ashamed, guarded way that also involved staring intently at the grains of red sand under his feet, as if they held the answer to these conundrums. His guardedness made me think at least part of him might have preferred being back on the old, safe territory of lying, secrecy and omission. I identified with him there.

Looking at him again, I wondered if the spy story meant he was psycho. A fantasist. A wannabe James Bond. And one I'd shared my home with, too. If he'd come onto me (he hadn't, thankfully, though at the time that had been disappointing) I'd probably have shared my bed with him, too. Thank goodness I hadn't; the idea now revolted me.

Was I even safe with him, I wondered.

We were outdoors in day light, admittedly, illuminated by no fewer than three separate suns, but no-one else was around and he was stronger, fitter, faster than me. Then again, if he'd wanted me dead, he could've killed me a long time ago and without too much difficulty. Or got his Aballonian police chums to do the job for him. The thought sent a chill of dread through me as I began to understand how much danger I must have been in. Unwittingly. Maybe the paper had been right to let me go; I hadn't a clue what was happening in my own life, much less anyone else's.

"Seriously?" Part of me kept expecting him to break into laughter, slap me on the back and promise to buy a round as he announced he'd fooled me, of course he wasn't a spy. As if preparing for my humiliation, an odd-looking bird at the edges of my vision, with a long beak and inquisitive eyes began making a harsh whistling sound. The notes sounded like a warning that hell itself was breaking open and we should leave – aye-sap.

For a moment, neither of us moved.

I turned back to Istvan, prepared for him to laugh at me. Yet, again, though, he surprised me by nodding and glancing up at me. It was odd, I realised with a jolt, him meeting my eyes at last.

Why hadn't I noticed before he wouldn't look me in the eyes? Maybe because so many others had often been even more aloof, more disdainful towards me. Him keeping his distance from me wasn't anything unusual.

"Please. I can't do any of this with you thinking I'm someone I'm not." He looked different, more humble than normal.

Less confident. I was liking him more.

But do what? What did he mean?

Feeling lost, I was beginning to feel sorry for myself until the curlew's renewed squawking dragged me back into the present and some kind of equilibrium. Still difficult to stop trying (in vain) to process what was happening, though.

Maybe Istvan being weird with me was something I hadn't wanted to notice before. Me admitting to myself there was a problem with him – a big problem – would've got in the way of everything. So, instead, I'd effectively shuffled my doubts about him into a dusty, hardly visited part of my brain, because they ran counter to the story I was so desperate to tell myself was true; namely, that he was my loyal, dogged fixer who stayed glued to my side simply because I paid him to do so.

Maybe, also, it'd have hurt my stupid pride to admit that he was only pretending to like me, that he was using me. Not a great feeling.

"Seriously?"

"Yes, seriously." He shuffled his feet as he spoke, which cast further doubt in my mind over how far I could trust him, red earth and sand rising up in little scuffles, puffs and flurries over his walking boots. He seemed suddenly aware that lying wasn't an honourable way to behave. Odd, really, double-dealing had never seemed to bother him before.

"So this whole project, us working together, it's all been a lie." For a moment I felt too deflated to be angry, leaden heaviness weighing me down, fixing me to the red sand. The bird with the weirdly long bill screeched again, its long and painful wail cutting through the dusty air.

"No, absolutely not. I'm fond of you and respect the work you do. But most of it, yes, I'm afraid so. Lying is part of our work. That's what we do."

He sounded a bit like a waiter announcing the lunch specials for the day: one or two honest chickens and a few mendacious ones. In fairness, though, he seemed genuinely upset over how he'd behaved, but that might have been just another stunt.

"I was only following orders, I want you to know that. It's all classic Karpman triangle territory."

Following orders, indeed; not much of a get-out. As for this triangle, I felt like suggesting some very rude things he could do with it.

Istvan's impact on my world was turning out to be like that of a child shaking the multi-coloured pieces of plastic in a kaleidoscope, twisting it round a few times so that the same tiny bits of plastic would appear utterly different, as if they were in another constellation. Without having actually gone anywhere at all.

"All the trouble I've had, tracking down Zoltan, getting nowhere on the story, the police turning over our apartment. That all down to you?"

He took a couple of paces back, perhaps afraid I might fly at him. The thought did cross my mind, but I'd the sense to drop it; he was much stronger than me. And had some kind of connection to the police.

He said nothing.

"Is it?"

His silence told me the answer.

"You caused all that trouble. You creep, you user."

"I was following orders."

Him and his orders. He could shove them.

I'd the impression he'd special discretionary powers over which orders he bothered following, as well as which ones he pretended he hadn't heard, not unlike how a recalcitrant toddler might have behaved faced with a tetchy parent.

"You must have wondered why Aballonian security wasn't more interested in you when we arrived, surely?" He looked like he was trying to guilt-trip me.

"Of course." The thought hadn't crossed my head, but I wasn't telling him that.

As far as I was concerned, the Aballonians had been on my case from the moment we'd first flown into their wretched orbital airspace.

"Obviously I kept tabs on their reaction to me, sure." Being vague felt like my only option. "I'm a professional, you know." Even to my own ears, I sounded pompous and clueless.

I tried to observe his reaction to my words without him noticing, but wasn't sure I managed. Mostly I'd just covered more basic stuff in my pan-galactic media training, falsification, extortion, lying, blackmail, amateur dramatics and theft.

"It never occurred to you they took a rather hands-off approach with you?"

Hands-off? Not how they'd come across to me.

"They broke into our flat, turned the place upside down, left threatening messages on the mirror. I wouldn't want to see them hands-on." I knew I sounded self-righteous, but felt justified – under the circumstances. Istvan's last-minute appearance back at the Earthen spaceport was now looking different, too.

"They left one relatively moderate message on the mirror, that was all."

"I thought you never got to see that little billet doux? That we left before you got chance?" Yet another part of the past to revise and reinterpret.

"They ran it past me before giving it to the men to intimidate you."

My heart was bursting on learning of his betrayal.

"You bastard. You utter bastard."

I couldn't hold back any longer. He'd hurt me too much. So I swung at him with an open palm, slapping him as hard as I could.

He looked unmoved.

"No, not an utter bastard, whatever you say. By Aballonian standards, we were gentle."

"Gentle? By Aballonian standards?" I tried to make a scoffing, dismissive 'pah' sound to indicate a knowing cynicism. It fell flat, my lips faltering in the middle, spittle dribbling onto my lips and chin. Furtively, I used the back of my hand to wipe it away, uncomfortably aware he'd probably noticed what I was doing.

"They'd have done a lot worse to you, and I mean a lot worse, if I hadn't told them you were miles off target, hadn't a clue what was happening. They'd have forced you into the food trials, if I hadn't put my foot down."

The sick part of me loved the idea of him dismissing me as clueless, daffy; welcome proof of how crap I really was.

It was unnerving, but I was also becoming aware of a growing attraction to him. How sick was I? My therapist back home had gone on at length, in her gentle but strong Finnish accent, about my tendency to love men who couldn't or wouldn't love me back. Even I could see falling for someone after I found out he'd been lying to me for the past few months from behind a false identity was, well, self-destructive.

"All this time, you've been taking money off me but working against me, destroying any chance I had of nailing down the story?" I wanted to swear at him, call him names, scratch his face with my nails, pick him up and throw him into a different galaxy.

Tears running down my face, I sank to the ground, allowing my body to collapse awkwardly against the earth, and sobbed. The anger diminished with the pain, the sorrow of the hurt. "Isn't that what those Germans said at Nuremberg? That they were just following orders? You might at least give me my money back, you thieving, dishonest prick."

"I'm a soldier, Cathy. I have to follow orders."

A soldier? To me, he was a translator and fixer.

"Why're you telling me this?" I really meant why was he telling me then but felt too dazed to explain. Shocked, I got up off the ground, using my hands to brush the dirt off my trousers, walked over and sat down on some old crates, the wood faded and discoloured by the different suns.

Again, the tortured expression; brow etched into deep furrows that would loosen and aerate the main root zone of his treacherous heart. That same feeling of Jekyll slugging it out with Hyde over whose face Istvan would use and when. The same absence of a core, or bastion personality. Instead, the discovery of nothing more substantial or lasting in him than a revolving and hollow carousel of clothes-hangers, all of them bearing different costumes made from the same tawdry, grubby sequins, attached to a dirty pink gown designed to seduce and entertain the gullible. People like me.

And it had worked, dammit, even worse luck.

Not knowing what to say, I stupidly hoped he'd be the one to break the silence. In vain. Although we were outdoors, the air felt stale, tired, a dull purplish hue hovering above the more optimistic azure skies below.

"I'm telling you this because I'm changing sides."

Changing sides?

"What?" My mouth gawped.

"I've had my doubts about the government for a while; now I've seen what the trials have done to people, I can't support them any more. It's inhuman, what they're doing."

Coming from someone normally as quiet as Istvan, this was quite a speech. And expressive, emotional too; qualities usually left to me to handle. It was all feeling a bit like the lines in that Carole King song, as if the earth had shifted under my feet. I was glad of the support offered by the blistered, splintering crates holding me up, even though one side was slipping down into the sand, leaving me tilting at an angle.

"I want to work with Zoltan and the rebels. To stop the government from doing any more damage to innocent civilians. This has to stop."

Uneasily, I shifted first my left hip then my right, trying to correct my posture so I'd be roughly parallel to the land. The bamboo around here was growing fast, some plants already several feet high despite being lopped down every day to prevent them taking over completely.

"You want to come over to the rebels? You really think Zoltan will let you?"

"I'm hoping you might vouch for me. Zoltan may welcome the chance to get an insider."

"Why should I trust you? Or believe anything you tell me? I mean, who are you?" I didn't mean the question rhetorically.

One thing was clear; he wasn't the flinty, jokey, calm, battle-hardened snapper he'd led me to believe, at least not if his latest announcements were to be believed. "How can I trust anything you tell me now? You've been lying to me for months." I tried not to sound self-righteous. "We've spent the last, what, five months together living a lie?" Yes, I was gullible and daft, but I wasn't the one peddling a collection of muddled half-truths and fiction.

"I knew you'd see this emotionally. You're very fond of drama when you're in pain, I remember that." He looked disappointed in my response to his revelation.

"Pain caused by you!" I screeched, scared he'd like to push me into whatever the emotional equivalent was of the trash folder on his computer's hard drive. "Do you feel less guilty if you blame it all on me? Does that work? All the awkward feelings go away?"

At least we hadn't slept together, I found myself thinking, slowly beginning to see his behaviour toward me differently.

"Is that why things never went any further between us?"

"Actually, no, my bosses felt if we became sexual with each other the relationship might fall apart. They were basing this on patterns observed in your previous, er, relationships."

"You were watching me? Working out what'd appeal to me? I trusted you and you were just using me."

"They simply observed you're fond of the kind of lover who throws you down on the bed, ravishes you, then disappears."

It was humiliating, hearing his take on my most private, most cherished experiences. I liked to think I loved – and lived – with a fierce, passionate bohemian abandon; hearing Istvan describe my love life so forensically made me feel shit.

He swallowed. Oh no, there was more. "I needed to build something longer term with you. We thought introducing sex to the arrangement too soon might derail our plan."

It was almost physically painful, hearing him so chilly, so impersonal. About us. About me. Except there wasn't an 'us', that had been another silly illusion.

"So all those times my head fell on your shoulder, when we chatted into the small hours, when I felt as close to you as I've ever done to another person, all that was just an act? Staged for work?" No wonder I'd felt so confused about him. Frightened, even. My mistake had been to think there was something wrong with me for not understanding what was happening. Everything he'd done had been designed to make me feel like that.He sat down heavily on a few other bamboo crates slickly wet with earlier rainfall, wiping his hand over his face. After less than a moment he got up again, his backside soaked through.

"Brilliant." He peeled the fabric away from his bottom, holding it from him as if disgusted by it, but an upward turn at the sides of his lips made me think he was happy for an excuse not to have to talk further about his deceptions.

It was unworthy of me, but I couldn't help feeling pleased. He couldn't be so superior with a wet bottom.

"At least you didn't get a splinter in your arse." It felt daring, using a word my mother would have described as 'rude', and my confidence was disintegrating faster than the reddish sand under our feet.

"I'm changing sides. I've had my doubts about the trials for a while and now I've seen the medical unit …"

I leant forward.

"I'd heard rumours about the trials. When this job came up …"

"Job?"

"Following you."

"Right." I was a job to him.

"So when this assignment came up, I decided to use it to find out more."

It wasn't exactly a surprise to learn he hadn't got himself the job because he was interested in fostering inter-planetary co-operation, but still disappointing. I tried to hide my wounded pride as best I could, refusing to allow my gaze to veer off sourly.

"You're not a photographer, though, are you?"

"No, okay, I'm not."

"I knew it." I'd never been sure, but had long had my doubts about him. He was no David Bailey, and, okay, I wasn't even close to being a Martha Gellhorn, but I was a journalist. If not a very good one.

"I've learnt to take the odd usable pic." He'd the gall to look cheekily proud of himself as he spoke.

"How'd you put that folio together then? You've got some decent shots in there, considering you're not a professional."

"We paid a stringer. He wasn't bad."

All that assiduous devotion to me, that hadn't been to me personally, no matter what I'd been daft enough to tell myself. This was work, at least as far as he was concerned.

Something, I suppose the kind of instinct that kept our distant ancestors alive long enough to procreate and protect their children, kicked in.

"So are the Aballonians on our trail? They must have trackers on you, surely? They sending in the storm troopers now? Just I better have a quick word with Zoltan, give him a heads-up. Especially since I'm the one who's been stupid enough to bring you here." I finished on a tearful snarl, angry at myself for putting the others in danger. I'd inadvertently betrayed their whereabouts to the scuzziest, nastiest regime I'd ever come across. Getting up from the crate, I started back towards the tents.

Unbidden, he followed.

"No. The Aballonians don't know I'm here. Unless they've developed trackers I don't yet know about." He looked as if I were the one at fault for not understanding his layers of deception.

I gave him a quizzical look. "When you say 'here', you mean out in the cold, at the end of the day, at the side of a dirty, dishevelled tent masquerading as a field hospital?"

"No, not just this afternoon, more broadly. Come on, don't pretend you don't understand."

"I'm hoping you haven't brought me here to kill me." I'd often got a feeling he'd be more than capable of polishing somebody off, if ordered. Or even just off his own bat. I felt sick at the thought.

"So, tell me." I tried to make my voice conversational, but it betrayed me, cracking up, quivering, forcing me to pause and swallow. "Why haven't you killed me? You've had plenty opportunity." While I'd been fantasising about him liking me. I was a fool, an idiot. "You just allowing me to stay alive so I lead you to the other rebel leaders? Give you a hand in all the lying, hurting, betraying?"

It felt as if the birds, too, knew that something potentially serious was up. They'd paused on the soundtrack of squawking and chirping, instead poking quietly about on the grass like guests at a dinner party when the hosts have had a public disagreement and everyone else is too embarrassed to speak.

"I told them you weren't getting anywhere on the story." He gazed off at the dim horizon. "To protect you. Throw them off the scent."

"Told who?"

"Aballonian security, of course. I told them you hadn't a clue what was happening, you weren't a threat. They were perfectly happy to believe me."

I said nothing.

A dog was barking somewhere, possibly at the different moons, which were becoming higher and more visible as they took over from the suns. I felt oddly sympathetic to the poor creature; I wouldn't have minded howling at something to express my bafflement, my confusion, my pain about being used as a pawn in a game I hadn't even known I was playing; a few yelps might have made me feel better. More likely, though, the poor dog was yelping because he or she was starving, like almost every human and animal I knew.

It was unusual, this feeling of humility, of admitting, even if only to myself, that I hadn't the proverbial about what was happening. As a journalist you were expected to prevaricate and lie, and do so convincingly enough to avoid getting caught. So this afternoon's honesty was oddly soothing.

"I'm sorry for how I've behaved. But your story set Aballonia ablaze. And plenty of other places too. We've been following you since you started working on this story."

"What, all those months ago? Way back then?" It was odd, I'd often had the feeling I was being followed, but had assumed it was my paranoia, maybe made worse by my drinking.

"Yes, we've had different teams watching you. Since we first picked up traffic around the food experiments."

Camp workers must have started cooking supper, an odd, recherché smell resembling food was travelling our way.

"Tell me you're joking. Please." I felt sick at the idea of foreign planets following my every move, tracking and monitoring me as I went about my shabby, screwed-up life.

"No, this is true. I want to help Aballonia, protect people. I have to stop the trials."

Over by the fire I could see a man cutting apart an old shoe, probably a woman's hiking boot going by the style, size and colour – turquoise. He was taking out the leather upper and sole like one of those old-fashioned cobblers used to do. Holding the dismembered footwear as if it were the finest silk or most beautiful flowers, he washed it carefully under running water, rubbing away the dirt on it with his fingers. Fascinated, I watched as he added it to a pan of boiling water, sliding it into the bubbling liquid with a tender care. It looked horribly as if a casserole of boot leather might be on tonight's menu, I realised with revulsion.

"It's true, what I told you." He spoke as if he and the truth normally had only the most tenuous of relationships, and I should congratulate them for striking up a closer, albeit fleeting acquaintance with one another. "Yes." He nodded to himself. "True." He seemed surprised at his own words, as if he'd never previously considered himself capable of honesty or he were a radio being retuned to a different frequency.

I found myself shaking my head, disbelievingly.

Was this the truth? Would I ever know? I craved a rest from it all.

"Are we eating shoe leather now?"

Istvan laughed in a dry, humourless way. "Hah. No, not quite. People are using it as flavouring." He paused, looking reflective. "Pretty sure if you could safely eat shoes, we'd all be doing it by now."

"No harm thinking laterally, I suppose." My mind wandered down a maze of dark possibilities. "Doesn't seem very hygienic though, all that sweat. At least it's not like we're talking cannibalism."

He gave me an appraising, knowing look as he spoke. "Oh, come on, you can't deny cannibalism is happening. We know it is."

My stomach lurched; I got the feeling I might be sick. It was odd, too, hearing him talk as if he were part of a much bigger organisation. We know it is. Hearing him speak of denial made me think again of the unfortunate people he'd insisted I hadn't seen that night back in the dog food factory. I finally understood why he'd disagreed with me – his job back then had been to keep the state's nasty secrets private. Maybe it still was . . .

The leaves were barely moving, not even a shiver of movement, except sometimes a trailing bough shifted fractionally sideways.

"I don't know what to believe." Although I wanted to believe him, it was too much to take in.

Hooting sounds drifted out, courtesy of the wood's bird populace, low and musical. A lighter twittering from smaller birds amplified the sound.

The world looked the same as it had before. Yet it felt like we'd landed somewhere even more alien than Aballonia – and any departures would be an uncertain kind of business.

"I'm telling you the truth." He looked almost unrecognisable in his new guise.

Listening to Istvan was making me feel like a player in a virtual reality game, I realised, one where all the pixels collapsed into each other at the end, whether you won or lost.

Reminding us both of what was at stake, the thickets of bamboo around us rustled noisily, the stems like a kindergarten game where toddlers slotted pieces together to practise hand/eye co-ordination.

"Now you've seen the human cost of creating the food, you can see why there's such paranoia around it."

"Can I trust you?" I felt stupid even just asking the question.

But when he replied simply that I could, I felt my body respond to what he was saying as something I could trust.

"Shall we go and find Zoltan then? Tell him he's got a new recruit?" I was joking to cover my anxiety about how Zoltan might react to the news.

"Let's go. And, listen, thank you for taking a chance on me. I know this must all seem very strange to you."

Walking towards the compound together, I glanced over at him again. Dappled light became him, maybe something about the mixture of light and dark in it.

I was probably getting carried away again; the guy had lied through his guts to me, sabotaged my last-ditch attempt to salvage my moribund career and actively undermined me.

How in the hell could I start trusting him now? He was probably about to double-double-cross me (again) and put the kibosh on my story. But I did trust him, instinct told me to hold onto that feeling.

As we trudged along, I looked more closely at the bamboo plants bobbing and inclining to each other, trying to work out how I felt.

Yes, he'd lied to me. Extensively. Maybe I was deluded in thinking he'd ever be honest with me.

"You're going to have your work cut out, convincing Zoltan you're on the level though," I said. "He'll be even more sceptical than me, you know."

"He'll believe me. Even you weren't all that sceptical."

He kept his gaze on the path as he spoke and might even have succeeded in hiding his anxiety from me, if it weren't for him tripping and almost falling over on a mass of bamboo stems spilling over onto his side of the path.

It was his uncertainty, fear breaking through his mask of affable remove, that told me he was, perhaps for the first time since I'd known him, taking the risk of showing me his true colours. Nobody else could have faked that level of anxious, inadvertent clumsiness, not even Istvan.

Eighteen

"HE'S OUR BEST bet of getting the story out." I felt as ambivalent about depending on Istvan as I guessed Zoltan must too, so kept my gaze lightly fixed on my erstwhile fixer in an attempt to disguise my fears. "Of beating the algorithms, I mean."

"I know perfectly well what you mean. No need to spell it out." In the same good mood as ever, that was our Zoltan.

"No need to be rude, we're here to help." At least, I was. It was still tricky to be sure about Istvan.

Wordlessly, he gave me a look that suggested disagreement with my assessment.

Through the open tent flap, I could see a rocket trailing a lazy burst of starlight whistle-arching across the darkening sky, before exploding noisily into a cascade of light, flashes of fire peppering the night and illuminating the lines of scepticism on Zoltan's face. Probably the work of the Aballonians, preparing for more trouble, or maybe another rebel faction.

"Don't be silly. How could he help us?" A hint of the old Zoltan's arrogance I remembered from that handful of ill-fated meetings back on Earthen. Maybe also an upturn of hope flickering at the edges of his mouth?

Zoltan's scepticism at my news didn't come off quite as he might have intended. A bit of anonymous-looking white fluff was caught in his greyish beard, diminishing his outraged self-importance.

"A guy like that isn't our best hope of anything. Except trouble." He picked up a bag of coffee from the table and emptied several scoops of it into a paper filter. "Even you must see that." The smell of coffee, synonymous for so long with friendship and chatter, began filtering out into the tent. We remained oddly silent, though.

"He's not who you think he is, he can help you." At least, I hoped so. Why couldn't things be more straightforward? Maybe famine and war inevitably complicated things.

"Him?" He jerked his head dismissively at Istvan, who was

standing awkwardly next to me, an uneasy mixture of determination and anxiety. "How exactly can your 'friend' here be much help to us?"

Pausing to gather my breath, I launched back into my story.

"Ah yes, that's the thing. My friend." Only as I repeated the word 'friend' did I realise that Zoltan was hinting Istvan and I were more than merely friends. "Oh, no, no." My skin crawled with embarrassment. "We're not . . ."

Zoltan looked amused and, refusing to meet my eyes, he instead inspected the coffee maker and scrutinised its grubby dials.

"I'm serious, Commander Zoltan. This is nothing to do with my private life. Give him a chance, he wants to help us."

Zoltan scrutinised me sharply, unblinkingly, making my insides turn to mush, (although the fluff in his beard was undermining the impression of stern authority I sensed he wanted to convey).

"Istvan here can help us."

Our host made a spluttering noise that made me think the coffee was getting close to being ready. Looking at the machine I felt disappointed. It wasn't even close. Probably more energy outages holding things up. Or our host's disbelief. Shaking his head dislodged the fluff in Zoltan's beard, though, which helped him in the gravitas arena.

"I thought Istvan was making his way home tomorrow?" He paused, looking a little irascible, before finishing drily: "Wherever that might happen to be these days." He paused, appearing to be taking in the two of us. "Somewhere on Earthen now, from the look of things. I'm sure he's told you a lovely story about himself, but he's not got the greatest track record, you know."

"He's here, right in front of you, and he wouldn't lie to me about this." But he'd already lied to me about so much else, I remembered, dimly aware that Zoltan too was probably thinking of my fixer's earlier twisting of the truth. Why assume his honesty now?

"I'm Aballonian," said Istvan, looking aggrieved. "And proud of that. This is my homeland."

I put a hand on Istvan's arm, hoping he'd try to stay calm. My fingernails were dirty, I noticed, the cuticles bleeding.

"This'll work best if you let me do the talking," I whispered to him.

"Really, Cathy, I can hear perfectly well what you're saying, you know." Zoltan wasn't lowering either his voice or his eyebrows, instead elevating his gaze towards a wind chime some kindly soul had attached to the tent ceiling, probably to make the desolate place more cheerful.

The chime's tinkling sounded forlorn, broken, a reminder of all that was missing in the way of connection, friendship. Home.

Shaking my head in frustration, and casting an exasperated look at the tent fabric above our heads, I resumed my normal voice. "Yes, so Istvan is working for me, true. He's got other, er, hats too."

Zoltan glanced at Istvan's fair-haired – and hatless - head.

"Has he now?" The older man sounded unimpressed by this talk of Istvan's headgear.

"In a manner of speaking, that is," I tried to avoid gabbling, but nerves had got the better of me; it was proving hard to know how to finesse the news. "He's also connected with the Aballonians. Or used to be."

On hearing my words, Zoltan reached behind him, without taking his eyes off me or Istvan, grabbing at a thermos flask and lifting it up in a pose that suggested he was prepared to wield it in battle. "What the hell? The Aballonians? I knew there was a problem with him."

"No, no, it's okay. He used to work for the Aballonians." I paused to check Zoltan's response. "He isn't any more, not now he's seen what they're doing to their own people. His people." I braced myself for Zoltan's reaction; instinct told me he might not see my news favourably.

"No, no, really, it's okay." I began patting at the air in front of me with my hands, my arm pits damp. "He wants to come over to us. To you, to the rebels. Now he's seen what the trials are doing. He is Aballonian and hates what's happening here."

"How am I supposed to believe any of this? Much less trust either of you? For God's sake, Cathy, even you don't look that sure about him. The guy's a spiv, he'll work for whoever's willing to pay him. That type doesn't scruple to double-cross, to betray, to lie and cheat; it's their bread and butter, surely even you can see that?"

"Yes, correct, even I can see the danger, the risks. But I've spent that last five months practically living with Istvan . . . I just think we can trust him."

"You'd better be right about this."

"We've just spoken together, spoken in a way we've never spoken before. I know we can trust him." Even as I said the words I began, silently, to itch at where the now-grubby bandage on my arm met my skin. I was aware of sounding like a love-sick teenager, too.

"Cathy, I know things here aren't great; not being able to get word out to the wider world sucks, it really does. But magical thinking isn't going to help us, trusting every smooth-tongued charlatan, it's just going to cause more trouble. The Aballonians could destroy this place in moments, they've got the firepower. We wouldn't even be a footnote in history, we'd all be dead."

"Of course I understand why you have to be so careful. But we're stuck right now, not going anywhere with the story. There's nowhere to take it. Comms are compromised, nothing coming in or leaving. Unless we get the story out we can't signal for help. And Istvan might be able to help us with that. Is it really such a big risk to let him try?"

"Why should I believe this?" His words weren't encouraging, but he put the thermos down on a plastic trestle table, where it began leaking an unidentifiable brownish liquid onto the surface, and sat down heavily on a folding canvas chair next to it.

"If he was going to grass us up to his Aballonian friends, he'd have done it by now."

"How can you be so sure? Maybe he's holding off on making contact with his old friends until he's clear of the camp, and can pick up his devices again wherever it was he left them."

"He wouldn't do that to us, I just know he wouldn't." But Zoltan's disbelief was fuelling my doubts too.

"How's he going to get the story out? The situation's dire. What can he do?"

"Yes, I am aware of what's happening, you know." Although it turned out I hadn't had a clue what was happening right under my nose.

"Horribly so, in fact."

"You can't seriously want me to trust someone working for the Aballonians? You must be joking."

"I totally see why you're sceptical. But now he's seen what's happening he wants to help us." I faltered. "Help you."

Zoltan remained implacable, arms crossed around himself.

"Don't make me regret bringing you here."

"You didn't exactly give me much choice over that, did you?" I looked at my broken arm in as pointed a way as I could manage. That reminded me, I'd need to take my next round of antibiotics.

"Not this again. We've already been over this. We're outlaws, we don't have access to all the fancy extras."

"Freedom isn't a fancy extra. Not in my opinion, anyway. I'd say it's a basic human right."

"Not here it's not. You know what you've seen, the scale of the suffering."

It was a fair point, much as I resented him.

"Desperate times, desperate measures." He looked sanctimonious as he spoke, sounding more and more like a Church of England vicar. "The Aballonians have pushed us into behaving like them, they left us no choice but to take you by force. They've degraded us morally."

I was fed up re-hashing the past. "We need to work out how to tackle them, stop this happening. Protect people, protect ourselves."

"How's he going to help us do that?"

"Istvan thinks we can get round the security cordon and get the story out, so the Inter-Planetaries know we're in trouble and will send help."

"We've already had the top comms people on the planet work on this, none of them have got anywhere. It's sewn up bloody tight."

"Which is why Istvan can help, he knows those systems from the inside. Even helped create some of them."

"What if he grasses us up to his mates in Aballonian HQ, soon as we let him near any comms equipment?"

I swallowed, my heart beating oddly loudly.

"You can't fake the truth, not really. Not ever. And I know, I just do, that he's telling me the truth about this. I saw the expression on his face when he saw the wounded, saw the latest intake earlier. He's genuine. I'll stake my life on it."

"And the lives of hundreds of others too, if he gives away our details?"

"What else can we do? Carry on offering palliative end-of-life care to survivors? Knowing that more people are being hurt in their idiot trials, even as we speak?"

"We do what we can for them."

I gave him a look.

"We do. We give them pain relief. Now, tell me, Istvan." Zoltan wheeled round to face him. "How are you going to help us? And, more to the point, why should I trust you?"

"I understand your reservations." Istvan looked solemn, which had the unintended (or so I thought) effect of making him look out of his depth. "A few of us have had doubts for a while. A crypto expert back in the capital is saying he might be able to circumvent the algorithms. Not a sure thing, but worth a go, at least I'd say so."

Another first, there. Self-deprecation was new for him.

He needed some back-up, I decided, aware I might soon regret helping him. "I mean, come on, you were going to let him go tomorrow anyway, your guys have already questioned him and found nothing. He's telling us this voluntarily, off his own bat."

"Sir, if I may . . ." Odd, hearing Istvan deferential. And to Zoltan, too.

"Go on." Zoltan looked as if he hated even the pretence of taking Istvan seriously, of being courteous to him.

"I'd like to take Cathy with me back to the capital," said Istvan. "We can pretend she's no idea who I am, and, as far as she's aware, I'm just her fixer taking her back to the spaceport, tail between her legs, to beat a retreat back home now the story's fallen though. In reality, we're going because all the best algo guys are based there. We'd like a hand with transport, if feasible. And identity documents too. We've got to assume the Aballonians are keeping a watch for any sightings of her, I don't think they've worked out about me yet."

"Really, Cathy, I hardly think . . ." Zoltan wasn't having much luck with his coffee that afternoon, he spluttered again, some of it dribbling onto his beard.

One of Zoltan's team wandered into the tent.

"What d'you think," Zoltan asked him.

"Keep them prisoner here." Not helpful.

Zoltan was hard to read, sitting fixedly and gazing out at the ridge of hills protecting us (or so I liked to imagine) from the darkness beyond.

Instinct told me now wasn't the moment to start asking questions, no matter how desperate I was to know what he was thinking.

"Okay," he eventually said. "You'll be mostly on your own once you leave here, you understand that?"

Trying to control manic, terrified grins, we both nodded, aware of a jubilant energy pouring through our bodies at the idea we might, at last, be able to do something to prevent any more people being hurt.

"We'll work out a route, stock up on what supplies we can and set off as soon as conditions permit."

Istvan and I went back to my tent before the event we still persisted in calling supper, even although I half-guessed the bowls of leather-flavoured water would bear little relation to old ideas of what the meal constituted.

"You don't have to do any of this, you know. You could stay here with Zoltan." He looked genuine in his anxiety for me.

And miss out on what could potentially be one of the biggest adventures of my life?

"No, I want to do this."

I prepared mentally for a disagreement, until I saw him begin to half-smile at me, and it was such a friendly, happy-go-lucky smile that the anxiety evaporated.

"Seriously, this idea is to protect you."

"I know, I get that."

"Relax, okay?"

I wanted to relax, I really did. At the back of my mind, though, was a crowd of vague, undefinable fears about what we'd be facing on this next leg of our journey – and, possibly even more worrying, who I'd be facing them with.

We were talked out. Acknowledging the need for silence, I let my head relax until I was curled into his shoulder.

And for some moments we stayed like that, sitting on the earthen floor together, patches of earth watered by my tears, neither of us saying anything at all, relaxed enough in each other's company by this stage to be comfortable in silence.

Nineteen

LIGHT CRADLED THE line of hills in its arms, unfolding along crenellations of land stretching across the horizon, bouncing and reflecting off their sloping green curves, and, for some moments, I felt stupidly optimistic about our travels, despite the shadowy obstacles we knew lay ahead. Underneath us rested a lining of placid and flat cloud cover, its soft and woolly appearance belying the presence of latter-day dragons we knew almost certainly awaited us out there.

Saying even a temporary goodbye to Oxie was difficult, painfully so, for both of us, but she eventually accepted the idea of being looked after by nurses from the field hospital for a few days while I travelled for 'work'. She was standing outside our tent when we set off.

"Come home soon, Cathy," she called, taking her thumb out of her mouth only long enough to speak before reinserting it. "Promise."

"We'll be home in no time at all. Only two or three sleeps. Be safe, my darling, I love you." I felt terrible for leaving her, terrible at the idea of staying, but knew I had to follow through on this job, or it felt like I did, if life were ever to be meaningful again. This was meant to be my resolution, more than that, my redemption; I couldn't give up on something so important, couldn't give up on myself.

"I'll bring you a nice present," I said, remembering too late there probably wouldn't be any shops where we were going; might not even be any food or clean water; we were bringing what supplies we could with us in nano-sized packs.

"Bring me some daisies, please. Do not worry about a present."

"What a lovely idea, of course." She broke my heart with the humility of her request, so modest and simple, so unassuming. Like Oxie herself.

Istvan's revving of the bike interrupted my reverie.

I turned to him. "Tell me again how we're going to find your stuff?" I asked, clambering aboard his bike with what grace I could muster. It felt awkward, swinging one leg then the other up and onto the grubby bike panels too, worried he'd see my period leaking onto my trousers, since towels and tampons were among the many shortages.

"Don't worry about that now."

"Just curious." Why shouldn't I ask about that?

"We can't get into that now, we'd better get going, hadn't we?" He gripped the handlebars, measuring his hold on them.

Normally I'd have been the one chivvying him on, things were reversed now. It turned out I'd never really been his boss, despite what I'd thought, but old habits died hard; I was used to thinking I was the one giving the orders – even if only in name.

I was just about sufficiently self-aware to understand that barking out edicts was how I buried my fears, too, except it wasn't really working that day. Hadn't ever worked. My nose was sniffly with pollen grains released by the warrior-like spears of ragwort that were making themselves at home everywhere you could see.

"Have this," he said, revving up the engine and handing me a sodden-looking handkerchief.

"Thank you," I said, as meekly as I could manage.

He busied himself checking our bags were stowed away safely. We weren't even in a relationship, yet he was already talking to me like a tetchy partner of many years' standing. It didn't seem right, but I wasn't sure any more what was and wasn't okay. Possibly had never known.

"It's okay. Don't forget they'll be watching us. We pretend that nothing's changed, I found you wandering out here on your own, remember, in distress and hungry, now I'm taking you back to the capital for a flight home, since the story hasn't worked out. So you need to be subdued, even disappointed. Not feisty and bolshie, okay?"

"Okay." Huh. I tried to inject a tone of disappointed compliance to my voice, but wasn't sure how convincing that would sound, coming from me. Was that how he thought of me? Feisty and bolshie? "What about Oxie, though? Won't they want to know where she is? By the way, do you want the hankie back?"

"If we're asked, we tell them she never left Platignall. That she managed to escape in all the confusion and made her way back to the house. And no, don't worry about the hankie. You hold onto it."

"Thank you. And my line is that I somehow managed to escape and survive in the wilderness on my own without food, drink or painkillers while at the same time nursing a broken arm? Bit unlikely, isn't it?"

"Not in the slightest, you're a tough and resourceful woman."

Speaking like that, he made me feel like a piece of Plasticene he was moulding into whatever shape took his fancy that fortnight. I didn't think of myself that way.

"And more than capable of escaping captivity." He sounded as if he believed him saying that would be enough to make it true.

I was liking this description of my new character, so much so that for a moment I forgot how unrealistic it sounded; at least, it certainly wasn't how I thought of myself, put it that way.

"You really think these stories have a chance of convincing them?"

"Course I do. Be casual, be confident. Use a telling detail or two."

"What's a telling detail when it's at home?"

"The kind of detail that only someone who's been through what you've been through could know about."

"Ah, okay." My mind had gone blank. Not okay.

The hills disappeared quickly enough, the diminution and crescendos of light and colour rising and falling into each other as we travelled past them. At first my helmet kept misting up with my breath, until I found a tiny switch on the dented, bashed, black-painted metallic side that allowed fizzles of air into the damp, foggy interior, and gained a view out onto our surroundings.

"We need to stop and pick up my comms equipment," Istvan told me on an early stop, leaning back with an attractive insouciance against a tree, one leg bent and pressed up against the trunk, the other anchoring him to the earth. Waves of colour blended bell heather with bugle, broom and bog asphodel; they were in alphabetical harmony, too, weirdly. I spotted the odd-looking birds' foot trefoil and their distinctive trifoliate pattern, it was a relief to be escaped from the oddly desert-like sandiness higher up, where we'd started, although I was still only beginning to understand the Aballonian weather systems in all their glorious complexity.

Glancing at him I felt a stab of physical longing so strong it was almost physically painful, and had to lean over to hide my emotions from him, breathing in and out slowly to recover my equilibrium.

"You all right? You look like you're going to pass out."

The words, no doubt harmlessly meant, were enough to break the spell.

Straightening up, I assured him I was fine, and walked back to the bike, telling myself to get a grip on my feelings.

We rode on for some miles, me trying not to think too much about having my legs wrapped around a man I found so attractive, as the embarrassment was making me flush. This was work, I reminded myself. It was also a hell of a lot of fun, maybe it was no wonder I got confused sometimes.

It was a shock when we arrived where Istvan said he'd left his kit. No wonder Zoltan had been so suspicious, I realised, looking at the banks of surveillance and communication crystals stacked untidily one on top of another at the side of the entrance to a narrow cave.

"You came prepared then, like a proper Boy Scout." I'd assumed he'd understand the joke, but he didn't, wheeling round to face me, brow and cheeks creased with lines.

"This is serious," he began. "People lose their lives, get maimed, disfigured when they slip up over details with their kit. Don't ever treat these things as a joke."

The one good thing about his tirade was I began going off him. Fast. He was turning out to be a little bit psycho, with ideas on travelling arrangements that multiplied obsessive compulsive to the nth degree. I'd better not let him see the insides of my rucksack, that packet of biscuits I added at the last minute had actually been open and the crumbs had gone everywhere, decorating toiletries, clothes and make-up, not that I even bothered with cosmetics, it would have seemed indecent with all the suffering in the field hospital to get dolled up there.

"Better just check my messages," he said, in the tone of voice that always left me wondering if he was joking or not.

"Of course," I said, aware I hadn't a clue what checking his messages involved. "I'll wait out here for you."

It was a surprise to discover how long it took him to listen to his messages, but he must have been in demand, since almost an hour passed with me sitting on a rock meditating and breathing in sunshine before he reappeared, looking (by his standards) rather shaken.

"You okay?"

"Yes and no. A lot of messages from various bosses in the service, asking where the hell I've gone, ordering me to report in and await orders at the earliest possible opportunity."

"Is that why you were gone so long?"

"Yes, it is. But that's not the point. My colleagues are seriously pissed off, they've been phoning every twenty minutes since they heard nothing back from me. They've sent out search and rescue parties to find me, they're scared I've fallen into enemy hands. They'll be out there now, in the Highlands, looking for me."

"Yikes. Have you made contact with them?"

He shook his head.

"So they can't know you've found me?"

"No, but they know I was hunting for you. And I've been doing this kind of work a while."

"I could hide out here for a while, couldn't I?"

"Not indefinitely, no. We'd do better to tough it out with Aballonian security and stick to the line you still believe I'm your friendly local fixer and you've got nowhere on the story, so I'm escorting you back to the spaceport."

"You really think they'll fall for it?"

"Don't see why not."

"How'd you find me, then?" Not exactly wandering lonely as a cloud.

"Tip-off from a local." A well-worn line.

"Who told you that though I may look like an unfit hack used to living it up on her expense account, I'm capable of surviving overnight on my own in the high mountains of Aballonia? I don't like to show off my survival skills; that's why I look bookish. Underneath the leggings and cardigan is the taut, highly toned body of an athlete."

He gratified me by smiling and giving a half-laugh. "You hide your athleticism well," he eventually said.

"Okay, you're my fixer, escorting me back to the main planetary port since I've given up on the story."

"Exactly. And we stick to that line, no matter the pressure they put on us."

"Okay," I said, aware I was feeling anything but.

"As far as we're concerned, the last twenty-four hours never happened."

I tried to imagine what we could say had actually happened, and pictured Istvan casting a forgetfulness spell on me while dressed in a spangly robe and pointy hat. The image was refusing to appear in my mind's eye as hoped, all I could visualise were crumpled robes lying on a floor somewhere, no wearer in sight, just a feeling of deflation and emptiness.

I'd no idea where exactly we were when we finally ran into the patrol I'd been worrying about – so much so it had been making my body tight with fear - since we set off. The cloud cover was gone, leaving a serene mistiness in its place that lent a deceptive softness to our surroundings.

They'd resentful, put-upon looks that clashed with the sun-baked grass and trees surrounding us as they walked over to us, deadbeat and surly after waving us down mid-air, as if the world should have been dancing to their orders but, inexplicably, wasn't, much to their disgusted annoyance. Behind them was parked their craft, a beaten-up looking planetary vehicle that almost made our appear sparkling and clean.

"Get your papers out," one of them began, gesturing at me with his arm with a note of barely repressed anger that made me think him someone no stranger to violence.

With sweaty palms – why did my body insist on betraying me? – I began digging in the bag slung across my body.

"It's all right, she's going back to the capital to get a flight off the planet, she's going home. You don't need to worry, we're leaving."

Istvan walked over to the senior of the two officers, showed him some papers and said something in Aballonian I didn't understand. Fear was rising in crescendo waves across my body, choking me; if they took me prisoner they'd probably force me into the drug trials. Or worse. I shuddered as I tried to force my features into an appearance of ignorant compliance. The effect was to make me feel like a village idiot from hundreds of years ago, dumb and 'simple'.

One of the policemen came up close to me, closer than I'd have liked; I could smell his rancid breath and struggled not to recoil, the back of my legs meeting what felt like a thick cactus as I involuntarily stepped back. Wasn't Istvan supposed to have influence with these people? But maybe they were being so hostile because they meant to be playing along with the fiction that he was just a fixer. Just a fixer. The clouds had risen high into the sky, lit up by the triumvirate of suns, giving the place the appearance of a western movie featuring shoot-outs with the local, indigenous inhabitants. I felt very small and stupid, under the cloud-mediated glare.

"Let me ask you a few questions." He sounded as if he'd memorised the line from a script for just this sort of scenario.

I tried to remember what Istvan had said to prepare me.

Just be yourself. Shame I wasn't yet all that clear on who that was, mostly just whatever or whoever someone else more powerful and forceful said I had to be, but no time to worry about that now.

Remember, you're female, your identity is based on who you are, rather than what you do. You want to please your audience. Making others happy, impressing them with your status; that's where it's at for you.

"How can I help?" I paused to smile, aware I wasn't opening my mouth properly, the best I could manage was more of a grudging smirk; he might know I was less than enthralled at meeting him.

"Let's see your ID then."

"Of course."

I dug in my pocket for the relevant crystals, took them out, waited for them to expand and begin to glow.

"How on earth did you find us out here? Hundreds of thousands of miles to search." The question was meant to suggest the police were awfully clever to find us, but they didn't look any less jaundiced by my clumsy flattery.

"We've a good sense of where people like you and Istvan might be found."

Except he hadn't managed to find us, I reflected gratefully, trying not to look smug as I watched a halo of light crowning the hills. People like me and Istvan, though. I didn't like that comment. He sounded like he meant ne'er-do-wells, criminals, reprobates; it was hateful hearing this clown talking about us in those terms. Privately, or not so privately, I was ashamed of considering myself superior to him, and maybe, aware of my disdain for him, probably that was why he was being so condescending to me. Anyway, he hadn't a clue how we'd found each other again, he was miles off course.

"You did well, surviving in the wilderness on your own like that." His tone suggested disbelief rather than admiration.

From far away a rumbling of diggers, mixers, drills and other equipment drifted over to us. We must be getting closer to known, charted habitation, the kind that actually appeared on the maps, unlike the rebel compound.

What to say?

"Yes, well, thank you, we're a resourceful bunch, us hacks." I tried to look unassuming, which wasn't difficult, with my wind-blown hair and dusty clothes. "We have to make the best of things, wherever we happen to find ourselves. Part of the deal, really."

"Well done." He didn't sound or look very impressed, barely bothering to turn away from me as he spat a thick-looking gobbet of something indeterminate onto the ground.

"Thank you," I said primly, feeling revolted by the spitting.

"Don't you go getting any ideas now," the officer said, blasting me with more gusts of sour and putrid halitosis. "You want me to let you carry on cavorting across our homeland, you'd better watch how you go."

I glanced over at Istvan, trying to work out how far he'd got the situation – or, rather, my interlocutor and his pal – under control, but he was doing his gnomic, affable look, the one where his mood never dipped below amused tolerance, presumably worried that an Aballonian goon might pick up on any unusual or inexplicable signals between us.

"What are you doing out here, then? Not just staging a re-run of famous religious figures enjoying a spiritual experience while wandering in the desert?"

"I've been here on a story." Not that I was giving him details of the story, how it involved revelations of a new miracle food and the cruel methods being used to produce the stuff.

"A story, eh?"

"Yes, exactly, that's it."

"And I have been helping her," said Istvan. "As her wingman."

The officer looked unimpressed; they must know exactly who he was, I realised, Istvan was one of Aballonia's own, after all. And they'd assume he needed to continue pretending to me he was nothing more than my friendly, local fixer. They couldn't be allowed to know I was aware his remit extended well beyond that of mere fixer. Sighing, I squared up to them again.

"What we'd like to know more about is what your fixer here has been up to," the guard spoke the word 'fixer' as if it had inverted commas around it. "More exactly, what your fixer here has been doing these past twenty-four hours."

"What he's been doing?" I was honestly confused, so said nothing, not even daring to give Istvan a look begging him to take over for me. The life of a spy wouldn't have been for me, I reflected, not for the first time, not that they'd have wanted someone as tactless and clumsy as me, anyway.

"I take my work as a fixer very seriously," said Istvan, sounding a little bit too serious, at least to my admittedly sceptical ears, to be totally convincing. But, then again, the Aballonians must already know he was one of them, they'd have that information readily available. It was only so we could pretend to them that I was still ignorant of his real identity and that he was still an Aballonian strong and stout (as their national anthem claimed of them all) that we were going through this charade.

"So where has your work as a fixer taken you these past twenty-four hours?"

"Obviously, when I discovered that Cathy here was missing I set off after her."

"Obviously," said the policeman, yawning, picking at his teeth and gazing out at the horizon.

"It took me a while to ask around, get some leads, a good few hours, I'd say."

I was so confused it took me some moments to work out what was happening. The Aballonians must have wanted to know where their man had been for the last day, but they could hardly come out and ask openly, not while I was around anyway, they wouldn't want to reveal his true identity (or one of his several profiles, it turned out, since he was notching them up at a fair old rate), to me, since I was meant to be kept in the dark. Lines about tangled webs refused to stop spooling through my brain, almost as enmeshed as the original threads in their disarray.

"It's taken me a while to find Cathy, I'd to trek into the back of beyond to locate her."

"And you couldn't take a single comms device with you?"

The policeman looked bored; he must have been aware they'd get a different – potentially, though not necessarily more honest – answer from him when they were doing a proper debrief later. For now, we had to stick to our parts. And mine was to play the role of baffled innocent, something I found myself taking to with a disturbing ease that verged on alacrity.

"Yes, so as I was saying, now I've found Cathy I'm escorting her back to the capital for her to get a flight home."

The policemen stepped away from us and conferred in lowered voices. Although I longed to know what they were saying, my Aballonian wasn't good enough to make it out.

They fell silent and walked back over to us.

"Make sure she leaves the planet, won't you," said the more sardonic of the two, breaking off from speaking something into his device.

"Don't worry about that," said Istvan. "Soon as we get to the capital we're heading straight for the spaceport. Might take a while for Cathy to get back to Earthen, what with flights being cancelled, but she's leaving us and moving onto her next project, whatever that might be."

I knew just about enough Aballonian by this stage to understand a hurried aside between Istvan and one of the police.

"We don't care there aren't any flights running to Earthen any more. Just make sure she leaves the planet. And soonest."

Istvan looked as if he might have liked to salute, but instead of putting his hand to his forehead he straightened up.

"First thing we'll do is get Cathy on a flight out of here, isn't that right?" He looked at me with an expression that seemed to ask for my confirmation.

"Yes, it's been quite an adventure here, and thank you for a wonderful few months. But all good things, and all that. I'm heading home now."

Twenty

HUNGER BECAME EVER-PRESENT for us again once we were back in the capital; cups of tasteless tea bought only limited time before the pangs renewed their gnawing. It was so bad I could take only limited comfort from my jeans becoming looser around my waist, bottom and thighs, a fact that would have normally delighted me.

When Istvan ignored the doorbell ringing twice in rapid succession, I felt cross, as well as ashamed of myself for being so grumpy. Feeling tired and weak all the time was my new normal by then and, not understanding malnutrition, I thought it the result of the journeys, the fear, the constant pressure. When I felt my temper getting hold of me, I started to think about how I never used to be so angry. Not understanding scurvy and malnutrition, I thought it must all be my fault for being a substandard human being. Breathing exercises helped – but only a bit.

"Aren't you going to get that?"

"Lady Muck, aren't you? By your leave, milady, excuse me, I'm only a humble gardener."

"Okay, sorry, I was out of order, speaking to you like that." He didn't sound like he was going to turn into a Lawrentian hero and ravage me in the woodshed, worse luck.

"You're not well, are you?"

For a moment, I thought he was going to accuse me of being mentally unwell.

"No, no, I'm fine, thanks. My arm hardly hurts any more, it's almost back to normal." I tried to stretch it out, but it refused to comply, going less than half the distance it had before. "I'm taking all my anti-depressants."

"I know what's wrong with you."

If he suggested it had anything to do with either my enforced celibacy or mental health, I would struggle to pretend to be okay with the idea.

"Malnutrition, from the sound of things."

"How would you know?" He wasn't a doctor, not as far as I

knew.

"It's happening all over the planet, I'm afraid. Scurvy too."

Christ. It sounded piratical – and not in a good way. More in the same vein as what happened to Long John Silver. And Long John Silver's leg.

"Malnutrition? Don't know how we're going to fix that. No fruit or veg in the shops that I can see." I couldn't feel the insouciance I was pretending.

"I've got some vitamin C, you'll be okay." He passed me a grubby, dirty-looking bottle that rattled with its meagre-sounding contents. "One of these, three times a day. Ideally with food, but that's a nice-to-have."

"The food? That we don't have. Never mind. Thank you for the vitamins, very kind." In vain I tried to make my eyes and mouth relax so he wouldn't notice my disgust at the state of the container.

"Don't worry, I know the bottle's seen better times. But the contents are still fairly sterile."

Fairly sterile? Was 'sterile' something approximate? I'd thought it a situation of absolutes, in which something was sterile. Or wasn't.

"Great, great," I murmured to myself, feeling as if I was not so much emoting as praying.

That particular morning the suns were low in the sky as I drank one cup of milkless tea after another, the tannins sharp and acrid against my tongue and mouth.

Only a sliver of blue sky peeped out from between dark and heavy bands of cloud intersecting with each other. They looked as if they were doing a fair job of compressing the sky together, squeezing out any light.

"It wasn't sensible to think global access might come back, just because we're in the capital again." Years of provincial childhood had given me a near-magical and stubborn, though misplaced faith in the superiority of metropolitan ways, in defiance of all I'd witnessed of the brutal criminality, pushing and shoving in capitals across the universe. Although I should have known better, I clung to the notion that somebody, somewhere had sussed the business of life, lording it over the rest of us from a capital city that reflected their own majuscule status. Sadly, or maybe reassuringly, if such a person existed, I'd yet to meet them.

"It's better if we stay on the move," Istvan said, putting on his giant anorak with a care that suggested it was a piece of medieval chainmail. He'd the anorak on before I'd a chance to say if I wanted to join him. "We need to track down my friend."

"Means at least we won't be inhaling fumes from that dead body." I tried to look as if I found my silliness amusing, which I didn't. We'd a running gag about there being a corpse buried under the floorboards, the joke enjoying a resonance from both of us being uncomfortably aware there might well be a horrible truth to our words, a corpse really could be lurking under the floorboards. We weren't planning on investigating further, though, to my relief.

"Only comfort is cannibals would have eaten him by now. If there was any flesh left on him before, there wouldn't be now," Istvan said, deadpan, aware our flagging spirits needed a boost. "Probably just a few old bones left."

"Jesus." I tried to sound as if I was joking, aware I wasn't.

"Hey, only telling it like it is." He was pretending to be offended, but sounded secretly delighted to have made an impression and scared me. I didn't fancy him at all when he was in this kind of mood.

"Anders here likes to keep people entertained, he'll be happy."

"Anders? How'd you know his name?"

"We were chatting before you woke up. Got a chance to introduce ourselves."

I couldn't manage even a half-hearted laugh. "Let me get my things."

The jacket was hanging on a wire coat hanger, the metal struts poking through the fabric like the bones of a poor, underfed animal (of which there were, sadly, all too many back), my jacket had lost much of its hippyish allure some months earlier. Now it was looking more forlorn than bohemian, and I could see my jeans weren't even close to being up to the job of keeping me warm. I took them off and put tights on underneath, before putting some leggings on those and the jeans back on again, then another jumper on top too. It had bobbly bits all over it, which weren't really meant to be there, but it would make the cold bearable. The bobbly bits might help trap some warmth.

Together, we trudged down the block's dirty steps, several of them missing chunks of stone, which seemed to have crumbled away under some mysterious pressure. On one of them I stumbled, felt my ankle begin to veer off at a different angle to normal, my body following the same, vertiginous path.

"Hey, you're all right." Despite his words, Istvan still seemed to think I needed support, grabbing at my waist with a swift dexterity that surprised me.

A little winded, I grabbed onto the aged iron banister.

We kept moving and, at the ground floor, there lay a selection of bikes and prams, not so much parked there as loosely abandoned to the gods of the stairwell.

"Who's this friend we're going to see? Where are we going?" I was asking this latter question a lot on this trip, and it was becoming harder to avoid feeling the confusion hinted at a deeper lack of bearings, of direction in my life.

"Thought you'd have already worked that out by now." He might have looked a little self-satisfied, it was hard to tell. Sometimes, though, his attempts at humour failed to translate into the desired merriment. Being with Istvan could be like tackling one of those five-thousand-piece jigsaw puzzles; you knew you'd never get to plumb its depths in their entirety, there'd inevitably be a missing piece somewhere.

"No, maybe you'd enlighten me." Determined to keep my voice neutral, I tried not to let him see how annoyed I was feeling, my irritation no doubt sharpened by fear and hunger. "Someone who can decode algorithms?"

He unlatched the front door, pulled it toward him and stood back, holding it open so I could go through first.

"Thanks."

Exhaust fumes from the highway made me pause, put my hands to my nose. Had it always been so polluted here? Hard to remember.

"I take it we're going to see someone who can help us break this comms deadlock then, right?"

"Yes, you've guessed right. An old friend, Steve. I've known him since university; we worked together for years. One of the best guys in the business."

"Okay." I wasn't sure it was or would be, but never mind.

It was a relief to escape the grotty bedsit and its stained bedding, even although both of us were sleeping on the floor to avoid the assorted bugs and dirt in the sofa-bed.

There were other advantages to sleeping on the floor, chief among them that we didn't have the awkwardness of sharing a bed. We weren't actually lovers, after all, and I wouldn't have felt comfortable at the idea of our limbs touching, tangling in the darkness, although the idea appealed too.

So we were kipping on the floor on a couple of rugs, with greasy cushions covered with dish towels for our heads. The room smelled of boiled cabbage, like most places in Aballonia, since it was one of the last foods available.

We walked over to where the space pod was parked. A brownish—grey covering of rain-smeared bamboo leaves lay on its roof.

"You think we can just turn up like this? No warning?"

"Of course. Anyway. Can't do it any other way. Messaging would just cause an alert. Right now the Aballonians think I'm escorting you to the airport, and we want them to keep on thinking that."

"Are they following us now?"

"Got to assume they are, yes."

Not a pleasant thought.

"I've a few ways of escaping surveillance teams." He glanced at the omnipresent bamboo growing by the side of the pavement, rustling in the breeze. "Don't worry, we can improvise."

"What's in it for your friend, though? Why would he want to talk to us? He must know how risky it is for him. And his family too."

"What's the plan for today, then?"

"We go to a few travel agents . . ."

"What, again?"

"Verisimilitude."

"Tell me what that is, again?"

"We have to make this little charade look real. So we keep pretending to make enquiries about how you can get off Aballonia."

"While looking for your friend with the secret algorithm talents?"

"Yes, right."

"Heard anything from them yet?"

"Not yet."

"Can't we just phone him up?"

"You don't understand how these people operate."

Me in the wrong again, not understanding. How could he expect me to know how Aballonian government agents behaved?

"How many more nights on the floor of this shit hole are we facing?"

"Don't know yet. I'm working on it. We can't phone him."

"Why not?"

"The Aballonians'll be monitoring all his communication, all his crystals. If they hear us they'll use that to track us down, and possibly algo man too."

"Oh. I see." Well, not totally I didn't.

Later . . .

We parked some distance from the actual house, and walked over to it together. Colonnades and pillars, tortured-looking box hedges and microscopically tended plants made me wonder how Istvan and this man could be friends. They seemed, at least on the face of things, very different to each other. Istvan's usual accommodation featured someone else's sofa, which he was then forced to leave under cover of darkness. A four-poster would have fitted into algo guy's place nicely.

Ringing the front bell produced no immediate answer. Cold biting at my cheekbones, I shuffled my feet around wearily, trying to keep warm. We couldn't give up, not now, not after coming all this way.

The door opened, eventually, but not to Steve himself. Instead, a woman with an apron tied round her waist looked at us suspiciously.

"How can I help?"

"Is Steve around?" Istvan peered into the interior as he spoke.

"No, he's not here." The woman's vehemence made me suspicious; too much energy was going into the denial for it to be convincing.

"Know where we can find him?" He didn't sound hopeful, too much bluster for that.

"There is no Steve here," repeated the woman, ignoring the question Istvan had actually asked, while sounding both exasperated and distressed at the idea of such a thing even being raised as a possibility. "Thank you, goodbye."

We turned away, walked back to the pod.

"What next?"

"Don't know yet. That's where he lives, with his wife and kids. I've visited them a few times over the years."

"With your wife and kids?"

He didn't reply.

"Please tell me we're not doing a stake-out." Like most things that sounded exciting, a stake-out was actually boring and hard work. Without enough loo breaks.

"Not exactly, no."

That didn't sound encouraging.

"Can we at least get something to eat first?" I had to bite back my imitation of Oliver Twist.

He gave me a pained, but comical look. It seemed meant to remind me of the central issue in all our lives – I hadn't forgotten.

"Sorry, I forgot." Why was I so socially clumsy? My endless apologies only made things worse, but I couldn't get out of the habit.

"Right, we'd better get back to the flat."

"Why's that?" My brain wasn't working quite right.

"You've got all that packing to do, remember?"

Packing? Did he want rid of me already? I'd been there only a day – and it wasn't his flat anyway, more a safe house he happened to have keys for.

"Not like that, relax."

At the instruction to relax, my shoulders automatically

tightened.

"Remember we're going to stage a tearful farewell at the spaceport so my esteemed colleagues think you're one less crusading, lie-busting journalist for them to worry about."

"Oh, yes, of course." In a naïve moment, I'd thought we were maybe going on a mini-trip together. A 'holiday' that actually was a holiday, without having to scavenge through anybody's rubbish bin.

"Right now, though, I'm going into the office."

"Isn't that rather risky?"

He shrugged with a nonchalance that was impressive.

"I'll be fine. They've no reason to suspect me."

"I thought they suspected everyone. That's how they roll?"

"Trust me on this one, even if you don't on much else. I'm not putting my head in the lion's mouth unless I'm fairly sure the lion's heavily sedated and my head will be coming out again unscathed."

"But why?"

"Because their comms people will be sweeping the planet for whatever the population are saying to each other. Steve may have managed to remain under the radar, but they'll be charting whatever they can get on him."

"And you're hoping this'll help us locate him?"

"Got to be worth a go."

"You take care while you're out there." I realised I wanted to hug him and, without pausing to think about it, moved closer to him, close enough that I could wrap my arms around him. So close now that I could feel his heart thudding and I became aware of the strength of the man, of my attraction to him. We stayed like that some moments, I felt the prickling of tears in my eyes.

He was the one who separated from me. Putting both arms on my arms, he held me and looked into my eyes.

"It would look more suspicious if I didn't go in, as far as they know everything's shut down and there's nothing to worry about. I know you worry, but don't worry about me. I've chosen to live my life this way, I trained a long time to do this job. I'll be fine."

"I'll cook up some seaweed soup for our tea tonight, then. Might head down to the shore after lunch and see what I can find."

"Lovely." I still couldn't tell if he was being sarcastic or not.

"Er, just in case I don't come back . . ." He hadn't the breezy cheer of earlier. "There's an open ticket in your name at the spaceport. Don't hang about here in town, just get out as fast as you can."

"You going to tell me there's a gun in a spaceport locker for me, too?"

"Gun? No, no, that's here. In an old wellie boot, at the bottom of the wardrobe. Keep it fully loaded and close to you at all times."

Not much danger, indeed. If we were toting powerful weapons capable of killing, then I wouldn't bet on a smooth and peaceful path.

"Okay, I'll be back early evening. Probably best you stay here until then."

"Fine, I can work on tidying up the story. Just on the off chance that we ever manage to publish it. At least we'll be ready."

I succumbed to my clinginess.

"Do you really have to go?"

"Yes, it's our only hope of tracking down Steve."

"Oh, okay." It was still hard to believe the man could be a real person, I wasn't going to share my disbelief with Istvan, though.

"Keep all the windows locked. Don't answer the doorbell if anyone rings. Pretend you're not here."

This sounded like hell. "Okay, of course. If the bell goes, I'll ignore it." It was going to be a long and lonely day.

"Okay, see you later."

The day went just as slowly as I'd expected, although I did make progress on tidying up the story. None of the Aballonian news channels were even alluding to the internet outages, or how they'd effectively stopped communications from reaching or leaving the planet. It felt not unlike John Cleese always reminding his unfortunate wife they should never mention the war.

The suns shone into my face when I sat at the kitchen table, so I closed the noisy plastic/metallic blinds as best I could, to stop the glare. It didn't go well, I got worried I'd broken them, but they were already so scuzzy and dirty, it wasn't easy to tell. I did manage to have a long chat with Oxie, though, which cheered us both up.

Cups of tea helped stave off complete boredom, as well as death from dehydration, but it was still a relief when early evening rolled round. I squirted on two goes of perfume as I thought we were getting close to when he might be home, then as an afterthought squirted another spray down between my breasts. I shouldn't like him, it was already all much too complicated, but there couldn't be any harm in the perfume.

From where I was sitting at the kitchen table, I saw Istvan pull up outside in his clapped-out old banger and got to my feet. Unthinkingly, I opened the door and stood waiting in the entrance to welcome him.

He didn't look too happy to see me, though.

"What are you doing out here? I told you not to open that door under any circumstances."

"But I could see you outside, getting out of the pod. I knew it was you." That third squirt of perfume was feeling like a mistake.

"They might have been planning to ambush us."

"Surely not. I haven't seen or heard a thing out of the neighbours since we got here."

"Nice perfume, by the way." He was slightly more relaxed now we were inside the flat.

"You haven't double-locked the door," he told me, looking pained, almost hurt by my omission.

"Does that really matter? I mean, the only neighbours I've seen have been fine. Except for the one who keeps banging on the door, saying something in Aballonian. Not a clue what any of that meant."

"We can't get involved in that now."

"In what?"

"In a falling-out with the neighbours. You didn't open the door to them, did you?"

"Of course not." Although the loneliness had been awful and I'd felt tempted. I just hadn't felt too keen on getting to know better the enormous Aballonian with three large dogs and some sort of medieval trenching weapon in his arms stood outside the door. Something about him and his leather jacket put me off wanting to open the door.

Something in his manner told me he knew I'd been tempted to strike up a conversation, but he said nothing more.

"There's some progress to report." He looked as if he would appreciate some praise, so I did my best to look impressed, while also hoping I wasn't going to be disappointed in what I learnt.

"Look at this." He handed me a piece of white paper folded over a couple of times.

Unfolding it, gazing at it, I felt none the wiser. There was a pompous-looking crest of Aballonia with bits of gold and other flummery on the top, underneath that were what looked like various codes and indices, though I wasn't sure. Then more text, written in the usual flamboyant Aballonian typescript, a lettering in keeping with much else I'd seen of the planet, that I couldn't fully understand.

"Is this ornithological?" I asked doubtfully, after seeing a reference to something that might have been an insult to women, or something about a bird's nesting habits. Or possibly both. "I'm sorry, I don't understand. My Aballonian isn't that good."

Istvan still looked expectant, as if confident praise for his efforts would be soon forthcoming.

"What does this all mean? Why does it matter so much?" If it really even did, that was.

"It's okay, I understand, you have your interpreter on hand to translate."

He confused me when he switched between roles like this, one moment the humble translator, the next a not-so-humble police spy.

"You going to tell me?"

"Yes, of course."

"That's good." As I tried to settle back on the sofa, I felt a frisson of unease run up my back. He was taking his time about telling me.

"So, go on."

"I've made great inroads in our investigation." He looked hurt, though, as if resigned to no-one else being capable of appreciating his achievements.

"What we have there is a coded message from Steve to his

wife."

I still didn't understand.

"What does it say?" I asked, privately doubtful of ever being able to understand the message. Not even if Istvan translated it into Earthen for me.

"Don't you see?"

I didn't but wasn't going to tell him that.

"Why don't you explain?"

"It's a signal Steve's sending to me, to tell me where I can find him."

Was it? "Okay."

"Can you not see what Steve's trying to do?"

No, I couldn't. And I couldn't help feeling that was hardly my fault, no matter what Istvan said to the contrary. In my agitation I noticed the scuffed and dirty footstool in the corner of the room crowned with the inevitable adornment of young bamboo shoots.

"He is saying that for the next five nights he will be in the bird enclosure in the zoo for half an hour from four thirty till five. Lombeks are our code for an emergency meeting there."

Of course they were, of course.

"Steve must be aware of what we're doing, and this is his only way of contacting me. Straightforward crystal communication would have been too risky, the Aballonians'll be monitoring all that."

"Which part is Steve aware of?"

"Trying to bring down the government, stop the trials, prevent any more people getting hurt, bringing help to people who are injured."

"But the Aballonians are monitoring everything, not just his crystalline, they've seen this message."

"Yes, true, but they haven't a clue what it means. All the stuff about lombeks, that's something only Steve and I and maybe his wife too would understand."

"You trust this guy? It could be a set-up."

"No, Steve wouldn't do that. Or not to me. We go way back, me and him."

Wouldn't he? I didn't like to say anything to the contrary, so tried to focus instead on wiping away fragments of dirty brown mud clinging to my crystal ring.

Twenty-one

THE PATH LEADING to the zoo's aviary house looked all but impassable, thanks to the thick blanket of bamboo, brambles and other weeds swaddling it, although we'd been that same way only the day before without any trouble.

The hills signalled red and orange traffic-lights with a halo-like haze they'd created above the undulating line trailing between summits, a spool of thread spun out across the visible landscape, tracing the dips, peaks and troughs, signalling by the change of colour, the dip in their orangey emissions, the mellowing, down toning, diminution, orange dipping and sinking, the blue edging further down towards landform, to bird life it was time to wrap up for the evening and head home, before the azure beams subsided into an inky black darkness that was already stealing some of the day's earlier intensity from the window display. The glow was disappearing, until all that was left was an orange rinse, a faint colour wash all but eroded by the darkness.

"Sure you want to do this?"

I nodded, glancing to either side.

Returning my gaze to the tangle covering the path, I tried to pull apart the thicket as best I could, my hands acting like a kind of speculum, pushing first at one side then another, tearing at tough, slippery stems. Branches sprang back into my face, close enough for me to hurriedly raise a hand for protection.

Grasping the thin branches of bamboo was a slippery business. I slipped off my rucksack, allowing it to land behind me on the cement path leading from the pod park, leant over, unzipped it and took out some gloves – ironically enough they too were, of course, made of bamboo – and slid them on.

"Is is just me or has this grown since yesterday?" I didn't mean the question rhetorically.

"You know it's grown since then. Like it always does." Istvan was there too, hacking away at stems and leaves, although using rather more serious gear for the job than me – a serrated knife. The space I left between us was generous.

"You think today's meet might actually happen?" I was embarrassed at sounding forlorn but this meeting might never happen. And without an algo expert, we'd no chance of sending the story out via remote transmission. We'd been there for several hours in the same appointed slot agreed with Steve every day for the past fortnight. No show by him yet.

Istvan shrugged. On this occasion, the shrug seemed to be saying that he felt deflated and anxious, too. Other times it could signpost a devil-may-care insouciance. Not, alas, today.

"I wouldn't be here if I didn't," he said, without looking at me and slicing at some fronds with an angry swipe.

Twice, I stumbled and nearly fell as we inched forward. Rubble from the bombing and the plant growth were making the going hazardous. It was less than a mile from pod park to zoo enclosure, but spikes of bamboo made progress slow, as they did everything else. Concentration narrowed my vision, tunnelling my view into a blur of leaf, branch and aerial roots.

Our delightful and hospitable hosts were only too keen to renew their acquaintance with us, we were aware of that. What we didn't know was whether or not they'd managed to locate us yet.

It was possible they already knew we were here, but were waiting to see more – most obvious being who we were meeting - before making their move.

How would Istvan respond if they turned up? Probably by insisting he was still loyal to them, was only with me as part of his 'fixer' disguise.

Then it came to me. For some moments, I couldn't think what was wrong. Only a few moments. It was birdsong. Or, rather, the absence of it. Something had quietened the birds.

Smelling fire smoke, I breathed in heavily for a moment, mentally reliving childhood bonfires, then bit my tongue as I saw the expression on Istvan's face.

"What?"

"You seen what they're burning?"

"No . . ." My eyes followed Istvan's gaze, tracking across a landscape of derelict enclosures encircled by rusting metal fences. A summit stood out against its darkening backdrop, four birds swooped and flapped across the foreground, wings beating in unison with each other, a coded symmetry passing between them that prompted them to move as one, the four moulded by their journey into a single unit dependant on each other, sharing with and being the other.

My stomach plummeted as I took in what he meant. Frightened of being sick, I took a sip of water from my drinking bottle, noticing the sun dip further towards the vanishing semi-circle in the west.

At first I couldn't make out what we were seeing, a mound, a something. Then, sickened, I understood. In front of us, was a tower, a tower made of still-bleeding carcasses. Dozens of them, slabs of bloody meat piled on top of bloody meat. Paving stones of the stuff. Pink, purple. Distended, aching. Hurt, waste, cruelty. The life gone. Not really 'animals' any more. Instead, the smells of putrid, rotting flesh. Flies buzzing overhead. My heart felt as if it were breaking at the sight, collapsing into a molten puddle of horror and grief.

"Jesus." I tried to swat away the flies that had seized on us as a new target.

"Yes, Jesus."

When humans were struggling to find food, animals – of course, even the best-loved ones – had it much worse. I shouldn't have been surprised, but was.

"Oh, this is horrible. Horrible."

"The poor things." Istvan gazed at the animals, his eyes wet with tears. "Such cruelty." Belatedly, I remembered how scrupulous, fastidious he was in avoiding eating meat and fish.

The Istvan I thought I'd known didn't actually exist. That person was no more permanent or deep-reaching than a carnival mask.

Welcome centre

We continued our walk, until we arrived at the so-called 'welcome centre'. It was a bleak, concrete building that did little to dissipate either the place's general sense of despair, or that in my heart.

Istvan took a key out of his pocket, inserted it into the door, twisted it, while pausing to check over his shoulder that we were clear of watchers.

Turning back to me, he nodded.

"It's okay, we can go in." He continued to look around before we went in and locked the door behind us.

In my anxiety, my hand went again to the locket. Touching its hard metallic outer surface with my index finger, I traced over an engraving on it.

There was already someone inside, a worker cleaning the floor.

"Don't worry, I know what you're thinking."

He couldn't possibly, but I forced myself to smile politely.

"What am I thinking, then?" I allowed a little cheekiness into my tone.

Saying nothing, he gave me a look that seemed to warn I shouldn't go too far.

All I knew about police spies was from watching mid-budget yarns on my crystal when bored or lonely. I'd watched quite a few of them over the years.

"Right," I said nervously.

Desperate to change the subject, I seized on the first thing to come into my head.

"What are lombeks, then? Never heard of them."

"Ah." He paused. "Yes."

The way he spoke made think he might be winding me up, like Eartheners did when they told visitors of a tiny creature called a haggis said to roam the moors and hillsides of the more remote planetary outposts.

We sat in the aviary for a couple more hours, playing word games with each other to pass the time. The only sounds were from the place's heating system and the cleaner.

Trying to brush aside my gloominess, I looked out at the enclosure where birds of paradise would once have lived. Dark, shadowy, hidden.

"Think he's even going to turn up?"

"Maybe." Istvan gazed at an information panel about birds of paradise.

He became shut off, inaccessible. Like his knowing.

"The longer we stay here, the more risk they catch us."

"Steve's our only chance of getting the story out and getting help."

"There must be other algo guys working here . . . It is the capital, after all."

"Sure, but he's the only one I trust. The others'd sell us out for a hamburger."

"You sure we shouldn't get out of here?"

"Make your own way home, if you like. You don't need my permission."

Until he said that, I hadn't doubted it.

Perhaps sensing my anxiety, he struck a more conciliatory note.

"Come on, let's give it another twenty minutes. If he doesn't show by then, we call it quits. At least for today."

At least to today. We were going to have to repeat the ordeal every day at the same time until we found our man. Or gave up on him.

"Sorry. Don't worry, I'll do whatever it takes to get help, make sure nobody else gets hurt."

In the background the same guy in a baseball cap was cleaning the place, working as best he could to uproot bamboo growing in the floor. With gloved hands he pulled out the plants, placing them in a large refuse bag. His back to us, he was sweeping the floor as best he could, given the plant growth impeding his progress. He looked so hunched, so put-upon, I felt sorry for him.

Silently, I wondered how much longer we should bother waiting for the mysterious Steve. It came as a surprise to us both when the cleaner sidled up, his posture unassuming and mild, gaze fixed on the wooden decking that served as flooring.

"You think I was a no show?" It was only as he turned to us that I realised I hadn't had a chance to see his face before under his cap. How blind I was to everything . . . In seconds the diminutive cleaner seemed to have grown about a foot taller.

"Steve, my man." Istvan got to his feet and embraced him in a powerful hug. "You got me going all right. Thought you were a no-show."

"Had to make sure I wasn't being followed." Steve grimaced,

presumably to mitigate the cheesy line he'd just delivered.

I looked again at Steve. Somehow, I just knew, in one of those odd intuitive moments of knowing, that I'd never be able to remember his features.

He looked, yes, this was the thing, he looked like a regular, normal guy with a job and a family and a mortgage and recycling bins that he filled and emptied in cycles decreed by others.

"Talk."

"Cathy here's a journalist, with a story about what's happening. With the food trials. The damage they're causing."

Steve looked upset, though that might have just been my imagination.

"I knew this mattered to you . . . Personally, I mean." Istvan was in fully-fledged human mode, neither fixer nor police spy. Just a human being, not unlike the rest of us.

"Well, that's quite enough of that. No time to get into any of that now." Steve looked into the distance, where the earlier blaze of light had subsided into a dull glow that looked close to going out altogether.

"Well, what do you think?" Istvan looked as if he was trying to prove he couldn't care less what Steve thought, which was difficult with him being the one asking the question and after us waiting there more than hour for Steve, while he'd been under our noses the entire time. We were on the back foot, it wasn't a pleasant feeling.

"As soon as I put up the code deluge, they'll be onto us, you must understand that." Steve looked as if he understood personally only too well what that might involve and it wouldn't be pleasant. "If they catch us . . ." He didn't elaborate.

"Where are you going to be based for this?"

"Here, of course." Steve gestured at the straw bales piled high, one on top of another, tips of errant straw poking out from them, determined to try and escape their confined, once living plants harvested and compressed into market-ready commodities.

"What do you mean, 'of course'?"

"They watch every move I make. Including all the ones I'd rather keep private, if you know what I mean. So, I've made myself somewhere to work here at the zoo. No-one bothers me, I'm left alone." He paused. "Mostly."

It sounded as if the bleak surroundings of the zoo suited him just fine. A strange guy, Steve. Difficult to understand, not unlike Istvan.

"I've set up some primitive surveillance. Mostly it's quiet, though. Bit of a mausoleum, I'm afraid."

"I've got the story on some encrypted crystal." I took the crystal out of the pendant and held it out to Steve. "The Aballonians have this pretty tight. It's gone nowhere, despite me trying to send it for several days now."

He took the crystal from me, cradling it in his hand as if it were the precious relics of a saint.

"What do you think?" Would the story ever see the light of day, was what I meant, or was it condemned to remain unseen, ignored, pushed aside? My career no longer seemed as important as it had before, not now I'd seen what the trial victims were facing, but I hadn't yet resigned myself to waving goodbye to it permanently. Even if I couldn't get my career back, I still wanted to help the Aballonians already hurt in the trials, and stop anyone else being injured.

"I've got a plan."

The words were music to my ears.

"Tell me more?"

"I've never done this myself, and never seen it done either. But I've heard of a technique that floods the algorithmic sensors governing communications. Floods them so they stop working and we get the space to send your story back to Earthen."

"Sounds good. Let's do it."

"It's not that simple." Steve scratched at some sore, red, scuffed skin on his legs, visible due to the cycling shorts he was wearing, although the weather wasn't all that clement.

"Isn't it simple?"

"Of course not."

The conversation was starting to feel like a call to IT help back home. Steve sounded as if he was pouring superhuman levels of strength into staying calm.

"Sorry, I'm not really an IT person."

"No, I noticed that," said Steve, sounded as if he'd suffered from disinterest like mine.

"It'll take a couple of hours. We need enough remote hooliganized power to topple the algo wall. Once we knock it over, the Aballonians'll be able to track us, but we should be able to get the story back to Earthen."

"This the only way?"

"Yep, afraid so. Only one I know of, anyway. And getting word back to Earthen is only one step in a much big process, as you must already know. Then the Eartheners have to get a fleet halfway across the universe to Aballonia before they can actually do anything about these moronic flesh-eating cannibals who disgrace the name 'human being'."

"But there's an Earthen fleet moored over at Eyelash, don't forget."

"Of course. What's the flight time to here?"

"Forty minutes."

"So we couldn't be in Aballonian custody more than a couple of hours?"

It wouldn't take the Aballonians more than a few seconds to kill us or inflict life-changing injury. Two hours was an awfully long time. Separate white clouds hovered, indecisive, delicate, fragile, over the hills, protecting what they could, aware of their tininess next to the darker, heavier gloom of massed cloudiness inching ever closer.

"Depends who wins this one, doesn't it?"

I'd been assuming, probably wrongly, of course, that Earthen forces would win the day. And without too much trouble.

"Surely Earthen'll walk this, no? Superior forces, soldiers who been eating regularly, better technical capacity?" I was trying to convince myself as much as Istvan, which he seemed to understand.

"True, but they'll have been on deep space rations for months, their stamina won't be that great. And they'll be foreigners here, don't forget. Just the sight of those three suns can disorient people."

"Don't despair," said Istvan, making me feel his words were honeyed gold, a balm to my knotted spirit. "We know Earthen has had us in its sights for a while now. They've had ships and men stationed on Tretravus for a while now. It's only a few hours from here. No big stays in Hotel Aballonia involved."

It wasn't long before a palpable smell of sweat began to filter through the musty air.

"Would you like some water? Or tea?"

Steve shook his head.

"How's it going?"

"Nearly there. Not long now. You sure on these access codes for the paper?"

"Yep. Checked them while I still had comms."

"We should be going live with this in about twenty minutes. Barring last-minute interruptions. Remember, as soon as this goes out the Aballonians'll be onto us. Get ready to run or to hide. It won't be pretty."

We'd hardly the luxury of time to indulge in chatter, but one more question needed an answer.

"Why? Why are you doing this? Putting yourself on the line? Risking your life to get this story out?"

"Because those fuckers have hurt somebody I care about. Somebody I love – loved - very much indeed. Somebody I've never been able to stop loving, even though she's not around any more thanks to those sadistic idiots. So I'm doing this for her. To sock it to them and stop anyone else getting hurt." There were tears in his eyes that I normally would have pretended not to notice, not today though. A man in this much pain deserved authenticity, so I wasn't allowing myself any social tropes of socially permitted, socially encouraged dishonesty, the man deserved better. "This is payback, where I get some measure of justice, however rough it might be."

What was it that drives all of us but a deep woundedness, I thought. The pain that whipped us on to strive against the impossible, to seek, to quest, to hunt, for something that would ease the pain. I wouldn't have embarked on the stupid journey if not to compensate for what I felt was my flawed, defective being. The crap-ness of me. For which I was prepared to go to extraordinary lengths to hide from, to convince myself I was some sort of semblance of an acceptable person, even when I knew how broken and desperate I felt inside. From that brokenness and pain I was managing to help others, to bring a small measure of healing to this troubled and fractious planet. Perhaps if my wounds meant I could help others, there was some kind of. a point to the agonies of self-hatred, the shame, fear and self-doubt I'd experienced for what felt like so long. Redemption song – the notes had never sounded too sweet to me before, even when they were just a memory, a foretaste of what was to come.

As if in a dream I heard Steve and Istvan confer briefly about the story. The window for the algorithms was open, I learned, which made it sound like opening the ground-floor sash window of your home on a sunny, early summer's day, unscrewing the security fixing, then putting index fingers into the apertures at the bottom of the window, tugging on them to allow glass to lift, revealing an expanse of cold, clear, idyllic sky ,aware that the odd wasp might make it into your room too, but focused on introducing the zest, the upswing, vitality, the freshness and verve, that energy and excitement you have only when life is still barely begun but lies largely ahead in stored-up promises of laughter and love and friendship. Before the friendships turn sour and the dreams rot away in a powdery trot of insubstantial nothingness, when you look back and can no longer recognise the naïve teenager as yourself, she seems so different.

Were we good to go?

"Yes, send it now."

Clicking on the crystal sensor to push the story onto the system, Istvan was concentrating.

"There, that's it. Done." He looked relieved, proud, but still anxious,

"Congratulations." I gave him a brief hug. He didn't relax against me, holding me instead as gif afraid of me.

"And to you too. It's your story, I'm just facilitating the distribution."

As if in a distant dream as the story spiralled out into the universe in a flurry of electrons and magnetism. 'Successfully sent'

read the vast, fizzing display of the screen crystal.
    The dance of delight began somewhere deep inside my chest.

Twenty-two

"WE NEED TO get out of here now." Istvan gathered some papers together and shoved them into a bag, not even bothering to straighten them first as he'd normally have done. "As soon as that window opened, they were onto us; we have to assume that." He put his glasses on before slipping a memory crystal into the pocket of his parka.

Wearing my brown coat and hat, bag strapped across my body like a piece of artillery, I scrambled up from my chair, heart racing. "Let's go."

"Good luck, Steve." Istvan and I chorused our farewell together.

Too busy to reply, Steve was hurrying to leave as well, cramming kit into his bag, sweat dripping from his brow.

"See you," he said, without turning back to look at us as he waved an arm at us.

Istvan put a hand to his hair, itched at it, ran his other hand over his face.

"We've got to go."

We scrambled out and into the space pod, wind-blown, exhilarated. Scared. Crashed down onto our seats, buckled up. My stomach readjusted.

"How long till the Eartheners get here?"

"Don't know."

The space pod lifted off, we were airborne.

"Where are we going?"

"A safe house. In the city."

Was anywhere safe for us?

Arriving at a downbeat block of tenements, we ran from pod to building entrance, hurrying along chipped paving stones. He unlocked the door, ushered me in.

The lift, elderly and protesting, took us to the fourth floor, where we trekked along lengthy, empty, dilapidated corridors punctuated with dusty, artificial plants until we came to the right door.

"This is off the books," he said to me in a whisper. From somewhere, we could hear what sounded like the steady hum of vacuuming, yet the air still smelt stale, fetid, like so much of the planet. It was hard to imagine living, sentient beings there.

He pulled open the door and ushered me in with an ironic pretended doffing of his (non-existent) hat. Unsure how to respond to his bravado, I grimaced at him in what was meant to be a self-deprecatory way. I was too tired for nuance.

Trudging inside, my feet sank into the cheap, rag-pile carpet. I watched as, without a word, he walked over to the Art Deco windows, pulled open the lurid orange curtains and gazed out at the annoyingly empty sky. After the hills and mountains, it was desolate looking at such a void. The space where hills ought to have been. Where we hoped to see rescue . . .

"Come here." He opened the window and looked out of it.

"What . . ."

"Just checking we're not . . . overlooked. Okay, good." His face remained tight, angry; he scowled.

"Let's go and wait on the balcony," he suggested.

I followed him through dirty, aged and unattractive acrylic doors onto a small space looking out at the city.

"Forty minutes from Eyelash." My heart rate speeding up, I held onto the balcony railing, the light-green paint peeling away from the wood spiky under my fingers. The scent of geraniums and jasmine did little to bolster my dwindling nerves.

We heard them before seeing them. Soldiers, by the sound of their practised march. A heaviness. An intent to their steps. An unstoppability. Destructive, heavy, heartless. The sound intensified as they got closer.

They rapped on our door, which shook in response. The line of shabby slippers and bootees with dirty, worn linings placed next to it trembled on the wooden floor.

"That's them." Panicked, I turned to Istvan, who looked fixed in his intensity. "They've found us. What do we do?"

"What people like us have always done. We wait." He didn't look like he was settling in for a long wait, though, more readying himself for the fight. He braced, tensed, hunkered down into himself, his eyes reading deep into all he saw, mouth clamped shut. "Then we fight."

"The door's holding," I volunteered, feeling idiotic. A cliché. There was no feeling in my knees.

"It is a safe house, it's got the latest in bamboo armouring."

Bamboo armouring? That didn't sound promising.

"Titanium-infused." He'd read my scepticism in my face.

The battering continued.

Infusions notwithstanding, the bamboo wasn't holding. Splintering, really. Shards were landing on the stairwell's concrete and on the carpet in the flat.

It was horrifying when I saw him reach into the back pocket of his jeans and take out something that looked horribly like a gun. How'd he hidden that from me for so long? I edged away from him.

"I didn't know you had a . . ." Most of the sky's light had migrated upward to the solitary band of cloud, but the nebula still looked vulnerable, embattled.

He didn't answer me.

With a mixture of disbelief, horror and abject gratitude I watched as he took the gun and walked over to the door. The frame was badly broken, it was a matter of seconds before they'd be in the apartment.

Jumping over the balcony felt like a better option than being captured and shot by Aballonian goons, or forced into their inhuman food trials. Only problem, I was too scared to do it.

The first one was in the flat, faceless behind his mask. Menacing. Inhuman.

Time stopped.

So did my heart, or felt as if it did.

The outside world receded. All that existed was my febrile brain.

Was this . . . it?

The end . . .?

I cursed my imagination. Only the band of brighter blue emerging along the top of the hills helped. It pushed back against the darkness, smaller than its enemy but still more powerful.

Two more men in black joined the first one in the flat.

Anonymous, hidden. Killers? Empty.

They spoke in Aballonian, I was just about able to understand them.

"What do we do with them?" asked one.

"They'd do well in the trials. Show them the rough side of life, do 'em good," said another. "Take 'em prisoner, get 'em signed up."

The smell of jasmine from that evening, sweet, cloying, enveloping, intoxicating, would always mark salvation for me from that evening onward, to the end of my life, although I didn't, of course, know that then.

"If I don't make it," I whispered to Istvan. "Tell Oxie I love her."

"Of course, but we're going to make it. Don't worry."

The men were crowding into the room. Our space. Our lives. Violated.

Istvan didn't say anything as he stepped forward. Didn't need to. The gun he was holding in his hands was doing all his talking for him.

"Back off, back off now," he ordered them, in a voice remarkably free of tremor.

"Oh, lover boy." The largest of the new arrivals sounded sneering. "Or what? Will you object if we hurt your girlfriend here? She might enjoy it . . ."

I've never liked violence. On principle. But a time can come in everyone's life when there are no alternatives to force.

My hands partly over my eyes, but still able to see, I watched in disbelief as Istvan used the gun to shoot the man through his right knee.

"You f-f-f-f-u-u-u-u . . ." The man grabbed at his knee as he collapsed onto the rag pile carpet, bleeding over that and the grotty slipper bootees. "You c-c-c-c-c . . ."

The other men swarmed towards us. Istvan turned out to be a good shot – at least he seemed to hit them in the places where he was intending to land the bullets.

I was dissociating from my body, trying to imagine myself in a different place as a different person. Stupid imagination. It wasn't much help. We'd no idea how much back-up the four men, (at least, I was assuming they were men, had), but they at least were down. No doubt about that.

Violence scared me, my hands wouldn't behave. Wouldn't stay still. Fluttering. Shaking. Tremulous.

The only sounds were groaning and cursing from the wounded.

"I'm calling for back-up," said one of them, holding his crystal, in what felt like a foolish decision to broadcast his intentions.

"Not so fast." Istvan moved quickly, though, as he strode across the room, seized the man's gloved hand, forced it open and grabbed hold of the crystal.

"They'll send back-up when they don't hear anything," said the same man, the one who'd tried (we hoped in vain) to summon help.

"You want me to shoot your other knee too?" Istvan sounded as if he'd have been only too happy to oblige.

The man whimpered and fell silent.

"What are we going to do with them?" Reluctant to reveal anything, I whispered as I spoke, wishing I could be more useful. Hoping I wouldn't have to get directly involved in the violence, cursing myself for my hypocrisy.

"Leave them. We're getting out of here." Istvan was remarkably cool in the face of the setbacks. "Come on."

I was already scrabbling for my things.

"Just leave them," he barked. "We don't have time."

My bag. My lovely, scuffed, leather hippy bag. It'd been everywhere with me. I had to leave it. The pain winded me.

I just had time to get my boots on and race over to the door. The men on the floor looked considerably less intimidating now they were prone. But still presented an air of menace.

Together, we rushed out, Istvan in the lead. Me trying to follow as close as I could.

It was only later, when we'd made it out into the street, that I really looked at him.

"What now? Where do we go now?" I hoped he'd have some ideas, because I hadn't a clue, although hiding out in the omnipresent bamboo might have been our best, if not only option.

"I don't know," he said, his humility disarming at the same time as frightening me. He was close to me now. Very close. His breath made mist in the air.

"If you don't know, we're most definitely in the brown stuff." I could hardly believe I was even trying to make a joke, however weak.

"I don't have any other ideas right now." He let his hands fall to his sides, as if defeated, but continued to look around, scouring the bamboo-infested landscape of broken cars and disused housing.

No ideas. I hadn't any either, but didn't like to say so.

We walked wordlessly over to a narrow alley that led off the street. Underneath the bamboo stems rats weee scuffling, skirting and shuffling. The sky was dark, almost as gloomy as my thoughts.

"We've come a long way, for things to end like this." I gestured with my head at the rats, graffiti and unchecked bamboo.

There was a box of grit, liberally festooned with bamboo, presumably for scattering the pavement and roads when snow or ice arrived. I sat down on it, the plastic bent, made a creaking sound, but didn't break. I watched him walk over to join me.

"This isn't over, Cath. Yes, they're probably, almost certainly, in fact, radioing for help. But we can still get out of this. Hell, we can sleep out here tonight. Use the bamboo for cover."

I wanted to laugh but felt too broken to make any noise except a heavy sigh. He was holding a soft, grey, woollen hat in his hands, I noticed.

"Its cold out here," I said, feeling ridiculous for stating the obvious. "Why don't you put that hat on?"

"But you don't have a hat . . ." This was the same man who had just shot those Aballonians. He turned out to have punctilious manners along with a ruthlessness I hadn't noticed or understood before.

"You need the hat. You wear it."

A breeze blew into the alley, stirring up the dead leaves mixed up with general rubbish and bamboo. Old coffee cups. Crisp packets. Paper bags. The light was almost gone, except for small pockets nestling above a distant line of hills.

Something about this small act of kindness touched me, even at the most wretched of times grace was saving me. Maybe I was selling out for too little, was too easily won, but his decency about the hat touched my heart, touched me at a time when I'd rarely felt more alone or desperate. He was still holding out the hat to me and as I took it from him our fingers touched. Glancingly. But an electricity sparked between us, struck a flame and didn't put that blaze out. I could barely see his face in the gloom, and the darkness, but knew him enough to know he must have felt that same spark. No, I still hadn't found a place where I belonged but perhaps I'd got my search terms all wrong. Home wasn't a place, for me it was a person. This person. This man. This man whose hand wasn't pulling back from mine, as I'd been half-expecting, half-fearing, instead moving further around mine, our fingers weaving into one another, our bodies moving closer too.

"You'll always have me," he whispered. "Wherever in the world we find ourselves, Earthen, or here, you'll have me. That's how this love thing works, you see."

Love? Was he saying what I thought he was?

I'd little experience in the matter of how love worked.

"If they catch us . . ." Images from the hospital tent refused to leave the projector in my mind.

The lights of a fleet of ships sailing across the sky came into view. Blue, red and orange-streaked skies, tiny spots of buzzing energy travelling toward us.

I turned to him.

"Do you think? Is this . . ."

"Is this it?" I meant salvation, though wasn't sure he understood. Stupidly superstitious, I didn't want to spell it out, fearful of wrecking the good news.

"Looks like it, doesn't it." He tightened his grip on my hand.

"We've done it. We've done it."

What was it I'd really been looking for when I came to Aballonia? I'd thought it was a chance to revive my moribund career, to return to a life of travel, booze and expenses. A member of the fourth estate that allowed its members to float above the constraints of other, supposedly 'lesser' people.

And I'd got it all terribly wrong. Now I was ashamed of ever thinking in that horrible way.

Contentment, purpose, a reason to keep going even in the face of brutality and cruelty, that was more satisfying than even the fanciest 'free' champagne. None of the real peace in life came from the cheap glitz of running away from anything that looked difficult, playing the perennial escape artist, avoiding responsibility and trying in vain to buy the lies I told myself.

What I'd really wanted, I realised, was love, belonging, connection. It wasn't why I'd come to Aballonia, but what I'd found there had brought those intangibles into my life.

At last.

It's been worth the wait.

Epilogue

SO, WE DID IT. We managed to get word out on what was happening on the planet, despite our fears and the best efforts of the censors. And the truth set a lot of innocent people free, as the truth has a habit of doing. When the allied ships we'd glimpsed in the sky that day landed on Aballonia they shut down the trials immediately. It was sad that it was too late for many of the victims, of course, but at least no-one else was being press-ganged into taking the poison.

That came too late for Oxie's parents, though, and all we could do was head back after the Allied troops arrived to find her as soon as the airways allowed us to travel. Bamboo had quite a time of it, with everyone focused on wider events, and it took some weeks to prune it back to manageable proportions.

It's taking Oxie a while, as you'd expect, to trust Istvan and I won't disappear on her like her parents, but we're getting there. Slowly. She doesn't suck her thumb anything like as much as before, when there was all that uncertainty about her mum and dad.

Zoltan was put in charge of finding an ethically sourced alternative new foodstuff, which he eventually managed to do after some months of testily complaining that people expected too much of him and everyone needed to follow laboratory protocols more closely. He's done it, though, and managed to create a new food stuff that didn't hurt anyone as it was being pioneered. It doesn't feature bamboo.

Now he's more or less walking on water, so his lab is every bit as sparklingly clean and pristine as he wants it. Everyone working there washes their hands a lot.

The paper admitted I'd been right in what I wrote, and apologised to me. They even published a story exonerating me and saying all kinds of nice things about me saving the day on Aballonia and halting the abuse. It was a good feeling, being vindicated, and so publicly too. They offered me my old job back, too, which was gratifying. Even more gratifying was when I thanked them and politely declined, though I tried not to be self-righteous about it.

Yes, my priorities changed after everything that had happened on Aballonia; I didn't want to spend any more time stuck in the dirty world of planetary media, hating myself and being out only for my hateful self, feeding off other people's misery. So I didn't. I didn't bother going back to Earthen but instead stayed on Aballonia.

Istvan and I run an organic farm together here, at the foot of the mountains. We produce vegetables, fruit, a few seasonal delicacies. It took a while for us to work out how we felt about each other, to work out who we really are and get to know the people hiding under the masks. We've discovered we wanted to spend the rest of our lives continuing to find out more about each other, since we know we won't ever get tired of spending time with one another. So that's exactly what we've been doing. Looking after the lambs is Oxie's job; she takes great pride in it and does the work well.

This new way of being isn't the high life I once mistakenly thought I wanted. No, it's much more prosaic, much happier and much more satisfying than anything involving travel expenses and hotels could ever be. Helping the people of Aballonia somehow gave me the self-esteem that'd been missing before, helping them made me think I maybe deserved a bit of happiness too. That's what Istvan says, anyway, and I tend to agree with him.

Being on our farm is something that gives me a lift of happiness every morning. Makes me happy when I wake up, breathe in the tangy, sharp, cold mountain air and look out the window at low-lying clouds folded in a misty soufflé over our fields. Some days, (though not all, obviously), I even manage to believe I might deserve all this happiness. It's an unusual feeling for me and one I confess I'm beginning to rather enjoy.

***

Printed in Great Britain
by Amazon